THE DALLAS DILEMMA

- Douglas Stewart -

Douglas Stewart's Books

Fiction
Deadly Hush
Deadline Vegas
Dead Fix
Hard Place
Hard Place - The Prequel
Undercurrent
Late Bet
The Dallas Dilemma
Cellars' Market
The Scaffold
Villa Plot, Counterplot
Case for Compensation

Contributions
M.O. – an anthology
Capital Crimes – an anthology
Death Toll 3 – End Game – an anthology

Non-Fiction
Terror at Sea
Piraten (German Language market)
Insult to Injury
A Family at Law

Non-Fiction under the name Brett Morton
Roulette – Playing to Win

Praise for Douglas Stewart's Books

"People just love your book ... you are getting an unusually high percentage of high rankings."
—M J Rose - New York Times Best-Selling Author

"A clever blend of villainy."
—Sunday Times, London

"Gripping, action-packed thriller."
—PETER JAMES - Voted *The Best Crime Author Of All Time.*

"A brilliant start to meeting Ratso. A story you can believe in and a gritty style of writing that works."
—Seb Barrow

"Stewart's writing is fast-moving and laced with that natural British sarcasm that comes so effortlessly. Tough to put down."
—Richard Marcus – Author

"Do read this superb novel."
—Sunday Independent

"In Dead Fix, Douglas Stewart takes you as close as you'll want to get to the high-stakes, high risk world of top-level match fixing."
—SIMON TOYNE - Best-Selling author of SANCTUS

"He makes us think but entertains us."
—Evening Telegraph

PROLOGUE

'It is hard to escape the feeling that they (the United Arab Emirates), along with all the other oil-rich shaikhdoms along the Arabian shore, repose in the still eye of a steadily gathering storm.' (J. B. Kelly – Arabia, The Gulf and The West, 1980)

The shimmering blue waters of the Gulf provided a perfect backcloth for the ceremonials. Today, at Jebel Ali, thoughts of war, of mines bobbing about to sink unwary merchant ships, of war-menace from the Khomeini régime in Iran and pressures of expanding Islamic fundamentalism were far from people's minds.

For the past two hours there had been an endless line of Mercedes and other diplomatic cars, disgorging dignitaries, who'd arrived from Dubai, Abu Dhabi, Washington, London and Paris. Last of all to arrive had been the President and Vice President of the Emirates who were now sitting in the specially created rostrum, along with the most privileged guests.

Today at Jebel Ali, history was going to be made. Today marked the official opening of the multi-billion dollar industrial complex, another symbol of the advancing technology along the Gulf shore.

The red and white awnings and the flags of all nations flapped in the gentle breeze which blew from the cauldron temperatures of the sandy, inland wastes. Beneath the canopy, which absorbed the worst of the searing, unrelenting sun, the spanking white of the cool dish-dashas, worn by the Arab leaders, contrasted with the hot formality of the western suits of the representatives of foreign governments as they sat perspiring in regimental lines.

One of the western diplomats was Henri Leduc, aged thirty-three and a rising star in the French Embassy. Impatiently he tapped his watch, willing time to pass so that he could move on to the more obvious pleasure of the Presidential banquet. He looked at his watch again. *Mon Dieu*! It was hot.

He peered forward from his seat, five rows behind the President and could just see the man's head as it nodded occasionally in approval of the speaker's sentiments. Then he glanced away to the massed ranks of the construction workers, lined up behind makeshift railings some forty yards away, where the speeches were being relayed by loudspeakers. Not for them the protection of red and white awnings against the midday sun. Leduc looked at his watch again. It was 12.30 p.m.

It was the last thing that he ever did.

At 12.30 precisely the massive bomb, planted under the centre of the rostrum, exploded with a roar of violent flame and horror, scattering a jigsaw of broken bodies, twisted seating and burning planks over a huge area. Screams of the wounded, panic from the onlookers filled the air. Karl Wontner, a steel erector from Hamburg was thrown to the ground by the blast and there he lay, forty yards from the rostrum, hands covering his head, hoping against hope that there would be no more blasts. As he lay against the ground, his cheek pressed hard against the scalding concrete, something landed on his back with a heavy thud and then rolled off. Still frozen with terror, he lay on the ground for several more seconds, paralysed by fear, unable to look at the devastation which he knew must be there.

Later Karl would tell people that he hadn't moved for minutes but, in reality, it was less than one minute before he and those around him eased themselves up, staring in disbelief at the burning, flaming red confusion where the President had been seated.

The Dallas Dilemma

Wontner looked to his side. He looked again, uncertain of what he had seen. Then came that moment of recognition and he screamed, hard and loud, harder and louder than he had ever screamed in his life.

Lying beside him was the severed head of Henri Leduc.

It was 12.31 p.m. Hurriedly he scrambled to his feet to distance himself from the mutilation. Overhead, a pall of black smoke rose to fade into grey against the otherwise endless blue sky. The remains of the rostrum stood like a pair of bookends with nothing between to mark the final chapter for both the President and the Vice-President. No more would the fierce, haughty look of the wise and far-sighted President be seen; no more would visiting diplomats and businessmen be subjected to the penetrating stare and acute brain of the Vice-President.

It was more than two hours later before their dismembered bodies, along with twenty-eight others, had been retrieved and removed from the smoking debris, as bomb experts sought out the cause of the explosion.

Rumours, exaggerated by the onlookers behind the barricades, suggested that the bomb had been triggered by a timing device. Others claimed to have seen a mysterious package. In truth no one knew. For sure, no one knew *who* was responsible for the outrage as information and disinformation circulated that day and on into the days and weeks that followed. While diplomatic pundits assessed the patchwork of conflicting liaisons in the Middle East, no group had claimed responsibility and there had been no obvious winners.

Influence through oil wealth was as fickle as the market place and the 1983 price crash had been a sharp reminder, not just to the Emirates but to all the Gulf States, that financial muscle alone had its limitations, not least with Khomeini expressing aims of further expansion of his intolerant régime and with the West becoming increasingly involved in the Iran/Iraq war. The Emirates were exposed and vulnerable to those with anti-Western feelings, whether at home or from abroad.

Long after the last funeral had taken place, around Embassies and Consulates the debate lingered on. Was the bomb attack part of an international game between Moscow and Washington? Was it the PLO? Or Khomeini? Or was it one of the people subsequently elected to replace their fathers as President and Vice-President? Shaikh Ahmed Bin Abdullah al Ghanem, son of the Ruler of Dubai, became President, and Shaikh Rahman of Abu Dhabi had been appointed Vice-President. Could either of them have contemplated killing his father to further his own political ends? It was not impossible, far from impossible in a land where hatred and blood feuds were strongly rooted and passionately felt. And neither man had attended the opening ceremony.

By the following February, five months after the attack, the identity of those responsible for the blast remained a mystery.

London

Harley Street, W1, still legendary for the quality of its medical consultants, was poised in that moment when the snow of a February morning had turned to slush, and now as darkness was falling, that slush was starting to freeze. Traffic was slithering in the treacherous conditions while the Met Office had warned of further snow ahead. The darkening skies of a London evening promised frustrated travellers, frozen points and disrupted trains in the morning.

The street lights had come on, making little difference to the occasional pedestrian, head down against the wind, wondering what he had done to deserve being out on a day like this. The early Victorian buildings were littered with the brass plates of the medical aristocracy such as that of Professor Hugh Waddington, FRCS, who had read medicine at Glasgow University before specialising in arthritic diseases at Bath. There he had taken up a professorship, and a few years later made the ultimate move to his present fashionable address. Despite the mass of letters after his name, his colleagues joked that Hugh Waddington still had more noughts on his bank statement, specialising as he did in the lucrative Arab market.

For twenty-five years he'd advised on arthritic problems, knowing the cruel reality that there was no cure for advancing old age, when joints started to complain after a lifetime of wear, tear and trauma. Almost daily, the major drug companies would pester him, tempting him with bribes or near bribes to bless their new 'miracle cure'. A trip on the Orient Express for you and your wife, Professor Waddington? Or how about some amethysts for Mrs Waddington? Or perhaps you'd prefer a fortnight in Cyprus? All you have to do is promote our latest arthritic product, bless it as a 'dramatic new breakthrough'. Occasionally there was a straight offer of cash but steadfastly Waddington had resisted, preferring to maintain his integrity.

Outside his consulting-rooms a taxi stopped. A slightly built man in a grey suit and navy-blue overcoat of expensive cut emerged to shuffle across the dirty white of the pavement. He mounted the few steps between the railings with difficulty, using a rolling gait, until he reached the door, which opened as if by magic and admitted him to the building. The taxi moved away, followed at a discreet distance by another which had tailed it from Regent's Park.

'Good afternoon, Your Highness,' Mrs Blythe greeted Shaikh Ahmed, newly elected President of the United Arab Emirates. She was used to greeting the rich, knew how to deal with the arrogant, the powerful, and understood the value of presenting a friendly face. That the President was among the richest men in the world meant nothing to her, though as she looked at him, she realised that she had been expecting to see a bigger man, more striking in appearance and probably dressed in Arab costume like most of the others who had come before him. Yes, come to think of it, she had expected him to be wearing his white dish-dasha, topped with the black overlay, gold-braided to emphasise his importance. But as she looked at him in the immaculate neatness of his grey suit, white shirt and blue tie, she merely felt sorry for him: February and a small man – cold, out of place, out of sorts and carrying every one of his sixty-five years, he seemed deserving of sympathy, despite all his ostensible blessings.

'Shall I wait in there?' The President spoke in precise English, acquired when he'd read economics at Cambridge after a previous education at Haileybury. Shaikh Ahmed was looking at the waiting-room from which a large, eighteenth-century grandfather clock was chiming four in rich, mellow tones, befitting the dignity of the building.

'If Your Highness pleases, but Professor Waddington won't keep you long,' she smiled. 'And you will take tea? Arabian style, of course, with mint?'

'Thank you.' The Arab laughed nervously, his small, slightly sad face, heavily lined with age, creasing even more as he did so. Disclosing a weakness was scarcely an Arabic tradition. For the President, a secretive man anyway, it was especially difficult to confide in a stranger, not least when his country was still recovering from the shock of the Jebel Ali blast. Only his trusted confidant, Jayed Adawi, his physician in Dubai, and Hugh Waddington knew the truth of Shaikh Ahmed's doubts and fears. Yet every extra person who knew was a threat, a link in a chain which could be broken by those who were out to destroy him. As he gazed distractedly at *Country Life* and the offer of a luxurious villa in the South of France, he yearned for escape, resentful that destiny had plucked him from his complacent obscurity.

Waddington's arrival came as a relief. The President looked up and saw the man, a mere five foot seven inches tall, aged about fifty, with wavy, silvery hair. His eyes twinkled out of a face to which laughter came easily and which in turn attracted the instant affection and confidence of others. Shaikh Ahmed felt relaxed at once and realised why this man had such a reputation.

Hugh Waddington was tanned, freshly back from a few days at his villa on the Costa Smeralda, and his voice when he spoke was Scottish, gently so, with the mellowness of the Pentland hills rather than the rocky rasp of the city of Glasgow in which he had been educated. The voice had the smoothness of a true malt, with a shade of deference to the power of his patients. 'Your Highness. A privilege to meet you.' Waddington held out a hand, the delicate length of his fingers disproportionate to the rest of his body. 'I'm sorry about our English weather.' As he spoke he was leading the President to the consulting-room where he seated him in the depths of a luxurious armchair, reminiscent of a thousand others in the clubs of St James's.

'Please do not apologise for your weather.' The English was almost pedantic in its perfection. 'When I was at Cambridge, I grew used to it. You see, I was here in 1947. I know what winters mean.'

'1947! That was a terrible winter.' The consultant paused, shook his head and turned, eyes dancing wickedly. 'I can *almost* remember it.'

'Almost!' chided the President, eyes sparkling with momentary mischief. He continued. 'If I ignore your English, or should I say British, humour, I can say that I shall never forget that year.' The sparkle went and the President's face became sadder than before, the moustache even more drooping, the corner of the eyes even more turned down until his face resembled a bloodhound with a cold. But then he brightened. 'Mind you, I learned one or two ways of keeping warm.' His eyes seemed to drift towards the corner cabinet.

'That, Your Highness, is what we call an all-round education. So the offer of a wee dram would not offend?'

'A large Scotch would certainly help.' He watched as Waddington poured generously from a fine cut-glass decanter.

'You'll not be surprised to know that it's my patients from the Middle East who do most damage to my stocks of Scotch. My English patients always refuse, trying to kid themselves – or to kid me – that they're not dependent on alcohol.' Waddington laughed. 'You're comfortable, I hope? I'm very fond of that chair. I picked it up at Sotheby's and although I shouldn't say it, I paid over the odds to stop an Arab buying it. I felt it was . . . too British to go abroad.' For a moment Waddington wondered whether he'd gone just a shade far but the Arab's reaction was one of amusement.

He'd found before that the Arabs, with their mixture of austerity and playboy, were quick to pick up the slightest nuance of meaning which made the difference between a mere jest, and a jibe which cut to the quick. He knew too that in public they were far more sensitive, ever watchful of the suitors for their country's wealth and favours. Not without reason had the Middle East been described as a Dashing White Sergeant of posturing politicians, dancing with an ever-changing array of partners, all wondering with whom they'd end up when the music stopped. Today's ally was tomorrow's stab in the back.

Waddington had taken his seat behind his desk. The President's medical records lay on the blotter where Mrs Blythe had placed them in readiness. 'You're lucky to be alive according to your medical history. It must have been quite an accident' he remarked.

'It was. I can remember the day vividly. It was a year after the bad winter. I was a passenger in a car racing back to Cambridge after a night in Mayfair – 23rd January, 1948. The driver was killed. I was dragged clear with seven broken bones and a fractured skull. They thought I would die. Since then I've had almost forty years of life but for the last year or two the pain has been beyond belief.'

'You didn't need to say that. You can't break a hip, both knee-joints and an ankle without trouble.'

'I've had fifteen years of increasing hell.' He stood up and walked stiffly and somewhat uneasily around the room, apparently studying some of the paintings. 'I'm finding it impossible to remain seated at meetings. Sleep is a luxury which I've almost forgotten. I don't know whether I'm better sitting, standing, or moving about. Before the bomb my health was *my* problem. I was out of the limelight, unimportant.' As Waddington looked at the Shaikh, he felt sure that there was a glistening of tears, a thought confirmed as his patient looked away, unable to meet his gaze. 'What I am going to tell you now is of the utmost confidentiality. Not even your secretary must know of it. My records must be kept most securely. Besides my closest adviser Jayed Adawi, no one knows that I am seeing you and I hope that no one has yet appreciated the rapid deterioration in my condition.' He shook his head. 'No longer is my health my affair. After the bomb blast I became the compromise candidate, the reasonable choice, as you would say in England. I was there to divide the two rival factions, one pro-West, the other a religious zealot called Shaikh Rahman, who is now my Vice-President and Prime Minister. His views are even more extreme than Khomeini's in Iran. Should he take power, the effects on my country, let alone yours and the Western World, would be devastating. With that type of problem I must be strong.' He sat down and then stood up again almost immediately. 'So I am here to be cured, to say goodbye to this crippling arthritic pain.'

Professor Waddington smiled sympathetically. 'I must be frank with you. The *hip* replacement you've had already. But I don't recommend such operations on your knees. We're learning fast and it may not be long, but the techniques are still unsatisfactory.' Waddington showed the President a drawing. 'This is the knee joint and that is the synovial lining. Once that's damaged, you've got real problems. There is no cure.' He leant back in his chair, fingers tucked into his waistcoat pocket. 'And to answer your other point – yes, I do know something of your country's political problems and I'd certainly heard about Shaikh Rahman. Quite a hothead.'

'That's right.' The President was serious, sitting down again, his wiry legs crossed for a moment. 'I'm now a tired man, a tired and weak old man. Is there really nothing you can do for this pain? Shaikh Rahman is plotting behind me, ready to overthrow me at the slightest chance. He's older than I am, you know, but in good health. If you could give me ten strong years without pain, by then a good man, Shaikh Hassan, will be the natural successor to the Presidency.' He shook his head. 'Today, he could never win a power struggle and could not resist if I were overthrown.' Pushing his knees with his hands, the President stood up yet again. 'Professor Waddington, if I am seen as a weak, tired and crippled man, hobbling down the steps of the Majlis, with two sticks and a retainer to catch me, what type of public image is that? Outside pressures are already building, stirring discontent and funnelling it through Shaikh Rahman. You may laugh but in every whisper I sense a plot.'

For a while both men were silent. Waddington stared at his blotter, deep in thought. The President, although given no cause for hope, looked expectantly at the Professor. Finally Waddington spoke, fixing his eyes firmly on his patient. 'I think it clear you are ready to risk much.'

'I have no choice.'

'I haven't mentioned this until now because I didn't want to raise false hope. But there is a new drug product which is *supposed* to be the miracle cure for arthritis. It's early days. It's come from America with extravagant claims. But then, I don't know any new drug which isn't a wonder drug according to the marketing boys. It's a long shot, but if it does work then you could be cured. If it doesn't, then I couldn't give any guarantee as to what the side effects could be. It just hasn't been on the market for long enough.'

'But if a drug company puts out products, surely they're safe?'

Waddington smiled ruefully. 'I don't want to sound cynical but the drugs industry is ruled by the profit motive. Improving human life is often secondary to all that. Of course, they must appear public-spirited and altruistic.' Waddington noticed an expression of alarm flicker across the President's face. He smiled, reassuringly now. 'And fortunately, it's also good business to market drugs which work. But anyway – what is safe? All drugs are a balance. As to this new drug, Lusifren, it certainly sounds revolutionary. If you want to try it, there'll be no guarantees.'

'I have no choice.'

'Well, the risk is yours.'

'So what does Lusifren do?'

'It doesn't merely remove the pain. It *repairs* the damage. There have been some good reports of it.' He shrugged his shoulders. 'It's an incredible formula. Drustein who manufacture it claim that it erodes the bony changes in the joints and activates stimulation of the synovial fluid. I hope they are right.'

London

'Morning, Sandie,' said Rob Laidlaw, his voice deep, rich and resonant as, with a casual flick, he pushed the office door shut. In almost a single movement he draped his jacket over a hook and sat down in front of her desk. The offices just off Berkeley Square were newly furnished, the air crisp with new paint, the atmosphere fast and modern in line with the image which Sir Victor Henderson, founder of the International Safety Association, had wanted to achieve.

'You look cheerful.' Ms Sandie Nicholl's voice hinted disapproval. It was an August Monday morning.

'I am and so should you be, but you sociologists are all the same – seem to *enjoy* carrying the world's problems on your shoulders.'

'Worse still, I carry the burden of you. You don't take anything seriously, you're too flip for this job.' Sandie, a graduate of Sussex University in 1979, although dedicated to the aims of the Association, *did* feel the weight of the job. She was tall and clever, but with a charm which, when challenged, would easily turn to icy intimidation. At University she'd put lecturers and students to flight with a contemptuously raised eyebrow or a decisively slow turn of the wrist. By instinct she was a loner and the abrasive edge of her tongue ensured that she was often alone, but Sir Victor, having personally chosen her as deputy director of his charitable International Safety Association, had been delighted with his choice. Her zeal for justice, her heart on the sleeve worthiness, had been selected to counterbalance the enthusiasm and sometimes inspired impudence of Rob Laidlaw. And she was particularly good at handling the media. Though the Association was in its infancy, Sir Victor had enjoyed reports of the electric crackles which their conversations had generated, though there were already signs after just six months that the more abrasive edges of Sandie's enthusiasms were being blunted, a change about which he had unsettled feelings. Laidlaw, the publicist, with a fast line in repartee, loved quick decisions and forgot the bad ones. Lured from advertising, his role of creating controversy had been second nature and though the salary of £40,000 per annum and a car had been attractive, more important than money had been the freelance, free-ranging role which Sir Victor had given him.

As Sandie flourished her ballpoint, Laidlaw glanced at the Charter, as he always did, to remind himself of what he had yet to achieve:

'IN THE FIELD OF MANUFACTURED PRODUCTS, TO FIGHT INJUSTICE WITHOUT FEAR OR FAVOUR IN THE INTERESTS OF MAN AND MANKIND.'

'A trifle pompous, our Charter, I always think,' he said to Sandie. 'Especially when you consider how much time we've devoted to tin openers which didn't open anything and to lids which wouldn't close. But I suppose we were doing our bit for man and mankind.' He'd ignored her suggestion that he was flippant but proved the point by throwing her a cigarette and, just as she was about to catch it, distracting her by tossing a lighter, so that she dropped both.

'You're just an overgrown schoolboy. For God's sake! You're thirty-four.' She puffed aggressively, feigning concentration on the file in front of her, but out of the corner of her eye she could see Rob's confident equanimity. She both resented and envied his apparent ease with the world. After an upbringing in Darlington where she had jostled daily with dereliction, poverty and unemployment, his was an outlook she could scarcely share. To her, Laidlaw's background of grammar school in rural Hampshire was as distant as if he had been to Eton. She knew, though, that he too had fought his own way upwards on merit; his father had been a railway guard with no money to establish his son in life. Was he then a street fighter? Was there really the resilience of a steel backbone, or had his success come simply from the comfortably laid-back style which seemed so natural?

Whatever she said, she'd come to admire his assurance, his bravado, though she was certainly not prepared to admit it.

'Sandie, my sweet, what you need are two things: a sense of humour and a real man. I don't mean one of the open-toed sandal variety with shoulder-length hair who join you on marches to Trafalgar Square. You're only five years younger than me but you've got so much to learn. Just look at all the left-wingers. Miserable bloody lot. No sense of humour. Half the world's problems stem from that.'

'Some people,' she retorted angrily, 'haven't got much to laugh about.' Her irritation was further fuelled when he just smiled, ignoring the challenge. He swivelled in the chair and flung a leg casually on to her desk as he spoke. 'If you've finished berating me, then perhaps we can get some work done. We are here to work, you know.'

'And if you'd get your bloody foot off my desk, maybe I could get on. *I* was here when the office opened.' She watched his reaction as he leant back, hands clasped behind his head. His fair hair was wavy and had been the envy of his straight haired younger sister, who'd always had to struggle for hours in front of a mirror before going to a party. As she often did, Sandie puzzled over this curiously languid man, casual and elegant and yet able to deliver blows to the unwary with devastating effectiveness. Tall, broad shouldered and carrying slightly more weight now that he had stopped his County-level squash, Rob Laidlaw enjoyed the benefits of physical presence. The charming smile, the melodious voice and wide set eyes were disarming, leaving listeners ill-prepared for the venom which he could inject into the conversation. But which was the real Laidlaw? Was his style something which came naturally or would the concrete crack under stress? She'd never seen him in a crisis, not a real crisis and she wondered how he'd cope then.

'Oh – you were here when the office opened, were you? Well, let me tell you, I was here when the office closed last night.' His eyes narrowed in mock fierceness. 'Don't look surprised. I was working late last night, on a Sunday no less. Against my religion. Never work when the wine bars are open. Never work at a weekend. But then Sir Victor is my new God. And he told me to move in a mysterious way which I did, all the way down to that new bistro in the Brompton Road where I chatted up the MD of one of Global Kitchen Ware's competitors. He gave me the lowdown about that kid who was scalded when the lid fell off one of Global's kettles.'

'And?'

'Child burned. Millions of kettles unsafe. Questions in Parliament. The least we should be able to do is get the kettle withdrawn from the market. Apparently Global are flooding the market with a cheap line imported from Taiwan. Just the thing for breakfast TV. See what you can do about getting me on the air. By the way, when do we see Sir Victor?'

'He's coming in around lunch-time, I think. I'll try to get the media interested before he arrives.'

Laidlaw went through to his own office, thinking of Sir Victor, the millionaire philanthropist who had made his money from property speculation and videos and who'd avoided the pitfalls of investment in CB Radio. But his money hadn't helped in the road

The Dallas Dilemma

accident when he and his wife, Lady Gwendoline, had been injured. That had been three years before, when she had been fifty-two. Her seat-belt had failed to work and she'd been catapulted across the Ml, suffering permanent brain damage. Unable to talk, subject to epileptic fits and permanently housebound, Lady Gwendoline led a twilight existence, while he had devoted himself to exposing the shortcomings of the seatbelts in a series of meetings with the manufacturers. But they would admit nothing and, even though his solicitors had launched proceedings, documents which he felt sure would show that the makers knew the belts were not always reliable, never came to light.

'You can cry stinking fish,' his solicitor had advised him 'but that doesn't prove your case. There's no *evidence* that the company deliberately destroyed the documents although I suspect they did. If we could see such documents or prove deliberate destruction, you'd win. You're the victim of a massive cover-up. These big boys always get away with it.'

The next day, while seated on the terrace of his Roehampton home overlooking the park, he'd decided to create an Association which would fight that type of injustice.

* * *

Taking his seat in his own room, Laidlaw opened the file on the kettles, wondering how best to make his impact, remembering Sir Victor's instruction that in the battle for justice 'Queensberry Rules are not to apply.' Though he'd expressed enthusiasm to Sandie, lids falling off kettles and scalded children weren't the answer. The Association needed something big, something larger than life.

Next door Sandie was dictating a memo but thinking that without Laidlaw, the room seemed empty, the walls much further apart.

His presence always lit a fast-burning fuse and she still found it unsettling. She put down her dictaphone and studied herself in a mirror, produced from a handbag which was more like a hessian sack. Why waste your time thinking about him? He's never shown any interest in you at all. Too late to say that. You've done it! Fool that you are! You've done what you said you'd never do: fall for someone who didn't want to know.

She looked again in the mirror. Maybe her style in clothes was too unconventional. Yet Rob was able to appear outrageous, casual, prop to the poor, friend of the mighty whatever he wore. He'd told her that in the advertising agency he'd been through the burgundy coloured velvet suit syndrome, the polo-necked pullovers and kaleidoscope patterned ties. Now, more often than not, he wore a blazer and flannels or an off-the-peg suit, sometimes three piece and usually in grey.

Yes. Maybe she'd overdone the sexless efficiency of her clothes and hairstyle. Yet she'd never lacked for admirers who'd praised her looks, appreciating the generous abundance of jet-black hair and the large brown eyes. Maybe it was her voice, her accent? She played back a bit of her dictation, heavy with the twang of the North East. Maybe there was room for improvement. She'd try a re-vamp. It might be worth it.

* * *

'Ah! Rob!' said Sir Victor looking at his watch. 'Good to see you.' He was not tall, the only large things about him being his voice, his stomach, his cigar and his generosity. 'I must talk to you urgently.'

'Does that include me?' inquired Sandie, who had come into Rob's room with Sir Victor. Her tone was strident.

'I'm afraid not,' replied Sir Victor. 'What I have to say is for the ears of Rob alone.'

'Well, *they're* big enough for both of us,' she snapped. 'If we're supposed to work together, then whatever you say to him you say to me.' As her face coloured with indignation, Laidlaw was watching her, admiring the way in which the flush of blood made her more attractive. Her eyes stared fiercely from beneath hunched eyebrows.

'Men's talk', Laidlaw muttered, smiling like a tiger after lunch, knowing she'd rise to it.

'And you can piss off too.'

'It's not men's talk,' intervened Sir Victor quickly. 'But still I must talk to Rob alone. It's not my choice Sandie, and I'm afraid I can't explain. Just now it has to be this way.'

Sandie was speechless, not expecting this from, of all people, Sir Victor. 'You too!' her enraged eyes suggested as she stormed out.

'Now, look what you've done,' Laidlaw commented once they were alone. 'You know what Sandie's like. She's got to be in on *everything.*'

'No choice, Rob. We've got something big, really big. An old friend from my Cambridge days is in trouble and considers our Association suitable for a new project. But the instructions are that it's for you to tackle. Not Sandie. And it's so dangerous that no one besides you is to know what's going on. Not even me. You will see a man called Jayed Adawi, from the United Arab Emirates. I met him this morning. He's due here any minute. I know nothing except that it's dangerous and the guaranteed fee for the Association is £100,000.'

'But why me?' interjected Laidlaw.

'Apparently Mr Adawi saw you on television and liked your style.'

'Sounds interesting. Must be arsenic in pork pies for export to Israel.' Sir Victor frowned.

'One last thing, Rob. In dealing with Adawi it would be as well for you to observe certain niceties.'

'Niceties?'

'A certain decorum in the way you behave.'

'I'm not sure I understand, Sir Victor.'

'Then let me explain . . .'

* * *

'Mr Adawi, please sit down.' As Laidlaw spoke he made an instant assessment of the visitor. Medium height, fortyish, he had a dark-skinned face etched with deep and even darker lines, his generous moustache matching the remains of shining black hair. Above all, the hawk-like nose not only dominated the Arab's features but also the meetings which he attended. In his full regalia he'd have looked even more formidable. As it was, in his London uniform of gold watch, tie-pin with inset diamond, Savile Row suit and white shirt with cuffs as crisp as icing, he still exuded power and commanded deference.

Laidlaw's request that the Arab sit down was refused. Instead the visitor prowled round the room, his eyes as restless as those of an El Paso gunslinger. 'The room has been swept?'

'Swept?' Laidlaw was about to make a joke about the cleaners coming every Sunday when he recalled Sir Victor's strict admonition: 'No jokes, no references to thieving Arabs. None of your remarks about stoning women or cutting off hands. Mr Adawi's sense of humour is refined, if it exists at all.'

'My dear Mr Laidlaw. By swept I was referring to listening devices, bugs.' The nasal voice sounded exasperated.

'Bugs? What an extraordinary idea! In my office? Why should there be bugs?'

'If you doubt it, then you can't have many enemies. If you have no enemies then you have no success. If you are not successful, then you are not the man for this project.' The words came in clenched, staccato bursts from between rows of even teeth, two of which were gold, creating the aura of a pirate rather than a statesman.

Laidlaw did not like being on the defensive. 'Look, Mr Adawi, this is England, this is my office. You won't find bugs here, even though we do have enemies. But if you're worried, check us out.'

'That I intended to do, even without your invitation.' Adawi removed a small sensor device from his black attaché case and, holding it at arm's length, walked all around the room. 'Yes. We can talk now.' Adawi sat down, adjusting his trousers as he did so, appearing anxious to avoid creasing the immaculate cloth.

Ordinarily Laidlaw would have added a comment, but he refrained, contenting himself with wondering what a super-spy from the Kremlin would have made of the kettle-lid scandal or his repeated phone calls for the Test Score.

Adawi spoke, his tone arch. 'My name is Jayed Adawi. I am personal adviser to His Excellency Shaikh Ahmed bin Abdullah al Ghanem, President of the United Arab Emirates. Despite my initial impression in here, my previous inquiries have revealed that your reputation, Mr Laidlaw, is sound for an enterprise which I wish to discuss.' Adawi's dark eyes were close-set and sheltered beneath heavy brows, while his voice was ugly and without charm. 'Your reputation is for straight talking, of adopting a high profile. But can you be discreet?'

'I do what I'm paid to do. If you want publicity, I'll certainly generate it. If you want discretion, then my lips are tight-sealed.'

'Secrecy will be essential.' The Arab's face glowered and

darkened and, as the perfumed features leant towards him, Laidlaw could almost feel the threat of the knife across the throat.

'Fine. Just tell me what I'm to do.' Laidlaw watched as Adawi got up without speaking and walked to the window looking out towards Berkeley Square. His eyes, which were forever on the move, reflected the fear of a whole generation brought up in the turmoil of the Middle East.

'What do you know of my country?'

'Sand, oil and camels. That's about it.'

Laidlaw watched as the Arab examined minutely a bronze statuette of a racehorse, a present which Laidlaw had received from a grateful client at the advertising agency.

'Don't you trust your gadget, Mr Adawi?' Laidlaw's tone was sardonic.

'I trust nothing and no one.'

'Not even me?'

'You will be told what you need to know, Mr Laidlaw.'

'I'm listening.'

'You may know that Khomeini and some northern Arabs want all Western influences to be stamped out in Middle East countries; want all private conduct and public policy to be set by the rules of the Koran and by the Islamic law called Sharia. As a fanatic, Khomeini must never be underestimated. He wants all Moslems to rise up and conquer their fear of death, so that they can take over the whole world. Our Vice-President, Shaikh Rahman, is much under his influence.'

'I hadn't realised that Khomeini's aims were so international,' said Laidlaw.

'You are not alone. Traditionally Dubai and Teheran have been good friends, great traders, and you will find plenty of Iranians working on the quay at Dubai. But things have changed, not just in my country but from Libya to Pakistan. Everywhere the fever of Islamic revolution fills the air. Even the Saudis are concerned at the indiscriminate power of Iran.'

Laidlaw was wondering what all this had to do with the Association but decided that Adawi would reach the point in his own way. The Arab returned to the desk and produced a black leather folder. 'In here is your ticket, first class return, to Dubai tomorrow. There are also some written instructions which you will study now and destroy before you leave this room.' Adawi noticed the surprise which had come over Laidlaw's face. 'You must leave tomorrow. You had no plans?'

Laidlaw resented the man's hectoring style – the assumption that the large fee being paid justified giving orders like this. He only just remembered Sir Victor's instructions. 'Plans? Me? Well, I did have matters of some importance to deal with, but I imagine other arrangements can be made.' Laidlaw enjoyed watching the dark eyebrows frown in some disdain. Thank God Sir Victor wasn't within earshot.

'You will need no visa. Doors will open for you. Everywhere. Your stay will be short but comfortable. You will fly back the next day. Time is not on our side. I shall meet you at Dubai Airport.'

Laidlaw fingered the expensive black leather folder and then opened it. There was a wadge of money, both Sterling and Dirhams, an itinerary and a page of detailed instructions. 'Sir Victor mentioned that the fee to our Association would be £100,000. I presume you will need me for many months?'

'No. Not necessarily.'

'Then why such a fee?' Laidlaw watched Adawi closely and saw the eyes reply before the mouth, but the answer came anyway, stark and uncompromising.

'Because of the importance and because of the danger. I put your chances at around 50%.'

'My chances of success?'

'Your chances of *survival*. You will be investigating a US Corporation called Drustein – a ruthless outfit. But the real dangers come from the political overtones and Shaikh Rahman. If what I am going to tell you leaks out, then you will certainly earn your fee.' He smiled for the first time, a sight which Rob Laidlaw hoped would not be repeated too often. 'Of course, you will not be around to enjoy it.'

'Tell me the good news. Tell me I don't have to eat sheep's eyes. Anything but that.'

The Arab scowled. 'I'm glad you can joke. You will need your sense of humour. There will be nothing to laugh about during this investigation. From today, five people in the world, including you, know what I am telling you. They are me, the President, his personal physician and a Professor Hugh Waddington. That is the way it must remain. You tell no one else, you understand that? No one.' Adawi's eyelids dropped heavily with sadness, the first sign that he was not without emotion. 'Our President will be dead within twenty-six weeks, maybe much less. You will have heard of the anti-arthritis drug called Lusifren. Professor Waddington prescribed him that drug six months ago, last February. It should have been a wonder cure for the arthritis suffered by His Highness.' Adawi's near despair became more apparent as his voice dropped to the point where his words were almost inaudible. 'Instead of that, Lusifren was a death sentence. The side effects from the drug have attacked his arteries, clogging those to his heart and to his brain. He has become indecisive, confused and forgetful. Within twelve months there could be a civil war, at best. At the very least, Shaikh Rahman will assume power and lead my country back into the dark ages of politics. Worse still, our country could become the battleground for outsiders wishing to exploit our troubles for their own political ends.'

The Dallas Dilemma

'I'm sorry. To know a friend is dying must be very hurtful.' Laidlaw looked solemn as the implications of the instructions started to penetrate. 'Lusifren has now been banned in the USA and throughout Europe. There are thousands who are suffering.'

Adawi nodded. 'I'd heard. And His Highness is angry. Your Association must find out why the stability of the Middle East has been threatened. Was it ineptitude by the manufacturers, or was it greed.'

'And a cure? Surely Shaikh Ahmed wants a cure?'

'Yes. But His Highness does not delude himself. Time is not on his side. Professor Waddington told me this morning that the damage from Lusifren was almost certainly permanent. However, I shall not tell that to His Highness. He must cling to his hope, if only to keep him alive as long as possible. The alternative may be a blood-bath in a return to Islamic idealism. The West will be the losers.'

Laidlaw played nervously with the folder of instructions. 'And overtime for the firing squad?' Laidlaw was being serious.

'Yes. And although I shall be there, it will not be me who is giving the instruction to fire.' Adawi saw the implications penetrating the unusually solemn features of the Englishman. 'Before he dies His Highness wants to know the truth. If you succeed – and you must not fail – then after his death, his unlimited wealth will be placed behind you to expand the work which you are doing.'

'Let me show you something.' Laidlaw produced an extract from *Family Circle* magazine. 'This is no high-powered publication, nothing technical. Each page here shows the dangers from well-known drugs. Any number of drugs taken wrongly or mixed with others in error can be fatal. Mix a blood pressure drug with cough mixture and you may never see dawn in Dubai again.' He put down the document. 'When it worked, Lusifren was great. I don't know how much you understand about the pharmaceutical industry, Mr Adawi, but a company such as Drustein Drug Facilities, Inc., of Dallas, which manufactured Lusifren, is motivated by profit. Just imagine that you find a cure for arthritis, Aids or cancer which seems to work. You've invested millions upon millions of dollars. You want to turn all that research and development into sales. You want to market it quickly, beat the opposition. Imagine the temptation to conceal any evidence of unwanted side effects, to convince yourself that more good than harm would be done by marketing the product.'

'And killing in the process. Make no mistake, Mr Laidlaw. This task is no usual one. What you are now involved in has direct repercussions on the politics of the Middle East, the politics of death.'

Laidlaw replied slowly. 'The time factor is a problem. So too is Shaikh Rahman. I see there are some notes about him in the folder. Would this be right? That if he realises the President is a weak man, a coup would be tempting?'

'We are working hard to keep the President's condition secret. I think we have been succeeding. But if Shaikh Rahman found out, then your appraisal would be right.' Adawi closed his briefcase. 'Shaikh Rahman would act at once. By tomorrow you must have a plan. When you see His Highness, you must give him hope. No one must deprive him of the luxury of hope.' Adawi stood up. 'Or the luxury of vengeance. That is part of our way of life. We do not forget. Ever. And he alone stands between stability and anarchy.'

And between you and the firing squad, Laidlaw thought to himself. He gave a half laugh which, because of his edginess, sounded more like a choking cough. 'You make it sound so melodramatic. I can't believe that the death of Shaikh Ahmed could be so far-reaching.'

'Do not presume to talk to me of my country nor of the Middle East. It is you who do not understand. Now that Britain, France and the USA have become involved in keeping open the shipping lanes of the Strait of Hormuz, the tension is mounting. The dangers for us all are enormous – and particularly for you.'

'But just one question then. Why come to us? Why not go straight to the USA?'

'Firstly, because His Highness is an Anglophile, educated at Cambridge and a friend of Sir Victor. Secondly the drug was prescribed here in London. Above all, he has no faith in Americans, believing them to be twisted people motivated by money alone. Even the politicians, he mistrusts.'

'I like Americans.'

'Then you are a fool. Trust nobody in America. Money has corrupted their very souls.'

Laidlaw saw the man out, his mind absorbing the talk of corruption and international politics. It was only beginning to dawn on him that this might be the major investigation the Association needed to establish its credibility.

'He was a right misery, wasn't he?' suggested Sandie as she and Laidlaw watched Adawi hail a taxi. He knew that she was fishing for information, and, with something of an effort, resumed his usual joviality.

'Lost his camel. That was one problem. Last seen at a parking meter in Hill Street. Got the hump when a traffic warden gave it a ticket.' He knew that Sandie was in no mood for a joke and so he continued. 'But he really called about pyramid selling. Or was it selling the Pyramids. I forget which.'

'I wish you'd grow up, Rob. Can't you take anything seriously?' Yet, as she looked at his face, bronzed by sailing off the Essex coast, she knew that he would never change. His casual arrogance was a pleasing irritation, an underplaying of his looks, his lifestyle and his attractiveness to women. If Laidlaw had any awareness of fashion, it didn't show; if he had a comb, it was rarely used, as his fair hair always flopped casually into place, covering his ears. 'Trendy' was a word in his dictionary but not in his life.

Laidlaw's face, always ready to respond to the mood of the moment, lengthened, the grey eyes narrowed and he pushed aside an ashtray to perch on the edge of her desk, his long legs swinging almost to the floor. 'You've got a lot to learn Sandie. I *am* serious. Deadly serious in my aims. There's nothing better than being underestimated.' He paused to watch her reaction. 'It's better to be detached. Joking about it helps keep everything in proportion. I just wish you had a sense of humour too.'

'I'm not impressed by your philosophy' she said crossly. 'What did this Arab want anyway?'

'A big job. Hush-hush.' Laidlaw looked furtive and put his fingers to his lips. 'Don't tell anyone on pain of ending up in the soup. Or did he say dessert? Or maybe he meant desert. Anyway, hush-hush. Don't tell anyone. Especially don't tell you.'

'Piss off, you great clown.' Her voice convinced him that she thought he was joking. 'Come on. What's it all about?'

'I can't tell you – not even you – Sandie of the Desert. Not a soul. Gave him my Cub's honour. Swore on this year's Wisden. There's no going back.'

'For God's sake! We pool everything.'

'Not this time. I can't even tell Sir Victor.' He moved round her desk, put an arm across her shoulder and then kissed her softly, ever so softly, on the cheek. She look surprised. 'I'm sorry. I simply cannot tell you. And maybe it's better for you not to know. I'm flying out in the morning.'

'Just when I've got you lined up for breakfast television, too.'

'I'm sorry but the great British public will have to start the day without the benefit of my company. It'll scarcely be worth them getting up at all. What a louse I am to let them down.'

Dubai

The Presidential Palace was far smaller than Laidlaw had imagined but no less opulent. As he waited with Adawi in a high-vaulted ante-room, the mosaic tiling on the walls and floors was so richly patterned that the effect was almost overpowering. On the floor was a scattering of tapestry rugs and the air was fragrant with a delicate blend of spices, a smell which took him back to Istanbul and the Sultan's Palace, which he had visited some years earlier. He was just admiring a lamp, its base encrusted with rubies and emeralds, when the double doors were opened and together they went into the next room, which was much smaller, more modest and furnished to Shaikh Ahmed's own taste by Harrods.

Sprawled almost sideways on a comfortable sofa, the President made no attempt to get up but the falcon, perched on the Shaikh's left arm, gave the tiniest flutter of its wings in greeting, the sharp alertness of its eyes in contrast with the near-glazed look of its master. Though Laidlaw recognised the Shaikh from the photographs which he had been studying, he was shocked at what he saw. This was not a man tired at the end of the day but a man who was truly sick, with not a spare ounce of flesh on his hand. It was easy to imagine the thin, sinewy arm leading to the frail and almost bird-like body.

Laidlaw fought to remember the etiquette. Don't show an Arab the soles of your feet. Pain of death. He remembered that advice from page one of the guide book. Should he bow, shake hands or offer some other peculiarly Arab greeting he wondered, till Shaikh Ahmed leant forward slightly, right hand outstretched. 'Thank you for coming here, Mr Laidlaw,' said the Ruler, his voice striking the Englishman both because of the correctness of his speech and the hint of tremor in its tone. The shadow of death was written large across the Shaikh's face: his cheeks were sunken and, though the dark skin was more wrinkled now, it was yellowing almost visibly, like old parchment.

'Your Highness, it's my privilege to be here and I am delighted to meet you' he said, with a positive smile as he spoke, although the presence of the bird of prey slightly unnerved him.

The old man nodded. 'Please be informal. In private, when dealing with people from England, I like to be English. You know that I studied there?'

'Yes. I was aware of that.' Laidlaw lowered himself into a chair a few feet from the Ruler.

'I can see that my falcon bothers you,' said the Shaikh and instantly one servant hooded the bird and removed it, while another produced some Arabic coffee, thick and bitter to Laidlaw's taste. As they spoke, mainly inconsequentially, Laidlaw's eyes kept returning to the Shaikh's hands, noticing how much coffee he was spilling as his fingers trembled.

Save for Adawi, they were now alone. 'No one knows why you are here?'

'No one.'

'My life depends on it. Or what's left of it. It is now nearly the end of the day and I am exhausted. In the mornings, I am better but I wanted you to see just what I have become, so that you will understand my bitterness, and will understand my desire for the truth and for revenge. You see Lusifren has damaged my circulation. Now my heart has to fight to keep the blood moving.' Laidlaw saw a glistening of tears in the eyes. 'I am resigned to my own death but never to the death of my nation. Tell me, Mr Laidlaw, do you begrudge me my vindictiveness? My fears of a coup inspired by Shaikh Rahman? My desire for the truth? Do you see me as a silly old man, vain and foolish, the King Lear of the Emirates?'

'No, not at all. You have a right to ask why. You and the countless other victims are entitled to answers. You will understand also that many of the victims need compensation for their shattered lives. Naturally, for you, compensation is unimportant but I can tell you my strategy.' For a moment Laidlaw was disconcerted as he saw that the President's eyes were starting to close from the fatigue of the day. 'I shall be brief. My plan is to conceal *your* interest in Lusifren by acting for as many victims as I can. Using them as my excuse, I will litigate in Texas, using the American attorney who's already started proceedings in Dallas against Drustein.'

'I shall be dead before that's finished.' The Ruler's face was serious.

'I don't agree. American process *can* be very swift and the point is that we shall be jumping on the back of the existing American litigation, which is already well-established. This will give us the chance to get at the documents, to cross-examine those responsible for unleashing Lusifren on an unsuspecting world.' On seeing the nod of encouragement from Shaikh Ahmed, Laidlaw continued. 'I shall also follow up other confidential enquiries, both here and in the USA. In short I shall do everything I can.'

The thin lips winced as the Shaikh changed position with painstaking slowness. 'Yes. I believe you will. You have the enthusiasm of youth. But go carefully. I have many enemies. If they think they can learn something to their advantage from you, then . . .' The Shaikh played with the walking stick which lay across his lap. 'I fear for you.'

'I shall be all right. But thank you for your concern.'

'Please succeed. Though I hope for a cure, I fear there will be none. Nevertheless, each passing day of my survival buys time. That gives Mr Adawi the chance to plan for an orderly succession. My legacy must not be to leave my country in civil war at the mercy of the extremists.'

The small eyes were starting to close once again and the interview was over. Moments later Laidlaw was in the giant black Mercedes, Adawi beside him, while the Arab chauffeur sped them down the Zabil Road towards the city centre. 'Your hotel's on the other side of the creek in the area called Deira. Where we are now is truly called Dubai and this is the Al-Maktum Bridge, linking one side with the other.' The contrast between the two sides was marked. They were leaving the traditional, two-storeyed buildings, the minarets and the wind towers, the labyrinth of the Souk and entering the fast-moving modern commercial centre where the old houses were dwarfed by the skyscrapers which jostled one another all the way to the water's edge.

As they drove along in the darkness, the lights from the buildings illuminated the creek which was alive with small boats and water-taxis, plying from bank to bank. Dhows, crammed with sacks, crates and clutter, were moored along the quay and the pavements were thronged with scores of people of all nationalities, pushing and shouting as the boats were loaded or unloaded ready for departure. Where once had been pearl divers and gold smugglers, there were now the crates of sanitary ware, chemicals and sacks of cement.

Here and there Adawi pointed out a landmark leaving Laidlaw wishing that his return flight was not booked for first thing the next morning. 'This is your hotel,' said Adawi, as the limousine pulled

The Dallas Dilemma

up outside the huge splendour of the Hyatt. 'I'm sure you will be very comfortable here.'

Laidlaw watched the Mercedes move off, before himself turning to enter the hotel. Had he waited a moment longer he'd have noticed another car pull up – a car which had been following discreetly all the way from the Zabil Road. He would also have seen the driver get out, enter the hotel and watch him check in to his top floor suite.

The next day, after an uneventful flight back to London, Laidlaw also failed to notice the powerful black 750 cc. BMW motorcycle which tailed him from Heathrow to his office.

His life was changing but he didn't yet know it.

Dallas

Marcus Schillen, President and founder of Drustein, approached the gold-lustred building which he'd created through twenty years dedication and a readiness to trample over friends and enemies with equal enthusiasm. As usual, he ignored the polite salute of the security man who raised the barrier to release him from the super-saturated artery of North Central Highway. Normally the sight of his headquarters elated Schillen. But not today. This morning, like a few previous mornings, his past had been casting shadows, shadows which came in the seductive shape of Inge Loftin, the tough Dallas lawyer retained to fight Drustein for compensation for Lusifren. Now she'd been joined by some Englishman called Rob Laidlaw and he was making waves across the Atlantic. A gentle wash or a tidal wave? He wasn't sure but he'd heard daily reports of the Englishman's TV broadcasts, appealing for victims of Lusifren to come forward and press claims in concert against Drustein.

This morning's meeting with his attorney and two key Vice-Presidents was going to be crucial. Trouble? For sure he could smell it. Yes sir, he told himself, there would be trouble. As he cruised up the long winding drive, trees on either side, through acres of green, he could see the distant tight cluster of high-rise buildings of downtown Dallas, its skyline symbolised by the massive revolving globe on top of Reunion Tower. Most days he'd appreciate the view but not today. He'd deny it but in truth both he and Drustein were beleaguered, fighting for survival against the forces of the media, the law, the sins of their own past. But hell, at the age of fifty-seven, who hasn't got a few sins to conceal? He swung the black Cadillac to a halt and leapt out, briskly for his age but in line with his punishing, ninety minute daily workout.

He slammed the door shut. Sure. All successful men had something to hide, even those like his long-time friend, Jack Hode, currently President of the United States and facing a November election. If the pollsters were right, Hode was likely to be returned for another four year term and then he, Marcus Schillen, self-made multimillionaire, would be invited to take up the post of Deputy Chief of Staff at the White House, a closely guarded secret known only to the President and to Larry Parker, his Chief of Staff. Just a few weeks, Marcus, and you will be at the seat of power. You'll be the nearest thing to the President, closer even than Larry Parker in day-to-day routine. He nodded to himself. It'll be the pinnacle of your career, a just reward for a lifelong friendship and generous donations to party funds. 'Marcus,' President Jack Hode had said from Washington three months before, 'you keep this news as tight as your ass. We don't want any stories leaking out, not with the election coming up. This place just runs on soirées for gourmets where the staple diet is gossip. If it leaked out that I was dumping the present Deputy, then all hell would break loose. After the election, with four more years ahead, I can ride anything. And Marcus, I really need you. I need a cool head.'

'Well thank you, Jack,' Schillen had responded.

'But just be sure there's no crap flying about at your end. I've been hearing stories about Lusifren.'

'Don't worry, Jack. There's nothing in them.' Yet, as Schillen thought back to the conversation, he wasn't as confident now as then, what with that bitch Inge Loftin firing off lawsuits and now a smooth-talking Englishman stirring up more trouble.

Schillen's pace was brisk, economic, as he walked beneath the searing heat of a cloudless sky towards the main entrance. This morning the gleam of the sun against the gold-tinted expanse of building lacked its usual lustre. He had once or twice described the building as a monument to himself, though one embittered executive had been heard to say that the building was indeed a reflection of the corporation's President, 'all glitter outside, all crap within.'

The bellhop touched the side of his face in respectful salute but as usual Schillen never noticed; only the occasional senior executive on an upper floor got the slightest nod of greeting. His secretary, Lucille Malone, was already in his office, the large room cool and fragrant, the colours subdued, the lighting subtle, his massive desk littered with the clutter of useful objects for the international businessman, though Schillen never used any of them still preferring a throwaway ballpoint to scribble memos on scraps of paper. There was also a pitcher of iced orange juice, a glass, a cup of coffee and a croissant, each precisely positioned, for Mrs Malone knew better than to get anything wrong. Mistakes were not tolerated and the bitter joke in the company was that, while unemployment in Dallas was low, Schillen was doing his best to change all that. Dismissals were frequent, violent, and though Schillen never raised his voice, his menace came from the penetrating brain and rough edges of his exchanges.

'Good morning, Lucille. Another lovely day.' Not even his wife had enjoyed such a friendly greeting. But his secretary was different. She'd told him straight on day one that unless he treated her better on day two, she'd leave. Not usually a man to succumb to threats of this sort, Schillen nevertheless had done so, maybe because he secretly admired her stand, maybe also because he thought she'd be pretty good in the sack. This morning, like most mornings,

The Dallas Dilemma

he admired the tight curve of her butt and the generous swell of her breasts as she adjusted the blinds. It was *unfortunate* that she'd found his advances resistible. But brother! Once he could tell her that he was going to the White House . . . Power! The irresistible aphrodisiac! At thirty-seven he reckoned that a woman's mind and a woman's body were at their peak and he'd told her more than once that this was a very good age for a woman to have an affair. But she'd only smiled at him. If he had but understood, it was a smile of contempt.

'Morning, Marcus. The room is all ready for the meeting. Security has checked out the arrangements. You're all set.'

'Thank you, Lucille.' He wondered when he'd graduate to calling her Lucy. Would it be *before* or *after*? Part of her challenge, part of the allure was her chilly off-handedness. 'Have Security do it again.' He watched her slip through into her own office and heard her issuing commands with immense authority while he flicked through his mail, just a handful of letters. Once, he'd judged his importance by their number. Now he reckoned that power lay in skilled delegation, a factor on which he'd congratulated Jack Hode, who ran the White House on just that basis. And after the election . . . more power to the Deputy Chief of Staff.

Even before Mrs Malone returned to confirm that Security were coming right on up, he'd read the letters, assimilated the contents, answered them or dismissed them from his mind. Nothing, but nothing, had to clutter his thoughts. 'Problems?' volunteered Mrs Malone.

'Maybe. Just a few.' He stroked his thin eyebrows which ran like stilettos beneath his forehead.

'Why? We're riding high on Wall Street. Is there any serious problem?'

'Nothing I can't handle with the right guys around me. But

do I have them? Do I hell!' He nodded his head in reflection, adjusted his gold-rimmed half-glasses and fingered the pencil-line moustache. 'Drustein only exists because I backed my judgement. Maybe I've made one or two mistakes, mainly with people. Take a rodeo. You watch a tight-assed cowboy ride a bronco. OK he may get bucked. Or maybe he won't. The good ones are always in control. One against one.' He shook his head slowly. 'Now Drustein's too big for that. It's not one on one any more. You get to our size, you've got to have goddamned Vice-Presidents, executives, each one a weak link. They can bring you down.'

This was not the Schillen that Mrs Malone knew and for a moment she almost liked him, though she'd as soon make love to a spider-crab as feel Schillen crawling all over her. The door opened and two men from Security arrived. 'I want the executive suite double-checked. You've got five minutes.' Schillen asked Mrs Malone to leave as he spoke to the senior of the two men. 'I want to be certain that no one has any record of the meeting. How can I be sure?'

'With my help, sir, it's easy.' Jim McCabe grinned as he spoke. 'I just leave this little fella here on the corner of your desk. Each of your guests walks past it to go into the executive suite.' He flourished a small box about the size of a travelling clock. 'If any of them is carrying anything with magnetic tape or a transmitting facility, the needle here will register. If they're clean, then the needle won't even flicker.'

'That's fine. You just do that thing then, er, Mr McCabe.'

'And if it registers? What do I do? Apprehend and search?'

'No. You put the name in a sealed envelope and ask Mrs Malone to bring it in. And you, Mr McCabe, if you value your job, will then say nothing.'

'You know me, sir. The ultimate Drustein man.'

The Dallas Dilemma

'OK, OK. I don't need a testimonial. Just keep your lousy mouth shut.'

* * *

Superficially, the meeting was informal. Shirt-sleeves were in order though the room was cool. Designed to seat thirty round the long, smoked glass table, the four men seemed almost incongruous, gathered at one end, a cloak of secrecy around them. Though the meeting had been in progress for an hour and the coffee-pot had emptied and been re-filled, the ashtrays at each place setting remained empty. No one ever smoked at a Marcus Schillen meeting. 'Keeps lives long and meetings short,' he'd once said, or so the legend ran.

They were sitting, two and two, facing each other, four men aware that their decisions would set Drustein on an irrevocable course, though only Schillen knew that if the scheme went wrong, he could unpack his hopes of a desk in the White House and the prospect of Lucille, eager and welcoming his advances.

Todd Kranski, who had once been bright and fresh-faced, looked worn. For ten years he'd been groomed to replace Schillen if the corporate Lear-Jet fell from the sky, but since the Lusifren crisis Schillen had grown scornful of Kranski's unreadiness to stick it out. Sure, Kranski's good qualities remained, Schillen thought as he stared across the table at the thirty-eight year old. The man was shrewd, fast thinking and his honesty was transparent. But for Chrissake! Who wanted honesty now? As a quality it was old hat, irrelevant to the business in hand.

No, Schillen thought, what Drustein needed was the poker-faced indifference of Julius Weissman, the nasal New Yorker in whom integrity had never existed. And Ed Bechrach too, the attorney, who had been corrupted by twenty years of working for Schillen. The attorney's past misdemeanours for Drustein had made him easy fodder for Schillen's Augean stables. The overheads of Bechrach's law firm, twenty-seven floors up on Main Street, were crippling and Schillen had only to emphasise the occasional discrepancy in the lawyers's affairs for Bechrach to follow him like a poodle on a spring morning. Now? Now, there was no instruction which Bechrach could refuse.

'Over to you, Ed. I suggest we look at this video from London.' Schillen's face broke into a smile and yet it wasn't a smile at all. 'Anyone feel lonely without a broad to fondle while watching a movie?' Only Bechrach laughed at the crudity, but then he was ever the chameleon ready to adopt Schillen's hue. He flicked a switch and the face of Rob Laidlaw appeared. To the watchers he came over as a natural, enjoying a sharp turn of phrase, a polished performer, ever so English, who kept his hands still and made his eyes dance to retain the viewers' involvement. 'And what is your Association's next aim?' the interviewer had enquired.

'That's simple. We're holding a public meeting for Lusifren victims. Relatives are of course welcome. Then my Association will spearhead the most formidable UK attack on Drustein in the history of the pharmaceutical industry. We shall join forces with a Dallas lawyer and Drustein, big though they are, powerful though they may be, will be unable to resist the onslaught which we're going to make. We have the funds, limitless funds, but beyond that, we have the determination, the single-minded determination not simply to seek massive compensation but also to find the truth as to how this drug came to be marketed.'

The interview ended and in Dallas none of the watchers said a word until Schillen insisted it be played back again. Only after the re-run did Bechrach speak. 'I told you we'd landed something real hot in Europe.'

'Who in hell's name is . . . Rob . . . Laidlaw?' said Schillen.

'Like the programme said,' replied Bechrach. 'He's a trouble-shooter, a Robin Hood without the green hat.'

'His arrows are sharp enough.' Schillen's remark struck home. Each of them, even Weissman, had been shaken by the determined strength which Laidlaw had demonstrated. 'He's got charisma. He's got that fixed determined look which will make people follow him to the ends of the earth. I guess he's trouble.'

'So we fix him?' Bechrach was testing the extent of Schillen's alarm but, on seeing no positive reaction, hastily backtracked. 'OK . . . we . . . compromise him?' Bechrach was searching for words to please Schillen.

'Maybe. We sure as hell don't start writing cheques for compensation. We admit nothing. The line which we've drawn stays. This English wise-guy changes nothing. We shouldn't over-react. Julius – give us a quick run down. Where do we stand?'

Weissman liked being brought in at this point, for it emphasised his increasing authority over Todd Kranski who was sitting slightly hunched, examining his fingernails in minute detail. 'I agree. This Laidlaw fella's nothing, pure hype and bullshit. Hell, we've got two thousand lawsuits being handled by Inge Loftin. She may look like a Hollywood extra but as a lawyer she's mean, real mean and yet we've held the line against her. So why panic over some loud-mouthed Brit.'

'But she's just about to see our research documents.' It was Kranski who had spoken, his voice calm, his intervention full of purpose. 'This is where she starts to score points. Am I right?'

'What do you think Julius?' Schillen's eyes gave away nothing of his own instincts.

'Look. Don't listen to Todd. He doesn't understand. *I* do because I've worked every night sifting through the documents. I'm satisfied that when sweet Inge has read what we've produced, when she's interrogated everybody, she's still not going to know what may have happened. Jesus Christ! If we start paying out compensation, our stock'll drop through the floor. It's almost impossible to get insurance cover as it is. If we call on our insurers to pay now, I guess we'll be uninsurable.' He paused to sip coffee. 'We can ride this one. We can drag out these compensation claims for so long, so goddamned long, that the victims will be dead. So will their children and their grandchildren too. We can hold this thing. I'm telling you Marcus, *I'm* not running scared.'

'Good. I'm glad.' Now that he'd heard from Weissman, Schillen wanted to make his own views known before Bechrach spoke, but held back. 'And you Ed?'

The attorney knew now which way to vote. 'Inge Loftin's tough. She and Laidlaw may give us trouble. I go along with Julius. We can ride it. Anyway, I don't like the alternative.'

'Schillen turned to Kranski. 'I'm sorry Todd. I agree with the others. However big the bomb, however severe the fallout, we'll be tucked up neatly in our shelter. Sleeping sweetly. We fight.' As he spoke, his thoughts were very much of the White House, the well-kept lawns, the fountains, the power. If Drustein were going to pay up, it was better to do it after the election. 'If we pay out now, those guys at the Food and Drug Administration may wonder why and carry on sniffing anyway. And I for one want to avoid a jail rap. As it is, they know *nothing*.'

'And we mustn't forget Max Gossop deceased.' Bechrach looked at Schillen and then Kranski. He saw the irritation on Schillen's face as an unwelcome subject was raised.

'Max? What's he got to do with it?' Kranski's face was furrowed. 'He was knocked over in an accident.'

The Dallas Dilemma

'Sure, sure. Let's stick to the point,' retorted Schillen evasively. 'Well I hope this isn't *your* Watergate. I'd hate to see us boxed into a corner.' Kranski lowered his eyelids. He was wasting his time. He knew it. Schillen, Weissman and Bechrach had turned into pillars of salt long before. 'Lusifren is banned in every Western country. Some side effects have been mind-bending, yet here we are pretending it's not our fault.'

'Todd, I for one don't need you as the keeper of my conscience.' Schillen's finger pointed in angry accusation. 'You take it or leave it. It's agreed we hold the line. Any occasional adverse reaction during testing was of no statistical significance. That doesn't make us liable to anyone. How are sales in the Third World?' Schillen's question was aimed at Weissman but it was Kranski who stepped in first.

'Third World?'

'Sure. We had to sell it somewhere and while you were on vacation, our sales boys found markets in South America and Africa. All the drug houses do it. You know that Todd. So don't try moralising. We're selling Lusifren to these countries because it's not banned. If they thought it was bad they wouldn't allow it in.'

Kranski's voice exploded and his face darkened. 'Don't expect me to swallow that crap. You think these two-bit regimes in barely civilised countries can form a view about Lusifren? In moral degradation, this is the pits. We *know* that Lusifren kills and maims. It's obscene.' He looked every inch the College quarterback which he'd been.

'*I* determine marketing strategy,' said Weissman. 'Anyway we need the money for further research.'

Kranski was really angry now; gone was his earlier diffidence. 'Unless you change your minds over this, you'll have my resignation after the weekend. I may well resign anyway.'

Even before Schillen could speak, Weissman had done so, the narrow face almost hidden behind the large black glasses. 'I vote you quit now.'

Schillen coughed into the back of his hand. 'No, Julius. I don't agree. I respect Todd's views. He should have time to think it over and so should we. You see, Todd, we have a superior duty to our stockholders to fight hard for what we believe in. Lusifren does work and selling to the Third World does make profits and it's not illegal. So think about it.'

Schillen was about to continue when his secretary entered the room. 'Yes, Lucille?' She handed Schillen a sealed envelope which he opened but he said nothing, simply refolding the paper and putting it in his top pocket. 'Todd, I think you said you were weekending at San Antonio.'

'That's right.' Kranski's voice was slightly breathless with emotion. 'It's our fourteenth wedding anniversary this weekend. Not much of a celebration now.'

'Well you go right on and enjoy yourself. Think it over down there. We'd like you in, but if you feel uncomfortable, then I shall accept your resignation.' He paused to stare cold-eyed at Kranski. 'I guess the way you're feeling at the moment you'd be happier to leave this meeting now.' The voice was silken.

Kranski nodded. 'Yes, it would be preferable.' He pushed back his chair and stood up.

'There's one thing. Before you go, I want you to leave your cassette recorder.' Schillen was still smiling as he spoke. 'I guess I'm a bit surprised at you, Todd. Thinking of writing your memoirs, were you?' The sarcasm was heavy. 'I said there were to be no notes taken.' His voice was not raised, though it contained the usual hint of gun-metal grey. Kranski blanched and stood uneasily, wondering how Schillen had found out. He fumbled in the breast pocket of his jacket and handed over a slim recorder. Then he rose without a word and left the room.

Immediately the door closed Weissman stood and smashed one fist into the palm of his other hand. 'That son-of-a-bitch. He was setting us up, trying to get us to incriminate ourselves on record.' He looked out of the window and watched Kranski reverse his Pontiac with more speed than prudence before accelerating down the tree-lined boulevard leading to North Central. 'But Marcus! For Christ's sake, why didn't you take his resignation?'

'No one can prove what was said today. If he had resigned and had got away with his recording, he'd have put out a press release. This way I reckon we've silenced him for the weekend. If he's going to talk to the Press, it'll be on Monday. But I don't see that as a problem.' He tapped the side of his nose and looked over the top of his glasses. 'Not if you *really* think about it.'

Weissman laughed. Bechrach's smile was rather forced. 'Point taken.'

'That's settled. Over to you Ed for that one. Let's just think about Laidlaw now.' Schillen glanced at Weissman. 'Any ideas?'

'I've got just one. It'll be enough. We can fix Laidlaw.'

'Right, Julius. Shoot.'

London

'Next time you think about going on TV, don't bother.' Sandie was not altogether joking as the taxi changed lanes en route to the public meeting. In the week since the broadcast, the telephone had never stopped ringing.

'I don't know. British Telecom shares are rocketing. What's more, Sir Victor's pleased. Overnight the Association has changed from puppy to bulldog. But we've achieved nothing yet. We're heroes without having even fought a war.'

'It's the press. They love a good story. And this is real *Boys' Own Paper* stuff. I see the *Mail* called you a 'knight in shining armour'. It shows how little they know you.'

'Rubbish!' He winked at her. 'It doesn't matter *what* you are. It's what they *want* you to be.' The taxi stopped at the hotel in Piccadilly. 'We've half an hour until the meeting starts. If you check the microphones and so on in the main room, I'll watch out for the other speakers.'

'Meaning the Professor and your lady lawyer from Dallas?' Sandie hadn't meant to sound jealous about Inge Loftin but it certainly came out that way. Why did this scourge of the drug companies have to be so attractive? The previous afternoon Laidlaw had noticed that Sandie had bristled at the arrival of the Texan honey blonde, resenting her looks which made her immediate centre stage. He looked at Sandie as she paused momentarily in the rain-flecked wind and realised that she had been changing her image, re-styling her black hair so that it caressed her cheeks. Gone too was the sack-like handbag. It looked as though she was coming out of the closet marked 'drab'. He was still puzzling over this as he left her and joined Sir Victor in the small ante-room. 'Morning Rob. This is a very proud day. The last week has made my wife's suffering so much less hard for me to bear.'

'How is she? Any change?'

'No. I tell her what we're doing – what you're doing. She understands what's going on. That's the cruelty of it. Can you imagine her? She'll be at home now, her brain a prisoner of a body which can't do anything. She can't move a finger, a toe, an eyelid. Just slumped in her wheelchair, waiting for me to come home and talk to her. The nurse is fine but I know that she recognises my voice and sometimes I like to think there's a flicker of a smile when I amuse her.' It was rare for Sir Victor to open up like this. He put a hand on each of Laidlaw's shoulders. 'This battle you're waging means a lot to me. Out of the darkness that surrounds me, you give me the glimmer of light.' The hands clenched his shoulders tighter. 'Don't let me down.' Laidlaw saw just a hint of watering at the eyes as the tycoon's emotion got the better of him.

Rob Laidlaw nodded, uncertain how to respond. 'Don't forget Sandie's role in all this. She's worked really hard.'

'I don't, but you're the spark. By the way,' he spoke confidentially, 'can you tell me before anyone else is around, is all OK with our . . . Middle Eastern friend?'

The door opened before Laidlaw could answer. It was Professor Hugh Waddington, who, at Adawi's insistence had 'volunteered' to be honorary medical adviser to the Association. 'Morning gentlemen,' he burred at them, his weathered face revealing that beneath the dour granite, he too had been touched by the atmosphere of the big occasion. After an exchange of pleasantries with Sir Victor, the specialist continued. 'Thank you for inviting me to be on the platform. There's been a lot of rubbish written in the paper during the last week. Lusifren's not all bad. For every person suffering, wanting a cure or seeking compensation, there's another taking part in sports thought beyond them, walking distances and living lives thought to have been lost forever – thanks to Lusifren.'

Rob Laidlaw's face showed his disappointment. It was the reverse of what he needed to hear, a sobering balance to the near gladiatorial atmosphere in the assembly room next door. The rising clamour of voices in the audience seemed to suggest that Laidlaw's mandate would be to tear the Drustein board limb from limb. 'Don't dishearten the audience.' He was concerned, and the peremptory instruction showed it. 'Remember, the press are here and remember Drustein will be reading every word that's said.' He was about to expand on the warning when Inge Loftin appeared, resplendent in a powder blue suit with a white silk frilled blouse. He knew from the previous day that her eyes were much the same colour as the suit. If anything she looked even more stunning, all the better for wearing a skirt rather than trousers, because now her shapely calves were revealed and she looked every inch of her five foot nine, her golden hair, parted down the middle, the ends flicking up just above her neck-line. Her jewellery, though simple, was magnificent – eye-catching without being ostentatious. Anyone thinking that Americans lacked class, had never met Inge Loftin.

Laidlaw took a few paces towards her and waited while she switched her small attaché case from right to left before shaking her hand, immediately aware of the cool, assured grip which she gave him. 'Good morning, everyone.' Immediately all eyes were on her, just as they had been on a thousand previous occasions. Her face was small, almost oval, and deeply tanned by the Dallas sun. The eyebrows were faint but fair, the lips coloured slightly with pink. Her eyes were generously wide set to match her mouth and, her nose was slightly aquiline yet anyone looking less like a hard-nosed American lawyer was difficult to conceive. As he watched her introducing herself, Laidlaw reasoned that she could not be less than thirty-six, if only to have acquired her national reputation, but the years did not show. Plenty of English lawyers, their faces battered by the daily grind and stress of litigation, would have welcomed the secret of Inge Loftin's durability.

Sir Victor, always one to appreciate glamour, and smiling broadly, took her hand. 'I'm the President of the Association and we do thank you for flying over like this at short notice. I hope you enjoy your stay.'

'I sure will. I really do appreciate the privilege of representing the Association, though please make no mistake: I'm not like Mr Laidlaw here, I'm no knight in shining armour.' Her smile came from beneath half closed lids and showed her pleasure in putting over the fact that she'd done her homework. 'While I have every sympathy for Lusifren victims, I did mention to Rob on the telephone about contingency fees. I get a percentage of the damages if we win. I hate mentioning it when so many people have suffered. I hope it doesn't sound too mercenary.'

'No, no.' Sir Victor was quick to reassure her. 'We understand that. No foal, no fee, and if what Rob tells me is right, you're prepared to take on these cases for thirty per cent of the damages.'

'That's right.' With her southern drawl, Inge Loftin made even that comment seem like a speech. Just listening to her evoked images of rolling prairies swept by warm breezes. In truth she was as sharp as a cactus needle.

'And if I read you correctly,' said Sir Victor, 'thirty per cent means you think we've a very good chance of success. For the bad cases you'd want a bigger percentage?'

'That's partly right. Thirty per cent also reflects that you sure are giving me a lot of claims. I'm well on with the main test cases against Drustein and so I do assure you there's no charity in my fee. I just believe, just know, I'm going to win. Nothing and nobody will stop me.' She spoke with disarming candour and, as he listened, Laidlaw felt drawn to her, captivated by the subtleness of her glances which punctuated the contrasting bluntness of her style. For a second he found himself wondering about her private life.

'Did I make it clear that we have full media coverage?' he enquired of Inge. The Texan shook her head. 'I didn't know that. I rather thought this was a private meeting – between friends, between the committed.'

'So it is but the Association needs all the publicity it can get.'

'I'm glad you told me. I'll water down the poison. I'm told your laws of libel are tough and Schillen's lawyers at Drustein wouldn't hesitate to sue.'

Anything else then, before we go in?' enquired Rob.

'Yes. Just one little thing.' Inge Loftin put down her grey suede case and flipped open the lid. Inside, everything was as orderly as the neat rows of facts, arguments and points of order which she always carried in her head. She produced a copy of the *Dallas Morning News* and pointed to an article which the three men clustered round to read.

DOUBLE TRAGEDY

Drustein's Vice-President Todd Kranski, 38, and his wife Rachel, 35, were stabbed to death while passing a romantic weekend, enjoying the San Antonio Riverwalk. Their bodies were found by Earl Sanders, 28, shortly after 11.00 p.m., Saturday, beneath St. Mary's Bridge. The couple had no children.

'He represented all that was good in our corporation and in the community,' said a shocked Marcus Schillen, President of Drustein, speaking from his headquarters overlooking North Central Highway. 'Todd's savage death is an indictment on the people of America. That such a valuable life should be taken for a few credit cards and a fistful of dollars seems unthinkable. Though I knew Rachel less well, to me she was just one wonderful person.'

San Antonio police are pursuing a number of lines of enquiry and have interviewed persons known to loiter near the bus stop on St. Mary's Bridge but no early arrest is expected.

'I'm surprised you didn't show this to me yesterday.' Laidlaw's remark was not chiding, merely direct and matter of fact. So was her reply.

'I wasn't ready to discuss it yesterday. Now I am. If you're in the wrong place at the wrong moment, you get mugged. When I read it, I believed that Todd Kranski was mugged. But I got to thinking. Most muggings don't end in death, especially not double murder like this. And I said to myself, "just suppose that they were murdered deliberately. Who would want to do it? and why?"'

'And the answer?' Rob looked deep into the blue of her eyes.

'The Drustein board is divided. Kranski was a dove, a good man. Now just suppose that he was too good. Just suppose that he knew something. In those circumstances his death would have been quite convenient to Marcus Schillen.'

'And is Drustein's board divided?'

'Sure. There's not much I don't know. And what I don't know I'm going to find out. You want to know the size of Schillen's shoes? You just ask Inge Loftin. You want to know who he's crossed? What his wealth is? His ambition? You just ask Inge Loftin. Then think about Todd becoming . . . inconvenient to Marcus Schillen. Finally, think again about Todd and his pretty wife Rachel. Think of them, with their throats cut.' It was a good closing line and she snapped her case shut, knowing that she'd removed the pin on the grenade with impeccable timing. It was the kind of crescendo to leave with a jury, lots of emotion and not much fact.

Sir Victor, face pensive at what he'd heard, looked at his watch and broke the silence – matter of fact as usual. 'It's time to go in.' So saying he led them through the doorway on to the rostrum, their arrival greeted by spontaneous applause and the flashing of bulbs from the dozen or so photographers who'd awaited the moment. Laidlaw looked at the throng of well over two hundred people. 'Nothing less than blood will satisfy this lot,' he muttered to Inge as they sat down to listen to Sir Victor's brief introduction. 'So without further ado, I will now call on Rob Laidlaw,' he ended.

As he stood at the podium, Laidlaw noticed that, unusually for him, his hands were shaking and, as he saw the upturned faces, he felt the full weight of his responsibility. As he started to speak, he mentally reassured himself that the best public speakers are nervous on important occasions. He could just see Inge Loftin from the corner of his eye and he wondered what impression he was making on her, the professional speaker, the professional manipulator of words and minds.

Gradually, he settled down, improving his timing as he headed for his conclusion. 'And so I can say that, though you may not think it, you are indeed the lucky ones. Let us not forget all those who have written to me begging for help but who are too unwell to attend; let us not forget all those who, despite all the publicity, are still unaware that we are here to help; let us not forget all those who are too sick to have the determination to fight any more.' He paused, his hands clasping either side of the lectern and leant forward as if he were looking at each of his audience in turn. 'Let us not forget all those who, since taking Lusifren . . . are now dead.' Except for the whirr of the cameras, the packed room was silent, not even a cough breaking the climax of the speech, until suddenly the moment was shattered as a voice from the middle of the room cried out. 'Then let's get the bastards! They killed my father.'

The interruptor was a mere lad, maybe eighteen, but certainly not twenty. From round the room there were mixed reactions – murmurings of assent mixed with tut-tuts of disapproval and Laidlaw knew that it was vital to pitch his comment just right. 'I understand how strongly you feel but today we are gathered in a concerted effort to obtain justice. We are on a *crusade* . . . *not* a witch hunt. We shall seek that truth ruthlessly and relentlessly. If we find that Drustein and its officers marketed the drug in good faith, then we shall say so. If we find corruption and chicanery then yes indeed, bastards they shall be called.' The audience loved it, clapping overgenerously, the feeling of a lynch mob subsiding. 'And I am now going to introduce Inge Loftin from Dallas, Texas. She's an expert in these claims with a reputation second to none. Better still, she tells me that she's had the privilege of actually *meeting* JR.' The audience were ready for a bit of flippancy and the laughter reflected an outburst of nervous energy. There was applause as Laidlaw sat down and she rose to her feet.

'Well, I thank you Rob,' she drawled. 'That was a most flattering introduction.' Her smile was broad and warm and the audience seemed to love her instantly, ready to laugh with her as she moved into her introduction, explaining about compensation and legal proceedings in the States, using simple, straightforward language. 'But if I can complicate things for a moment, I must mention a Latin phrase because it is the right one to use. "Forum non conveniens" is a maxim which we have in the States. People who were prescribed Lusifren in England will be met with arguments from Drustein's lawyers that the litigation should take place in England. They will say that London is the convenient *forum*. Why will they do that? Not because it is more convenient. No sir. I'll tell you why.' She waited for her moment. 'They'd rather litigate in England because damages are far less. An award of £100,000 in England could well be £4 million in the States.' She nodded as she saw the stunned looks around the room. 'What's more, the procedures which we have for getting at Drustein's documents are tougher than yours. If a corporation wants to conceal the truth, then it's easier to do it in England.' She thought of the laws of libel and added a sweetener. 'But no corporation, including Drustein, however innocent it *may* be, likes to have its affairs investigated and its documents examined, so naturally the question of *jurisdiction* has to be considered. My view is that even although you were prescribed Lusifren here in England, since the research was done in Texas, you have the right to file suit in Dallas.'

Laidlaw realised that he'd been staring at her almost non-stop. Inge Loftin sat down. 'Brilliant, wasn't she,' whispered Sandie, anxious to conceal her confused feelings. Laidlaw nodded before rising to introduce Professor Waddington who was, in contrast, dry and matter of fact.

The Dallas Dilemma

When Laidlaw finally stood up to thank the Harley Street specialist, he felt deflated. Given that it was Waddington who had prescribed Lusifren for one particular patient, it was hardly surprising that he should be defensive. With hindsight, Rob wished he had talked Sir Victor out of asking the professor to speak at today's meeting, or failing that, that Waddington had spoken before Inge Loftin so that the occasion could have ended on a higher note. Too late for regrets. 'Today, we have been conducting our affairs in a goldfish bowl and I suggest that you elect a committee of five who will join with us to meet in private to supervise your claims and jointly we shall keep you informed of what is happening. We ought not to be discussing our tactics any further in the public eye. However, before electing a committee, I now ask for questions from the floor. You've heard plenty, I'm sure you've got plenty to ask.'

And they had. The questions varied from the inane, inept and inappropriate to the bitter and vindictive, with all shades of the spectrum reflected in the middle. Of hostility or antagonism to the platform there was none until a mean-faced man with pebble-dash glasses rose to his feet. 'Mr Laidlaw, this American lawyer has told us that litigation USA style is not like having tea at Claridges. Would we not all do better with a *man* as our lawyer.' He sat down abruptly to roars of disapproval. Laidlaw was about to respond when Inge Loftin touched him on the arm, motioning that she was going to reply herself.

'If I understand the gentleman's point, he wants a man for a lawyer – a man who can deliver. To him I would say just this.' She smiled across twenty yards of faces at him. 'I certainly had to deliver the goods to earn my reputation. And by the time the Lusifren case is over, you'll be agreeing that I fight as hard as any man – maybe harder.'

* * *

Lunch was over and everyone had gone, leaving Laidlaw and Sandie back in his office, able to mull over the morning's events. 'You won't thank me for saying it, Rob, but, while she's a great lawyer, I reckon her private life would be no different from her public image. The strengths which she shows in public will be weaknesses in her real self.' As Sandie sat, face and eyes downcast, it was easy to dismiss her views as partisan. She looked so young, so forlorn.

'Sandie, you're probably right but it's no good lecturing me. I'm a sucker for her and, rightly or wrongly, I'm taking her out to dinner tonight. Why not come along? You might change your views.'

She tried to smile but the muscles in her face were too taut to relax and she shook her head in refusal. 'Be the gooseberry? You go ahead, Rob. Treat her like a lawyer and you'll be all right. Treat her like a lover . . . and there'll be disaster.' Rob could see her temples throbbing and, as he looked into the young, uncomplicated face, he hated the way he was upsetting her. 'I'm sure you've misunderstood her. Please come along.'

The response was firm, almost vehement. 'No. I haven't misunderstood anything. Y'all be sure and have a good time.' She broke into an exaggerated mimicking of the Texan drawl and immediately regretted her display of bitterness. Laidlaw felt uncomfortable and, after smiling uneasily, left without a word.

* * *

'I've just had *the* most won-der-ful afternoon here in London. I saw the Palace, Trafalgar Square, had tea at Fortnum and Mason's, shopped in Harrods, then back for a hot tub to relax. And you're taking me to . . . I don't know where. But wherever it is, it's going to be great.' So enthused Inge Loftin as she sat in the darkened cab as it sped along Bayswater Road towards Queensway.

'It's a pity you're going back tomorrow. What time's the flight?'
'10.30 from Gatwick. By mid afternoon, Dallas time, I shall be there. With a full desk awaiting attention.'

'And with a full bank account needing no attention.' Rob Laidlaw saw that she was amused and her response was to rest her hand gently on his arm and so he added: 'you American lawyers have it made.'

'The money isn't easy. As you'll see when you're over. We really put the hours in. Ask Harvey.'

'Harvey? Is he your husband?'

'Sure. He's not the rabbit! I'm married to him but the divorce will soon be through. Meantime we have what in Dallas is known as an open marriage.'

'Open marriage? What does that mean in London?'

'Well, I don't know. It means we each kinda drifted into a situation, probably on the rebound from someone else. And it was OK but no more than that. Harvey's a senator, spends most of his time in Washington. Occasionally he telephones, that's when he isn't chasing all those females who hang around Capitol Hill. Secretaries, they're called. Power groupies, I call them.' It was said without rancour, a deadpan report on a dead marriage. The cab was slowing up outside the restaurant now. 'I guess that's what you'd call an open marriage. Here or anywhere.'

'And your part in that?' Laidlaw awaited a response but Inge said nothing, just tightened her grip on his sleeve, judging that there was no need to answer as the cab stopped and Rob settled up the fare. 'And this,' said Laidlaw, changing the subject 'is the Restaurant Chateau D'If. It's not the best in London but who can say which is? It's French, classically French and I don't suppose you have anything like that in Dallas.'

'You may be surprised when you come over. It's not all

cow-pokes and spitoons. What we don't have in Dallas . . . nobody has.' She made a most convincing commercial as they entered the small reception area and their coats were taken. Moving down the stairs they descended into the semi-gloom of a timeless atmosphere where, as they sat in the plushness of red velvet, vodka tonics appeared almost before they had placed the order. 'Is it night? Or is it day?' she laughed.

'You don't know down here. But then maybe neither did the people who worked here before it was a restaurant. This was an old bakery. You can see the oven in the wall. I bet you don't have bread ovens like that in Dallas?'

'Sure, they'll be made of plastic and have adverts for Coca-Cola across the front. Sure, we have everything in Dallas, everything, that is, but the natural chic of London or Paris. Now, that's something we *really* envy.' They ordered Dover sole and a Montrachet to go with it before demolishing another couple of drinks, almost without noticing.

'You know a lot more about Drustein than you've told me so far?' said Laidlaw.

For answer she leant forward and placed a hand on his hand, bringing her face close to his in a conspiratorial movement. Laidlaw wondered whether all women lawyers were as tactile or whether it was just those from Dallas. He could smell her perfume, almost feel the flutter of her eyelids, could certainly sense a vibrancy which crackled through her. 'Lawyers volunteer information only on payment but, if *you* ask the right questions, you may get the right answers.' The hand on his stroked gently, creating deliberate ambiguity in the comment.

Laidlaw's clean shaven and open face creased in surprise and then laughter. 'Let's go through. They're ready for us. We'll carry on this conversation there.' They followed the waiter through to the small table with pink linen and white chairs, where they were seated face to face. 'So what do you know about Drustein . . . which you didn't tell me today . . . or yesterday come to that?' he asked.

'I didn't tell you that their lawyer, Ed Bechrach, is unscrupulous. I couldn't announce that to anyone. Ask most any lawyer in Dallas, they'll tell you. He wasn't always dishonest. Just got corrupted, defiled by clients like Marcus Schillen until, bit by bit, he was sucked into the swamp of their deviousness. Now he'd do anything, fix anything, for the annual million bucks guarantee which he gets as his retainer from Drustein.'

'A million dollars!'

'Their President, Marcus Schillen, is a multi-millionaire. He fought to create the corporation and his defence of Lusifren will be ruthless – that is unless we can pin something on him. If he's got half a chance of escape, he will. Drustein has been issuing routine press releases, you know the kind of thing . . . "every drug is dangerous; every drug has side effects; it's a question of *balance* and Lusifren falls on the right side of the balance. That's why the FDA approved it; that's why the FDA were wrong to ban it; that's why the FDA are facing a suit from my company. They were *wrong* to ban it. Every day it's banned, more people suffer more pain because they have not taken it. Drustein regrets the occasional ill-effects but asks that it be judged in perspective." And so it goes on. Even with a cold I could smell a skunk and boy, believe me, there's some strange smells wafting over North Central from the Drustein camp. Security there is very tight but the murder of the Kranskis has convinced me. If we keep on digging, we're going to unearth not just a skeleton but an entire burial ground of deceit.'

Laidlaw smiled, before turning to the chilled soup, shaking his head slowly as if in disbelief. 'So you really do think that Schillen and Bechrach could have set up Kranski's murder?'

'Sure. Puppet and puppet master. Kranski was a threat, the guy with the halo, surrounded by shysters with cloven hooves.' She extended her long brown arms which were bare from the shoulders of her black, sleeveless dress. Again she stroked each of his hands, completing a magic circle which tingled all through him. 'But understand, I've only got pointers; that and my gut feeling about the Drustein empire. That's what guiding me.' As Laidlaw listened, he wondered why he didn't bridle at her self-confidence. Others might have found her vain. To him she came across so naturally, but then maybe the mellow pinks and whites of the room with the greenery hanging from the walls neutered the bluntness in her style. 'Anyway we've spoken far too much about me and Drustein. What about you? You look too happy to be married. Am I right?'

'I hadn't thought of it like that. Just call me happy.' He thought about it. He usually *was* happy but Inge's presence seemed to have given him extra zest. 'You're right. I've never been married, though I've drifted dangerously close. I'm in no hurry.' He smiled at her as he added the commercial. 'And there's no one around at the moment.' Inge was quick to notice the muscles round his eyes tighten just a fraction.

'Come off it. Married to the Association? And what about Sandie? She's real cute and I saw the way she was looking at you.' Laidlaw tried to avoid her gaze but couldn't and was glad that he would never have to be cross-examined by her. 'She's crazy about you.'

'Maybe she is. I don't know. We have a love-hate business relationship but nothing more. That's the way I want to keep it.'

'OK, Rob, if it's not women then you're sure holding out on me about something. Shoot.' Her eyes gave him a dressing down and he knew that she wasn't joking.

'Holding out?' he blustered. 'No. Nothing I can think of.' He knew that he was blushing and couldn't control it. God! How he wanted to tell her the real reason why the Association had taken up the Lusifren claims but there was no way that he could tell her about Shaikh Ahmed. 'I'm not gay, an alcoholic or a leather fetishist.' He joked his way out of her question.

She laughed but was not fooled. 'My instincts are invariably right. They tell me that you're holding out. So remember, Rob Laidlaw, if you want the best out of me, then you've got to trust me. You'd better believe it.' She smiled but the smile was less warm than before, more a warning smile, intent on telling him that fun was fun and business was business. And that she hadn't believed him.

'How did you enjoy the soup?' he changed the subject but thinking of Inge's speech that morning . . . there were women and women. There was Inge . . . and there was Sandie. Each of them women, each of them desirable for different reasons, yet for Sandie he felt no such desire. Why?

'The consommé was great. Strange girl, Sandie,' said Inge, as if reading his thoughts and almost ignoring the question. 'She hangs on your every word.'

'You think so?' said Laidlaw thoughtfully, glad that she'd attributed his secretiveness to Sandie rather than divining the real reason.

'I know so.' Inge leant across to emphasise her closeness to him. 'So don't mislead me about that. I'm not in the business of hurting people like Sandie.'

'Me neither.' His cheeks dimpled in the breadth of his smile as his open good-naturedness showed through. He was rewarded by a cool, appraising look which gradually softened.

She moved her glass and sipped with appreciation. 'I could enjoy sitting here forever,' she said. 'So often back home we forget that a meal is an occasion, that it's really not about food but about people. In Dallas you'll see folks eating fast food real fast, just so that they can go somewhere else. To a bar maybe. There, they'll plan the next bar and end up in a hamburger joint on Greenville Avenue. That's where tomorrow's yuppies hang out. Me? I prefer the easier pace. That's why I enjoy an evening like this. But I love Dallas. So will you. But here . . . I just feel there's nowhere else I want to be, nowhere else I want to go.' She saw his eyebrows rise just a trifle and her eyes danced in a moment of amusement. 'Or not for a while anyway'.

'There's no hurry while the coffee and conversation are flowing. This last week I've lived for Lusifren, telephoning here, meetings there.' He stopped abruptly as he remembered something. 'Oh Christ! I really can't get away from Lusifren. You wanted those papers to take to Dallas. We'll have to go via the office.'

'Sure. That won't take long. And then where to?'

'My flat's close to Chelsea, not far from Cheyne Walk. Just the width of the river away. They call it Battersea.'

'I'd like to see it.'

London

As **the taxi** sped past the bright lights of Marble Arch the difference between day and night disappeared. Endless lines of cars met and intertwined, jockeying for position before the sprint down Park Lane. Only when the driver turned into the streets of Mayfair did night return with dark empty pavements and heavily curtained windows. The occasional vehicle ferrying between the gaming clubs and the expense account glitter of the Park Lane hotels broke the stillness.

During the drive Inge had found it hard to keep herself from clasping him, stroking the nape of his neck as he sat close beside her, his arm loosely draped across her shoulder. A real hunk of a man, she told herself as she glanced sideways at his profile. She shouldn't be feeling like this, not so soon after splitsville with Harvey. Forget it. Like it or not, she'd stumbled on someone who sent waves of rampant desire through her.

She kissed him lightly, aware of the hint of expensive aftershave on the smooth cheek and he responded with a smile and a slight tightening of the arm across her shoulder. Fine, his looks, his melodious English accent had always been obvious but it was the clarity of thought and his underlying determination which had really struck home. When she'd read the press cuttings on the flight, she had seen him as all glitter, all surface, the usual PR creation. Their first meeting had changed all that and she'd been instantly impressed by the thoroughness of his research and the directness of his questioning.

'I don't think it's worth you waiting, Cabbie,' Laidlaw said as he paid off the driver and he and Inge stood in Hill Street outside the time-blackened building, the first floor of which housed the Association.

'Don't you find these old buildings kinda spooky?' Full of ghosts?' said Inge as he swung open the heavy door into the ground floor reception.

'No ghosts. Just history. Probably, up until 1914, this was one family's home, with the servants in the basement.' He pressed the timer switch which would light the way upstairs for two minutes, while underfoot their progress on the thick carpet was silent.

On arrival at the Association's suite, Laidlaw was about to insert the key when Inge saw his jaw tighten, his facial muscles flex and his eyes flash out concern. He motioned her quiet with a jabbing chop of his hand. She stood silently, watching his brow furrow as he stood, ear now pressed against the door, listening for the slightest movement. Instinctively she stretched out to hold him, wanting to feel part of him, as she leant forward to listen. Then she heard it, the faintest rattle but instantly identifiable as the noise of filing cabinet runners. She shuddered as she looked at him, her eyes wide and questioning but from him she saw no fear reflected – just resolute determination. It came as no surprise when he signalled to her to stay where she was while he gently slipped the key into the lock.

From inside came the further sound of movement. Unsure whether this was the Middle East connection, or Drustein undercover work, for a moment Laidlaw wondered whether to call the police. No. Adawi wanted confidentiality. He'd have to deal with this himself. Only for a second did he waver as he recalled Adawi's warnings of danger. Instantly, his throat was dry, his palms wet and he wondered whether, if alone, he'd have been as brave. He looked at his watch. In about twenty seconds, he reckoned, the timer would extinguish the lighting. That would be the moment to go in. He waited, watching the hand tick round until, with a click, the lights went out and the darkness on the landing became impenetrable.

Their thudding hearts seemed to intrude massively into the silence as he pulled her to him, so that he could whisper in her ear, the fragrance of her perfume seemingly highlighted by her fear. Against his neck he could feel her breathing, hot, short and excitingly close and, for a second he felt the urge to search out her mouth and kiss her in the fierce intensity of the moment. Speaking to her softly, yet in total command, he said: 'whatever happens, don't come in. Stay here in the dark. Only if things sound bad, fetch the police.'

'No police?' she wanted to comment but said nothing as he turned the key slowly, almost imperceptibly, until the door to the office was open. The sound of the intruder was more audible now as Laidlaw stood in the doorway, adjusting his keys so that the sharp edges of three of the Yales protruded spike-like from between his fingers, an instant knuckle-duster. Familiar office smells clouded his sense of danger: stale cigarettes, a touch of perfume, a hint of lemon from the office cleaners' air freshener and the cloying aroma of new carpets. The half-seen sights were familiar too and he could make out the receptionist's desk, the VDU and the silhouette of the word processor. To the left was the door to Sandie's office and next to that his own and Sir Victor's, the result of a neat sub-division of a room which, in the previous century, had been filled with Victorians, probably thirty or forty of them, banqueting greedily with a flurry of flunkies. The noise seemed to come from his own room.

Fist tightly clenched on his bunch of keys, he edged forward, avoiding the low coffee table and heading for the half open door into his room. There he waited, concerned that the sounds of his own fear were reverberating a tom-tom message to the ears of the intruder. If they were, there was no sign as the rattle and scrape of a filing cabinet drawer could be heard yet again. Adawi's warnings about security didn't seem melodramatic now. Not when he could see the dancing light from the torch which the person was using. Judging by the rustle of paper and by the changing silhouettes on the wall, the man was shining it on the files, picking out what he was looking for. Not that he'd find it, thought Laidlaw. Not if he were looking under 'A' for Adawi or 'A' for Ahmed.

How had the man got in? Not through the front. Not possible. He must have come up the fire escape which meant he had to come out of this door to get back to it. So what to do? Tackle him or wait till he emerged?

He'd wait.

The decision made, Laidlaw edged into the shadowy patch to the right of the door, well-positioned to grab the man from behind. Silently he inched sideways, so that he could stand unseen, but just as he'd got there, his right arm struck something, something which he'd forgotten about. The receiver on the wall telephone tumbled, dropping the length of its flex, clattering against the wall and swinging unseen like a pendulum beside him, while the whine of the dialling tone seemed as penetrating as the arrival of a police squad car.

The reaction from Laidlaw's office was instant. The torch was extinguished, the sound of search terminated. Divided only by the thickness of the partition, Laidlaw judged that he and the intruder were only three feet apart. He could imagine the man, equally scared now, silently wondering what to do, uncertain as to the significance of the sudden noise. Laidlaw, however, was quick to realise that his main asset, surprise, had gone. Now it was him and his knuckle-duster against a man armed with God knows what.

A stiletto?

His stomach churned at the thought of a knife slashing out in the darkness.

Neither man moved, Laidlaw out of fear and indecision, the intruder waiting for a further clue before acting. An interminable minute passed like this, then two and then three, before Laidlaw realised not only that he was cornered, but the whine from the phone was telegraphing his position. He had to move at once, get onto the landing, lock the external door and make the strike at the foot of the fire escape. With this in mind, he eased his way leftwards, knowing that, in a couple of feet, he would be beside the dividing door. After that he would be safe and able to scurry away. For those vital seconds he had to hope that the man on the other side was not himself moving.

But he was.

Impatient to see what had caused the noise, the man had crept to the door and just as Laidlaw was in front of it, he switched on the torch so that, although Laidlaw was not directly in the beam, nevertheless he felt as naked as if caught by a searchlight. As the torch moved, for an indelible second, the shape of a gun appeared like a picture from a black and white movie silhouetted on the distant wall of Laidlaw's office. Its edges blurred, its snub-size magnified, nevertheless, its menace was stark and clear.

Could he slam shut and then lock this door? Cut off the gunman on the other side? And then run like hell?

No, the key was on the other side. He was sure of that. But yes! Wait! Think! Yes . . . there was a bolt at the top of the door. On this side.

Right! Slam the door! Then bolt it and beat it.

He crouched down and moved the last sideways pace, hoping that the beam of the torch, if it suddenly swung in the right direction, would be aimed too high for an instant pick-out. He was ready. On the count of three he would spring, grab the handle and slam the door shut. And bolt it.

But he never reached the count of three, had barely reached two before there was a swift movement and, immediately in front of him was the burglar. The man's last step had been short but sudden as he'd swung the beam of the torch directly through the doorway, no doubt the gun also aimed in the same direction. Without further thought Laidlaw sprang, aiming for torch and gun, the keys still in his right hand, so that, with his left, he grasped the man's wrist and pulled it downwards, at the same moment slamming his head hard towards the man's midriff. Deafeningly close to him, the gun went off, the bullet searing into the carpet close to Laidlaw's foot.

If his head had struck the man where intended, they'd have both fallen, Laidlaw on top and the intruder disadvantaged but it hadn't been like that, the blow striking the edge of the rib cage so that the man, fit and lean as he was, met its force with only a temporary rocking on his heels. Now it was Laidlaw who was disadvantaged, one hand unable to release the grip on the wrist for fear of being shot, his head muzzy from hitting the man's ribs. All that was left was a bunch of Yale keys clenched in his hand and, with a short vicious jab, he aimed at where he suspected the man's genitals would be. The intruder let out a gasp of surprised pain, or perhaps it was a word in an unfamiliar language, as his head and shoulders sagged forward in reflex, while his arm tried to shake itself free.

For a second or two Laidlaw clung on but then the torch crashed down, fourteen inches of heavy rubber full of battery, striking Laidlaw on the right side of his skull. The room spun and his grip loosened as he slumped to the floor. The other man stepped over his body and ran.

When Laidlaw came round, his disorientated eyes and brain

saw two blurred faces. As focus returned, the lumpy throbbing pain remained and he recognised Inge and saw the anxious face of a young policeman. Through the window came the intermittent blue flashing of further emergency services arriving and, as he rose to his feet, unsteadily and with support from the policeman, the ambulance crew appeared with a stretcher.

Laidlaw leant against the wall, gingerly feeling his head. 'I'll be all right. I'm just a bit shaken.'

'I think you ought to go to hospital,' said the policeman. 'You've had a nasty blow. The bullet missed you though, did it? I was told there'd been a shooting.'

Laidlaw shook his head and wished that he hadn't as a wave of nausea swept through him. 'The bullet missed. I'll be all right.' His breath came unevenly between each word. 'Just need a few minutes to sit down,' he panted. With uncertain steps he moved to his desk and sat in the chair as the room continued to fill with more police officers arriving, including a Detective Sergeant Watkins, to whom he gave a thumbnail sketch of what had occurred. 'I must check to see what's missing.' He was aware of Inge hovering beside him while a doctor bathed the purple lump on his temple.

'I don't expect that he took anything,' said the detective. 'He's left his camera. Looks like he was photographing whatever interested him. He's picked the locks on the filing cabinet. Professional job, I'd say.'

Laidlaw saw that the intruder had worked methodically from bottom to top of the filing cabinet. All the Lusifren files were stacked neatly on the floor. 'We'll get the film developed and see what he photographed but do you have any idea what this is all about? Something to do with you being on the TV this morning, was it?'

'Possibly. If he were after the Lusifren files then the

manufacturers, Drustein, had the most to gain though I can't imagine any reputable company acting like this. So I wouldn't want to blame them.' Laidlaw's speech was slow and precise. Don't mention Adawi, he kept telling himself.

Watkins was making a note on his pad as Inge intervened. 'Well, let me tell you something,' she drawled. 'Back home I wouldn't put anything past Drustein. Boy, do some of these drug companies know how to play it rough. Even Machiavelli would have felt uncomfortable with some of them.'

Watkins looked unimpressed. 'Unless there's some hard evidence here to link the intruder with Lusifren, your theory, or maybe your wishes, will remain unfulfilled. No one saw the man's face. You say he left on a motor-bike, having gone down the fire escape.' He stopped to light a small cigar. 'He left his camera and there may be some fingerprints if we're lucky. Perhaps the ballistics boys may get somewhere but it's not exactly promising for imminent charges.'

Inge looked at him without saying anything and Laidlaw wondered whether Watkins was going to get a tongue full of scorn. But no. 'You win,' was all she said.

'Thank you.' Watkins then turned to Laidlaw. 'I want a statement from you. Would you like a lift down to the station?'

'No, don't bother,' Inge responded. 'We'll make our own way.' It was a command. Laidlaw looked at her with some surprise but said nothing, content to give his pounding head a rest, though there was not much chance of that as he discovered, while he walked with Inge through the chilly night air. From an upstairs window Watkins watched them disappear into the square, Laidlaw with his arm round Inge's shoulder, she with hers around his waist. And he could see that the woman was doing the talking and he'd have given anything to know what was being said. One thing was sure – Laidlaw hadn't been telling him the truth. Not all of it anyway.

'That was very brave. But very stupid,' she said to him and was rewarded with a sheepish look and a shrug.

'I was lucky. I never thought about a gun until it was too late.'

'But there's something else, isn't there Rob? That's why you went in yourself, why you wouldn't let me call the police. You're still holding out on me.' She forced him to stop so that she could face him. 'You know more about all this than you're saying. You think it wasn't Drustein, don't you. Won't you trust me? Can't you tell me what it is that's bugging you?'

'Of course I trust you but I'm under an oath of secrecy and I just can't tell you. Please don't ask me again. You've got to trust *me*. One day I may be able to tell you. But not now.' He leant forward to kiss her, trying to provide reassurance, but achieved no more than a bout of dizziness in himself and an icy rebuff from Inge.

'Aren't I good enough to confide in? Perhaps you'd rather talk to Sandie?'

Rob Laidlaw turned and put a hand on each of her shoulders. 'That wasn't worthy of you. I've told you there's nothing between Sandie and myself. And she doesn't know anything of these fears, these burdens of mine.' He pulled away with a sigh. 'The burdens are . . . all mine.' He started to walk away and then stopped, poised to tell the truth. Why be awkward, he asked himself? No. He couldn't risk it, couldn't break his pledge to Adawi. 'Don't you see,' he pleaded. 'I need you, I need your help. In my own way.'

'Oh, Rob. I'm sorry. I guess I'm too emotional. I just want you to feel you can confide in me. That's all. I want you to treat me as a friend, not as a lawyer.'

'When my head stops aching, that'll come easily and when I can tell you everything, I will.' He put an arm across her shoulder and they set off in step towards the police station.

Washington DC

From the window of the Oval Office, the President looked across rich green lawns in the direction of the soaring pinnacle of the Washington Monument. Soon the leaves would be down and he'd be able to see it again, though, for a moment, he wondered whether this was the last year that he'd enjoy Fall in the White House. A three point lead wasn't much but if the Democrats continued to tear themselves apart over tax reform, South Africa and disarmament, then his re-election for another four year term was assured. A successful Convention behind him, a sound but unobtrusive Vice-President on the ticket and most Americans *feeling* better off, even if they weren't, were good ingredients for another spell at 1600 Pennsylvania Avenue, Washington's most exclusive address.

For any bystander who knew no better, peering through the railings at the clean brightness of the building against the blue morning sky, the White House had the air of a small country mansion where single-minded enthusiasm for hunting was more likely than the double-talk of international politics. Sometimes he might see a flurry of activity as the President came or left by helicopter – but now the scene was calm, the fountains playing timelessly as the early morning visitors queued for a tour of the public rooms.

But the power lay there all right. President Jack Hode thrived on it, had grown into the job, proving his critics wrong. They'd said that he was just an orator, a Frank Sinatra without music, a rabble-rouser who could bring an audience to fever pitch with his rhetoric but who lacked the mettle for the harsh, uncomfortable decisions which the Presidency demanded. Yet he'd eye-balled the Russians, outflanked the Europeans and had routed the Democrats time and again back home. Still, three percentage points weren't much to show for it. He drummed his fingers nervously on the Waterford paperweight, a gift from the Prime Minister of Eire.

A Sun-belt politician from Dallas, now aged fifty-seven, Hode still felt in his prime, though his physician thought him too tubby for a man of five foot ten. His weakness for waffles and pecan pie was concealed only by the skilful tailoring of his double-breasted jacket. 'Hmm,' he mused as he glanced at the headlines in the Wall Street Journal. 'Should still be OK, despite the shake-out in oil prices. Barring unforeseen disasters, I ought to be returned.'

'Yes, Charlie,' he murmured, this time not to himself but to one of his six grandchildren, a three year old toddler who, out of earshot, was flourishing a kiddies' baseball bat over by the Rose Garden. Behind him the telephone rang and he turned from the French window, flanked by the national flag to his right and the Texan flag to his left. 'Your call to Mr Schillen, Mr President,' said his secretary from the next room as he sank into his swivel chair.

'Hi! How are you doing Marcus, you old son-of-a-bitch?' The President spoke on a top security line.

'I'm good, Jack! It's been a while. How's life in the madhouse?'

'I could get used to living here. Another four year term would suit me real fine though there'll be other changes come January. Boy, you'll be a real strength! Bob Freegard's been a great disappointment to me as Deputy Chief but the media loves his high profile, so we must be careful. No-one, and I mean no-one, must know of this change before I'm returned. For a start they'd be asking why I was getting rid of him and, if they found out, I'd be sitting on a verandah in Dallas for the next four years, writing my memoirs, a Texan Jimmy Carter.'

'Trust me, Jack, though I sure would like to know what Freegard's done wrong. His boots are going to take a lot of filling.'

'If you've got a fortnight, I'll tell you that after November 6th. Then it won't matter. There'll be some crap flying around when I announce that Bob's out but soon there'll be a better story and his sacking will be history. Meantime, every move I make is analysed, re-analysed and ultimately misinterpreted. It'll happen to you. They'll be in-depthing you, checking your tax returns, your sex life, your business affairs, your *everything*. They'll say I'm swinging to the right and paint you as an ultra-hawk. Or if it suits them, they'll say I'm swinging to the left and that you're a dove. You can't win in this place. You appoint a black man, they say it's a charade, a sop to the media. You appoint a white man and they call you a racist.' Hode chuckled, revelling in the fact that, despite it all, he was on top, ahead of the game.

'I expect all that. I haven't forgotten how the press crucified Geraldine Ferraro or Gary Hart.'

'I'm glad you understand.' Hode's tone was serious. Very. 'I guess we've been buddies a long while, Marcus. You don't get much time here to think of the past but, just occasionally, I get to remember the great days we had at college at Austin. Life was simple then.' He sighed. 'Sure, we're going to be a great team. I just wish I'd appointed you first time round. But I'll tell you why I'm calling, Marcus. Nothing that serious, I guess. Just that I'm reading too much about Drustein. You'll have seen this morning's Wall Street Journal?'

'Nope. But I can guess. All this crap about Lusifren.'

'So what's the fast track? You've got real problems? I can't afford to be tainted.'

'Jack, Jack!' Schillen sounded hurt. 'There *are* no problems. None whatsoever.' Schillen was firm, assertive in his denial. 'It's just real sad. Lusifren is the greatest breakthrough since penicillin. So, OK, it had side effects in a tiny minority of cases.' Hode could imagine Schillen shrugging his narrow shoulders. 'But Jack, you name any drug which can't upset *someone*. I tell you – you couldn't do it. We marketed Lusifren in good faith, had it passed through all the tests, had your FDA boys gooey-eyed at the prospects. Wall Street loved it and our stocks soared. I'm telling you, Jack, Drustein can ride it. Our attorneys tell us we can win these lawsuits, kick the claimants off the park.'

'I'm glad to hear it.' Jack Hode spoke with precision and those who knew him well, like Schillen, would have recognised the hint of cynicism. Schillen did understand. It wasn't the words: it was the timing, and the listener could imagine Hode's bland, weathered face puckering just slightly as he had spoken. 'Marcus, after forty years as buddies, I sure wouldn't want to see you up shit-creek. I really mean that.' Hode waved an arm to dismiss an aide with a worried look and a sheaf of papers. 'Washington is a political fish tank – I'm telling you it's full of piranhas. I don't want anyone dredging up sludge from your past. Friendship is one thing, politics another. I guess you understand.' Hode let the warning hang in the air for a moment before inserting the lance. 'Say, I just remembered: kinda tough about that guy of yours down in San Antonio. Your Vice-President.'

'Todd Kranski? That one really hurt. Tore me up. He was one helluva guy. If he'd wanted he could have been quarterback for the Dallas Cowboys. His brain moved fast, real fast. I reckoned on him to take over when I moved to Washington. What the hell the cops in San Antonio are doing I don't know. They haven't caught the muggers.' Schillen felt a flush, was sticky and uncomfortable, despite the air-conditioning. Was there *anything* that Hode didn't know? Mixed in with all the affairs of state, Iran, Nicaragua, the Middle East, arms deals with Russia, the fight against unemployment, to say nothing of the election campaign, he'd still picked up and remembered this detail.

'Just so long as you're right, Marcus. S'long! But don't forget, keep out of the papers. I want your butt lower than a Skid-Row bum.'

No sooner had the President rung off than his secretary, Jackie Woodall, entered. 'Your 10.30 meeting. Joe Wickens and Bob Narey have arrived Mr President.'

'Have them brought in. By the way make sure that article on Drustein is put on file. Oh yes! And make a transcript of that last call. There's real trouble with the Brits over Lusifren: questions in Parliament and even their Prime Minister is involved. That I can really do without. That woman! The way she talks on the telephone, no wonder the UK's got all kinds of internal problems. That Downing Street phone bill must be bigger than my wife's clothes allowance and that's really something.'

'You're worried about Drustein then?'

'I don't give that,' Hode clicked his fingers, 'for Drustein or for Schillen. My duty is to the Presidency. We had a foul-up when I appointed Tyler. Now we have the Bob Freegard problem. I don't want another.'

Jackie Woodall, secretary and trusted confidante left the room, smiling in recollection. Only after the President had appointed Tyler as CIA Director had the press produced evidence of Tyler's involvement in a Detroit insurance scam. Though they had known for a while, they had waited their moment to cause the maximum political discomfort. Tyler had resigned after three weeks. Jackie had learnt a thing or two then and the President had learnt a lot

The Dallas Dilemma

more. It still rankled. The thickness of her file on Marcus Schillen bore abundant testimony to that.

'Come in,' called Hode. The door at the far side of the Oval Office opened to reveal Joe Wickens, fresh from a tour of the Gulf States, and Bob Narey, tired and drawn from his long hours as Director of the CIA. 'Good morning gentlemen,' Hode advanced to shake hands warmly with each of them, his face fixed in the mode he usually reserved for TV appearances. It was his 'everybody's favourite uncle' look.

He showed each to a low-slung, wicker-backed chair, neither of which was designed to make the visitor feel at ease. In contrast the President looked thoroughly relaxed as he leant back in his own swivelling recliner and invited the guests to help themselves to coffee. Hode poured orange juice for himself a mechanical movement done without thinking, before flipping open the slim folder on his desk, the only paperwork visible, a lifelong habit in the interests of security. 'I'm real glad you boys dropped by,' he said as if either man had exercised any choice in responding to the President's summons. 'If you don't mind Bob, I'd like to hear from Joe first.'

Wickens had rather hoped that he would speak second. Although Secretary of State, he was still nervous when in the Oval Office, felt in awe of the history of the room, intimidated by the sheer power of the Presidency. His nervousness showing in his faltering start. He wondered for a moment how he'd coped so well with the brittle and sensitive Arab leaders during his whirlwind tour of the Gulf States. 'Well, Mr President,' Wickens' voice was uncertain. 'The purpose of the mission, as you will recall, was to get the feel of our current position out in the Gulf, particularly with Iran knocking hell out of Iraq in the War. The second objective was to find out what we should do in the light of that assessment, and finally to establish which of the Gulf States would co-operate with us. No one needs reminding of the strategic importance of the Gulf, nor of the Strait of Hormuz in particular.'

'Right. That seems a fair summary of where we'd gotten to at the National Security council meeting, when we decided to send you. So what happened?' There was something testy in Hode's voice as if he could have done without the preamble, but Wickens had needed that to get used to the sound of his own voice, to talk himself into the real meat of his report.

'I can keep the rest of it short, Mr President. In not one of the Gulf States did I meet resistance to the hypothesis that each was in danger from Iranian-inspired Islamic fundamentalism or, as an equally dangerous scenario, exposed to insurrection fostered by Arab terrorists. Each Shaikhdom seemed to accept that Iran was winning despite the billions of dollars being paid to support Iraq. They also knew that the Ayatollah would then be looking to the southern shores of the Gulf and to the richer pastures beyond – Saudi Arabia. I got a particularly sympathetic hearing in Bahrain, which has a large Shi-ite Moslem population. As you know, we've already got what we euphemistically term a *facility* there. I found sympathy too in Kuwait. Ever since the bomb outside our embassy, the Kuwaitis have realised just how vulnerable they are. Our efforts to keep open the oil supply lines through the Strait of Hormuz is much appreciated as well.'

'But?' The President knew Wickens well enough to know that the problems were about to be stated.

'There are two buts. The first is that, however nervous these Shaikhdoms are, they don't want to be *seen* to be in the pockets of the West, and Washington in particular. Remember the attempted coup in Bahrain? Right. There's also unrest in Kuwait, and the United Arab Emirates, under Shaikh Ahmed, remains unstable. These Rulers know that, if they are *seen* to be Western lackeys,

The Dallas Dilemma

then forces outside will stir those within for a return to Islamic principles.'

'In other words, publicly booting the West up the ass.' It was Bob Narey's first intervention and, as usual, his blunt appraisal was accurate. 'Whilst still wanting our financial, political and military support when it suits them. Naturally.'

'That's right.'

'So let me ask you this,' Hode enquired. 'Do these Shaikhs want to be left naked? Do they want to pretend that it's never going to happen when all the signs are that it is? Look Joe, if I'm reading you right, we need more than mere *facilities* in the Gulf. We need a real and obvious presence for, if we're not there, who the hell will be? The Brits withdrew in 1971. Our friends in Tokyo need the oil from the Gulf but are powerless to protect their own interests. If we don't have a *real* presence, who looks after them? Will no one let us have a major base?'

'Each Ruler appreciates the need for us; each of them actually wants us but equally each needs to appear to be strong and independent both to their people and to outsiders. The Gulf Co-operation Council takes itself more seriously than I was able to do.'

'I can understand their reluctance.' It was Narey speaking again. 'At the moment they may not sleep easily but at least they sleep. If we store ammunition there, have troops and a vast fleet patrolling the Gulf, based say in Kuwait, in Dubai and elsewhere in the Emirates, then the northern Arabs will move in fermenting trouble. Result: loss of sleep.'

'Or the Big Sleep if they don't co-operate,' responded the President. 'These small Gulf States will fall like dominos, with or without the Gulf Co-operation Council. The GCC may be enough to inhibit a disorganised coup but against anything more concerted, it would be helpless.'

'I said there were two "buts". The second concerns the UAE. Besides meeting their Minister of Defence, I met Shaikh Ahmed himself. Of all the Shaikhdoms, the one where we need the greatest help is that one. Dubai would be a perfect base. The Brits have a low-key special arrangement but are reluctant to do too much after the Falklands. It's got all we need for maintaining a fleet and it's well positioned for patrolling the Gulf. Shaikh Ahmed was sympathetic, let there be no misunderstanding as to that, but of all the Rulers, he claims to be the most vulnerable to an anti-West reaction if he is seen to co-operate. Historically his family and his Emirate of Dubai are friendly with Iran. That friendship may have worn thin now but Ahmed, while not admitting it, feels threatened by his Vice-President, Shaikh Rahman. To the rest of the world, he is nothing; to Ahmed, Rahman is a constant reminder that he has the influence, the drive, the power base and the jealous bigotry needed to fire the people in a Khomeini-type of Islamic purge against the West. Only last week, he was the guest of the Libyan Government, was in talks with the Syrians at Damascus. Shaikh Ahmed is very fearful of a coup and. . . .' Wickens' voice trailed away.

'And what?' The President stepped in smartly.

'And I got the impression that he was not a well man, was fuzzy and forgetful, no longer up to taking *any* decisions, especially ones which would encourage Shaikh Rahman to contemplate a coup. Look at the uneasy situation with the coup in Sharjah. Fine, the Sultan has been restored but the volcano there is still simmering. No one is resting easy in the Emirates.'

'Any observations on that from your quarter?' the President asked the Director of the CIA.

'Nothing specific. Reports reaching me from Dubai suggest that Ahmed tires easily. He's given up any appearances in the evening but he sometimes attends the Majlis during the day. He's also stopped travelling. He used to be a great one for jetting around, particularly to Pakistan with his falcons before he became President. His lifestyle's changed in the last few months. More of a recluse now. Could be that Joe's right and that he isn't well. That spells danger.'

'Bob,' said Hode, 'I want your man out there to report back within seven days on every decision which Shaikh Ahmed has made in the last six months. And I mean decisions which *he's* made. And I want to know what's bugging him. And I want a briefing on Shaikh Rahman. Is he really a danger? Has he the ability to overthrow Ahmed and then lead the Emirates into an anti-West position? But tell me Joe, did you feel that I might persuade Ahmed to let us have a real presence at Dubai?'

'Maybe. He's considering it. But, Mr President, I think he's going to *consider* it for longer than we want.'

'Consider it, be damned. What about a survey? A feasibility study? A few of our experts out there making contingency plans. Let's make a start. It could be done discreetly.'

'I'm afraid not Mr President. Shaikh Ahmed is running scared. He's only prepared to *consider*.'

'Well, goddammit, is there anything we can do out in Dubai?'

'No. Not politically. Maybe his "consideration" will accelerate if Kuwait falls. Or Bahrain.' The wry smile said it all. 'But UAE apart, I've got consent for the occasional goodwill visit round the Gulf and have secured agreement for deployment of our military fighters in *an emergency*. You'll understand the deliberate looseness of the language. As I said, the only real problem's in Dubai.'

'That's fine – as far as it goes. We need more than that. Think on. We'll meet next week. I'd like to help Shaikh Ahmed but I guess matters may be beyond that.'

After the visitors had gone, Hode called Jackie Woodall and handed her the papers. She laid them next to the dossier on Marcus Schillen, the nexus between the two files unknown to the President . . . or, come to that, to Marcus Schillen.

London

A week had passed since the break-in, a week in which the police had got nowhere in tracing the intruder. Detective Sergeant Watkins had reported that the film in the camera had not been used, leading to the conclusion that the man had not found what he was looking for. There had been no fingerprints and the ballistics report was inconclusive without the gun. In Laidlaw's office the only reminder of the incident was the bullet hole in the carpet by the doorway.

Outside in Hill Street, the autumn rain was falling steadily and, with overcast skies, the lights from the offices were reflected in the glistening wet surface of the road. As he stared moodily out of the window at the drab scene below, Laidlaw's thoughts drifted to Dallas, as they had done so often since Inge had left. His thoughts had been dominated by her, almost obsessively so, and on several occasions Sandie had entered his office, only to find him staring aimlessly across the room, his mind far from the project in hand. Once she'd chided him, convinced that his distraction had something to do with Dallas, an impression which she still held, despite his over-brisk denial.

He forced himself to study the agenda for the Lusifren Committee meeting, but found he was trying to recall what Inge looked like. The overall impression was all he could manage. It irked him. Her softness of touch, sharpness of brain, barbed humour and brevity with fools – these he could savour, but recapturing that look in her eye when she had gone through the departure barrier was impossible. With a sigh he checked his watch. Too early to ring her yet. In Dallas, dawn would just be breaking. 'I bet it's a bloody sight hotter there than here,' he muttered as Sandie walked in the door.

'Talking to me?'

Laidlaw looked embarrassed. 'No. Talking to myself. Just moaning about the weather. On days like this it's easy to understand why places like Vancouver and Sweden have such high suicide rates. Wet and dark, endless gloom. Makes you want to put your head in the oven.'

'Come on Rob. Snap out of it. It's not a bit like you. We all know you're in love. For the past few days you've just been a bloody nuisance round here. It's about time you stopped mooning about like a lovesick parrot and started thinking about all these Lusifren victims. It's probably raining where they are too. The only difference is that some of them can't even see or hear whether it's raining or not. Some of *them* would like to be able to walk to a window, even if only to see black clouds.'

'Sorry. In a way you're right, though it's not just Inge. It's the inactivity. I feel so impotent, so frustrated. Up until the public meeting, it was all great. Telephones ringing, press, television, the hero of the moment but, more than that, I felt I was achieving something. Now I'm sitting around waiting for something to happen. I've got MPs working on it, I've bearded the Committee on Safety of Medicines and I can't think what to do next. I want to make things happen. I'd like to prove that doctors and testing houses were bribed by Drustein to endorse Lusifren.' He flung the agenda across the desk. 'Worse still, Hugh Waddington has turned up nothing and despite his dreadful show at the conference, we have to believe he's really trying to help. For the moment we've got no choice anyway.'

Sandie, much more feminine in her dress, put her carefully manicured hand on his shoulder. She forced a smile from him. 'I'll tell you what. We'll have lunch after this meeting. It'll be a long lunch. We'll get smashed. And out of it we'll get some ideas. That I guarantee.' She smiled at the surprised look on his face.

'A drink-tank? How could I refuse? Thank you.' He smiled his appreciation, hoping that he hadn't given her more encouragement than he'd intended. He was about to add a facetious comment as the telephone rang in Sandie's room and, when she returned, she told him that the Committee members had arrived.

'Shall I bring them in?'

'Yes. Democracy must have its day.' He didn't sound enthusiastic. 'My ideal committee would be two. Just me and my ego.'

The elected three came into the room, led by Charles Fane, their elder statesman. They all wanted to see the hole in the carpet and then, as they sat round the table drinking coffee and munching chocolate biscuits, Laidlaw brought them up to date. Apologies were read out from the two members of the Committee who could not attend. 'That seems clear enough', volunteered Fane at the end of Laidlaw's report. A retired diplomat, he attributed his arthritis to falls at polo though his wife was sure it stemmed from excessive drinking while stationed in Singapore. 'But what I don't understand is how the drug got marketed. What about our CSM and the Americans' FDA?' He sounded calm, knew that he had to keep calm on doctors' orders. His advancing heart condition was due to Lusifren and he had been warned to avoid all stress.

'The Food and Drug Administration is known as the FDA. However, its nickname is the DFA, the D standing for "do".' Laidlaw laughed. For a moment there were blank faces until only Gordon Rose, a retired schoolmaster from Godalming, hadn't seen the point and Fane explained the joke to him.

'Is the FDA incorruptible?' enquired Sandie.

'I've never heard it suggested otherwise. Having said that, everyone has a price. The FDA's only as incorruptible as its weakest part. If there is corruption then my view, shared by Inge as well, is that it's in the presentation of the papers *to* the FDA. If Drustein invents a new drug, it follows the NDA procedure, which stands for New Drug Application. Before the drug can be sold to the public in the USA, it must get FDA approval. The application will run to thousands of pages, incorporating the results of the tests carried out by the manufacturer and the medical profession. That's where the corruption normally arises. They start with tests on rats or monkeys. If there are no adverse effects then they are authorised to move on to human guinea pigs, firstly on a limited volunteer basis and then on substantial numbers of the public. The results, supposedly *all* of them, are published and are lodged with the FDA to obtain the licence.'

'Sorry. Tell me what happens if there are adverse findings during the tests,' insisted Fane.

'The drug company must report *all* adverse reactions. The system breaks down because there is no one to monitor whether *all* the tests are brought to the FDA's knowledge. Obviously Drustein lodged evidence which enabled the FDA to grant the licence. The question is whether their tests were lucky or whether they fudged the paperwork.'

'All that sounds fine,' said Sandie as she stubbed out a cigarette and smiled across at Fane. 'But I'm sure what Mr Fane wants to know is, if the drug goes through all those phases, how can an Lusifren disaster happen?'

'Drustein could say it was just bad luck, that the victims of side effects are just a statistically insignificant minority. A less charitable view is that Drustein, like other drug companies, has forged documents, destroyed *inconvenient* documents, used slush funds to bribe testing houses and doctors into providing dishonest reports.'

'Regardless of the consequences?' enquired Gordon Rose.

'Certainly. The corruption of some major US drug houses is legendary.' Laidlaw leant back and opened his arms in an expansive gesture. 'Inge Loftin is now working on the legal process known as discovery which means she's calling for documentation and will be cross-examining the officers of Drustein on deposition. If she's not satisfied with the documents disclosed she can go to the Judge for further directions.'

Fane lit his pipe despite his doctor's warning that he should cut it out. 'I find it incredible. Do you mean to say these drug companies really manipulate the system?'

'Oh yes.' Laidlaw flourished a tome which Inge Loftin had left with him. 'Following a similar drug disaster, a US Steering Committee reported in March 1976 that there were "devastating deficiencies" in the practices and integrity of a well-known drug corporation. Trust me, there have been too many examples of drug giants falsifying records and concealing deadly or dangerous side-effects. These things really happen. And in England too.'

The third member of the Committee, Peter Shaldon, who had said nothing so far, made his first contribution. 'There's no evidence of fraud by Drustein? Just suspicion.'

Laidlaw nodded. 'Just suspicion.'

'And this break-in? There's no evidence against Drustein?'

'None. But Drustein are an obvious front runner.' As Laidlaw spoke he was very aware that Sandie was interested in his response. He looked at her knowingly and noticed how quickly she lifted her eyes towards the high ceiling. She wasn't convinced. 'Any other questions anyone?' he enquired.

'Yes.' Again it was Peter Shaldon speaking. 'I'm interested in this fraud aspect because, if that's proved, you said we get extra compensation. Let me tell you something about myself.' He shifted awkwardly in his seat. 'Five years ago I was smashed up on a building site. I've never worked since then and I got no compensation, as the accident was my fault. I was left with so many fractures that even a rag and bone merchant wouldn't have taken me away. I lost my HGV licence. I'm not an educated man. Driven a lorry delivering bricks all my life. I was unsuitable for a desk job, for driving or for heavy work. Then along came Lusifren. I was prescribed it in the hope that it would get my joints working freely again and I thought I'd be able to get a job, perhaps get my HGV licence back.'

'To make matters worse, I suppose you have a family?' asked Laidlaw sympathetically. Shaldon produced a photo from his pocket.

'I've got a wife and two kids. How am I supposed to feed and house them?' His already bitter face twisted in discontent. 'Now, thanks to Lusifren the joints aren't any better but I've got a heart condition as well. I'm forty-two, living on Social Security, riddled with debts and the Building Society threatening to sell us up as we're behind on the mortgage.' He looked across the table at Laidlaw. 'Now do you see why I want as much as I can get? Yes, I'm bitter. Yes, I need every penny I can lay my hands on. I've learned a thing. Look after number one. That's what I say.'

Amid murmurs of sympathy, Laidlaw nodded his head in reassurance. 'If anyone can get you that extra money – punitive damages – Inge Loftin is the person, but it'll take time, unless she uncovers details of backhanders, free gifts, slush funds. Besides that, she's looking for minutes of meetings and anything which suggests that other sensitive papers may have gone to the shredder rather than the FDA.' Laidlaw stopped for a moment and debated whether to add anything. He decided he would. 'I should also say that she's investigating the murder of Todd Kranski, who was a Vice President of Drustein. Let me explain.'

* * *

Half an hour later the meeting broke up and Laidlaw and Sandie were alone. 'I'm starving,' said Sandie. 'I've got a table booked for 1.30 so we'd better be going.'

The restaurant was full as they took their upstairs table, all around them the prosperity of expense account business people. 'The obscenity of capitalism – not quite your scene,' chided Laidlaw.

'I'm learning fast,' she replied looking round to make sure that her lemon-coloured cotton shirt and calf-length skirt were suitable for the surroundings.

'Seen the light, have you? Like the mob in the Kremlin. More capitalist than the capitalists. Girls, booze and their dachas at weekends.'

'I was *never* a communist,' she bridled. 'I was brought up in a background where there *was* injustice and by parents who could see injustice. University furthered that outlook.'

'We all change, although sometimes I could run a contrary argument to that too.' He took a sip of his vodka tonic. 'I was a Young Liberal once. I could put up with their abstinence lunches but when they voted to sell the snooker table and send the proceeds to Biafra, I decided to move on. I realised my talents had been wasted.' His style was jocular but Sandie took him seriously.

'So what did you do?' she enquired.

'Joined the Tropical Fish Appreciation Group – fascinating, if a trifle dangerous.'

Sandie laughed, wondering now if perhaps he had been joking.

'Have you chosen?' he enquired.

'Yes. I'll have lobster bisque, followed by the sole.'

'The lobster bisque sounds a good idea. I'll join you. And then the turbot I think. But if you like squid, I can certainly recommend that.'

'They do it well here, do they?' Sandie was very unsure of herself, anxious to do and say the right thing. 'If you're really recommending the squid, then I'll try it.'

'I can't vouch for it here. It's a long while since I tried it.'

Again Sandie fell for it. 'When was that?'

'After I resigned from the Tropical Fish Appreciation Group and emptied my fish tank.' Though she knew now that he had been joking, it was still hard to tell. You had to watch his eyes and eyebrows rather than his mouth and, even then, it wasn't always easy.

'And all that about the Young Liberals and Biafra?' she asked. 'That was a joke?'

He nodded in acknowledgement. 'Anyway,' he continued, 'what did you make of the meeting then?'

'It went well,' she said. 'Glad all five of them couldn't attend. It would have got even more rambling.'

'I particularly liked Charles Fane – very sound. Gordon Rose was a bit of a bore. What did you think about Peter Shaldon?'

Sandie thought for a moment. 'I didn't like him. He's entitled to be bitter but I couldn't warm to him. Mind you, for an uneducated man, his questioning was pretty sharp. One loose answer and he'd be on to you like a cat from a catapult.'

'Gordon Rose could have saved himself the train fare for all he contributed. A real cold fish, talking of which, here comes the turbot. You could tell he'd been a schoolmaster by the patches on the elbows of his jacket and I do believe that I could smell chalk. Quite nostalgic.' He eyed his plate. 'This looks good. Now all we want is the inspiration which you promised.' Laidlaw looked over Sandie's shoulder and watched a diminutive Japanese attack a sixteen ounce T-bone as if it were a snack.

'I've been thinking about Todd Kranski. What I had in mind was a blend of the classic ingredients of money and publicity.'

'So? What is your idea?'

'Put forward a reward with massive publicity for anyone giving information about the deaths.'

'Great idea. Except where do we get the money?' Even as he said it, he knew the answer. Adawi. He could always provide the money. If there were no other source. Not that he could tell that to Sandie.

'My guess is that Kranski and his wife would have had life insurance. Put yourself in the position of the relatives. Wouldn't you want to see the killers caught? Wouldn't you be prepared to use some life insurance money to get to the truth? With your connections, I'm sure you could hype yourself into a talking point on Texas television. Someone's memory may be jogged. As they say, money talks.'

Laidlaw was silent, thinking through the possibilities, assessing the downside. 'It could be done. We'd need a reward of say fifty thousand, or maybe even a hundred thousand dollars – something sensational to interest the media. I'll phone Inge and see what she thinks.' He could see that Sandie was bubbling with enthusiasm. 'It could be just what we want. Even if it doesn't work, at least I'll be doing something.' He raised his glass towards her. 'Thanks again, Sandie. We're quite a team.'

Sandie gave a diplomatic cough. 'OK then team member: tell me what the burglar was looking for?'

Laidlaw's laugh tried to be friendly and dismissive at the same time and he had a nasty feeling that it sounded like neither. 'I don't know.'

'What do you think he wanted?'

'My cheese sandwiches in the filing cabinet, maybe? Filed under M for mousetrap.'

'Come on Rob. It could just as easily be something to do with Mr Adawi as Drustein. Whatever Adawi wanted you to do was dangerous. Within a few days you nearly get shot. It's obvious.'

'That's an exaggeration. If the burglar had wanted to shoot me he could have done it. He just wanted to get away.'

'Was Mr Adawi from Saudi Arabia?'

'Pass.' Rob had both his elbows on the table, leaning forward looking her deep in the eyes. 'If I'd known we were going to play *"Mastermind"*, with me in the hot seat, I'd have arranged for the big black chair to be brought here.' He could read frustration and disappointment in her look.

'So much for our team. Twelfth man again.'

'Please Sandie. You've got to believe me. If only I could share the burden. Just this once, think the best of me.'

'And you've told no-one?' Her voice was defensive, uncertain. He emptied his glass of Louis Roederer champagne and topped up both their glasses and, as he looked at her, he decided it was not the wine which was getting to him. She really was changing her style. From the tough, boiler-suited tyro, she was becoming altogether gentler, more girlish. These were not the qualities which had caused Sir Victor to employ her. 'If you mean have I told Inge, then the answer is no. I've told no-one. That's in your best interests and maybe, just maybe, in the interests of whole nations.' He wondered if it sounded melodramatic. It did – but so what. It was true. Reading reports from the Middle East, he'd quickly realised that the kaleidoscope of countries stretching from Libya to Pakistan was a mare's nest of contradictions, ever-changing in ultimate allegiance.

For a fleeting second he visualised the fast-fading Shaikh

Ahmed, his Emirates vulnerable to a hostile environment. Now it held a key role in the Gulf and was in danger of being torn apart.

The short fuse was getting shorter. The risks were becoming more real. Without being aware of it, his brow was furrowed as he recalled the intruder and the fierce crack as the gun had been fired close beside him. That danger hadn't gone away and now he'd be going to Dallas to take on Schillen, a man who, if Inge were right, had stopped at nothing, not even the deaths of Todd Kranski and his wife.

'You're day-dreaming again Rob,' she said, 'though it looks more of a nightmare.'

'You're right. Maybe it is. Let's change the subject and have some coffee. And a couple of glasses of port.' He smiled at her, just a touch sadly, and she responded in much the same way, her eyelids half lowered, staring sideways at nothing in particular. 'You've been a great help to me.' He lowered his voice and searched for the right words, acutely aware of the increasing emotional element in their relationship. 'Don't think I haven't noticed the way you've changed and don't think I'm not very fond of you, but you must understand there must be no involvement. The beauty of our relationship is that element of detachment. I know we can't work as closely as I would like over Mr Adawi but on everything else we can achieve so much. I think you know what I'm trying to say.' He looked at her again, his grey eyes responding to the well of sympathy which he was feeling. 'I just don't want you to get hurt.'

She raised her own eyes, as large as harvest moons. 'I understand everything you're saying but I think it's too late.'

Maybe it was the champagne – perhaps the port. Whatever it was made him stretch out a hand to clasp hers. 'You're indispensible to the Association. Perhaps in time you'll be indispensible to me too . . .' As he spoke, he saw the reaction in her eyes and regretted at once that he had said so much.

Dallas

The lion on the tailplane of British Caledonian's London flight roared notice of its arrival in the sweltering heat of the Dallas-Fort Worth runway, before taxi-ing to a standstill. Rob Laidlaw had left Gatwick Airport, grey and drizzly, nine hours ago, and was now standing in the mid-afternoon sun awaiting a cab to take him to the Hyatt Hotel in the heart of downtown.

In the cool of the air-conditioned Oldsmobile, its interior nearly as battered as its exterior, its driver as battered as his cab, he tried to relax as the man steered with one finger on the massive and busy highway. 'First time y'all been to the Metroplex?' enquired the driver.

For a moment Laidlaw was lost and only when the man repeated the question could he get the drift of the laconic drawl. 'If you mean is this the first time I've been to Dallas, then yes.' Laidlaw was aware that his voice sounded terribly English.

'Y'all Australian?'

'No. From London.' Laidlaw was puzzled at the confusion, imagining that everyone recognised an English accent when they heard it. But BBC English played no more part in this man's life than did the news in Chinese. His was a day of garbled messages on a crackling intercom; his was a routine of endless hysterical DJs introducing even more hysterical music. 'But what's the Metroplex?'

'Y'all never heard of the Metroplex?' The driver shook his head in disbelief. To him, the Metroplex had been the world for the past forty-five years. 'It's all this.' He lifted his little finger from the wheel, so that the Oldsmobile was steering itself down the fast lane. His arms flourished right and left. 'It's Dallas. It's Fort Worth. It's DFW. It's the bit between them. Time was when Fort Worth was real cowboy country. Giant stockyards. Y'all better go there – it's real neat. Then Dallas became the new commercial centre but the folks in Fort Worth, now they want to keep up. So Fort Worth's changing fast man, real fast. And with the airport in the middle, the two are joined together. Fifty miles of it. And so the whole area, Dallas, Fort Worth, man that's called the Metroplex. And y'all better believe it. Dallas is America's fastest growing city. Full of young guys moving in all the time, moving in from the North, from Buffalo, Chicago maybe. Moving from the cold winters and unemployment. Here there's sun and hope.'

'And money?'

'Don't come my way. But sure. T. Boone Pickens. The Hunt family: even now, after their troubles, there's not many richer than that.'

'Do we pass any of the big houses?'

The driver shook his head. 'Nope. Not unless y'all want to make a de-tour.' He broke the word very much in two. 'For that y'all need to go to Highland Park, just off North Central. We're on LBJ Freeway. Up here we join North Central.'

Laidlaw's heart had quickened at the mention of Highland Park. So Inge lived in millionaire country. Interesting. She'd kept that quiet. 'Man, this traffic sure is a problem.' The driver brought him back to the crawling jam of North Central, to the forest of massive hoardings which lined the route. 'That's Drustein's over there. That gold building. Some landmark, huh?' The driver took his solitary finger from the wheel to point to Schillen's monument to himself, its four storeys of glitter looking like burnished copper in the afternoon sun. Driving past, Rob noticed that the drive leading up to the building was conifer-lined, the parkland surrounding it seemed without end. Even the name emblazoned by the arched entrance was massive and Laidlaw realised the bedrock solidity of the empire he was trying to shake. For a second he felt intimidated. The feeling passed. Hell, no! Respectability was just a charade, a front. What were all the major corporations paying you for when you were in advertising? Corporations just like Drustein? They paid you to peddle respectability, to puff up souffles of desire from rotten eggs.

The debate raged in his mind through the rest of the journey. Marcus Schillen, he convinced himself: you've got more to worry about than me.

Oh sure, just tell that to Todd Kranski.

His response to himself echoed in confusion round his mind.

The cab pulled up outside the hotel. 'Here y'all are. Be sure and take care now.'

Fair warning.

* * *

The Hyatt Hotel and Reunion Tower penetrated the skyline. Though not the tallest buildings, they were the most spectacular in the high-rise world of downtown Dallas. From his room Laidlaw could enjoy a wide panoramic view over the city. In his suite the silence was restful after the drive from the airport, for though the freeways far below were full of vehicles it was as if he were watching a silent movie, except for the profusion of colour. And at least this was something for which he could thank Adawi: there was no way that Sir Victor would have paid for his stay at this hotel but Adawi had been quick to give authority for a little cosseting.

Laidlaw was about to unpack his suitcase when there was a knock at the door.

'Your lucky day sir,' smiled the young man from room service as he swept into the room with a bottle of champagne on a tray. Beside it was a note. Somewhat bemused Laidlaw tipped the boy a dollar and read the message. 'Best cure for jet-lag I know. See you at 7.30. Inge.' Feeling as skittish as a kitten, he decided to put the champagne in the fridge to await her arrival while he unpacked and changed. London seemed a long way off as he showered lustily before sprawling in the veloured comfort of the reclining chair in front of the television. Between the torrents of adverts, or 'messages' as they were called, there was the occasional snippet of programme, loud, brash and sufficiently banal to send him to sleep despite the noise. Only the knocking on the door awoke him from the deepest of slumber and, as he hurried to it, his movements were zombie-like, his brain telling him what to do, his legs unready to respond.

He fumbled clumsily with the lock and when at last he mastered it, he saw her once again, standing cool, elegant, one eyebrow raised quizzically, one foot almost tapping in impatience. 'Rob Laidlaw,' her voice was stern and scolding. 'Have you finished that champagne already?'

'It certainly feels like it.' He took an uncertain step backwards, letting her into the room and then closed the door. 'I'm just drunk with exhaustion. The last thing I remember was seeing the weather forecast for the third time. Then I flaked out.' He shook his head slowly, aware that he wasn't presenting quite the image he had intended. On looking down he saw his bare feet, incongruously white compared with the deep brown of her legs which disappeared beneath a short white dress, loose-fitting, gossamer thin and apparently covering the scantiest of clothing underneath. He stretched out to put a hand round her shoulders and he felt hers in turn rest lightly on his waist. For a moment they stood face to face, eyes meeting and exchanging messages to which words could do no justice. He moved towards her, his arms slipping down her back, pulling her closer to him so that he could brush her cheeks gently with his lips and then hold her, even more tightly, with an intensity which he could never have anticipated.

'I've missed you, Rob,' she said. 'It's been no time and yet it's been too long.' He could feel the softness of her cheek as it rubbed against the nape of his neck, could feel the rise and fall of her breasts as they pushed against him, could feel the urgency in her hands as they clasped him firmly, pulling closer together, as if the physical bond were necessary despite the instant rapport.

When at last he felt her draw back so that she could see him, her lips, delicately pink, parted in an emerging smile, her face showing her happiness. 'If I'm to believe you, there's still the champagne, so we'll drink to us and to my divorce. Harvey's at last agreed terms.'

'Amicably?' Laidlaw enquired, though feeling that this was not the time and place for a detailed discussion.

'Sure. We'll remain friends. We chose each other for the wrong reasons, though they seemed good enough at the time. Anyway, that's history, let's hit that champagne. I've had one helluva day.' She kissed him, barely touching his lips, before killing the blare of the TV while he removed the cork from the bottle with a satisfying phut and proceeded to fill the two tulip-shaped glasses. 'Sorted out Drustein today, have you?'

'Yes and no. Mainly no. I've been trying to get something, make something, out of all their documents. So far nothing. I don't like it. Only you and me know the strategy, yet it's as if Julius Weissman can read my mind, as if he knows the questions I'm going to ask. I could see their smart-ass lawyer Bechrach gloating.

The Dallas Dilemma

You know, Rob, he was so smug, his shifty eyes glinting at me across the deposition room.'

'Does that surprise you?' Laidlaw replied. 'You didn't expect Marcus Schillen and the rest of his boys to be stupid. They'll have checked out your strategy in previous drug compensation cases. You've given them a map which is easily read.'

'Maybe.' Inge sat down beside him on the recliner but, from the pensive look on her face as she sipped the vintage Krug, it was obvious that she was unconvinced. 'I just wonder if we've got a leak or if they've got us bugged. The whole thing stinks. The documentation is too perfect.'

'If I'm right, what you should do is turn things upside down. Look for some line of questioning which you've never pursued before.'

She sucked in her cheeks before nodding in agreement, a gentle waft of Givenchy filling the small gap between them on the sofa. 'Maybe I'm a little stale. Too predictable as you say. So what do you suggest? You were in advertising. You're an ideas man.'

'You said Schillen fires staff at random. What about asking for personnel records and then follow up some of the staff. Find someone with a grudge. They might talk. What about finance? Have you got that covered yet?'

'Any slush fund is well hidden beneath a mire of offshore trusts. Got nowhere on that yet.' She helped herself to a handful of nuts and absent-mindedly studied them. 'I prefer your other idea. I'll call for personnel records. I've never done that before. And England? Have *your* police traced *your* intruder yet?'

'No. They've got nowhere.'

'Any more thoughts about who set him up?' Her voice was always a drawl, the words always evenly spaced with long gaps between them but, on this occasion, Laidlaw noticed that her speech was even slower, her voice deeper than usual. He wondered if it were a technique which she used when questioning witnesses. He certainly felt as if he were being interrogated, perhaps because he knew he was hiding something.

'There's no hard evidence at all. It has to be linked with Lusifren.'

'Sure, I can't argue with that, but Rob, you're still not giving . . . not giving at all.' For a moment a flicker of irritation showed that the soft contours of her oval face could have all the raw sharpness of a broken bottle.

'Something I'm not telling you?' Laidlaw repeated her question, playing for time, uncomfortable under her stare. He swallowed hard and examined the condensation running down the side of his glass. 'I've told you everything you need to know. Remember what I said that night in London. You've got to trust me.' It was an evasion and he knew it. And she knew it. He could see her disappointment but she made no challenge.

'Well, I guess you'll tell me the full truth when you're ready. Just so long as it doesn't prejudice what I'm doing.' She wagged her finger in warning but then took away the admonition with a wink.

He gave her a watery smile as he re-filled her glass. 'No, it won't prejudice what you're doing.' He spoke with more confidence than he felt. 'What else have you been doing, besides fixing a divorce?'

'Well, I've had Ed Bechrach watched. Twenty-four hour surveillance for ten days. My agent has also bought the contents of his trash cans. Result – zilch. Plenty of odd things but nothing I can pin on him.'

'What's all this about trash cans?'

'You mean you don't do that in England? Hell, how do your

lawyers expect to win cases?' She looked at Laidlaw's incredulous face and realised that further explanation was necessary. 'Buying up rivals' trash had become such a boom industry that most big corporations now shred everything before it goes off for collection. Backalong you could pick up old computer data, profit runs, cash flow analyses, designs of vehicles, results of marketing tests. You name it. I thought we'd check out Ed Bechrach but his stuff all goes through the shredder – just like Drustein's.'

'I don't think we worry about our rubbish in England. We're just *so* naive. I'm naive. Or I was. We try to pretend that industrial espionage doesn't exist. It does. It's not much use pulling our bowler hats over our eyes and shrouding ourselves in a Union Jack of smug isolation.'

'Are you suggesting that going through Bechrach's trash can is wrong? If so, are you talking about morals? Is it morally wrong to try to prove the truth? To expose a scam?' She gripped his arm as she spoke, pressing her point, her bare thigh rubbing against his leg. As usual she was as direct as a lance.

'Well . . . put like that.' He nodded in agreement. 'Anyway let's take a look at the Kranskis. After all, that's why I'm here.'

'Is it? I'd hoped you'd come here to see me.' Suddenly she wasn't Inge the lawyer. Now she was Inge the temptress, coquettish, her voice playful, the crossing of the thighs beneath the cotton dress suggestive, the hurt pouting look an act for his benefit.

'The thought had crossed my mind.' His smile was diffident, the underplay typically English. 'But business first. I'm glad you liked the idea of appealing for information on TV.'

'It may work. It's not every day that the people of Texas are treated to a crazy Englishman putting out an appeal about a murder in San Antonio. Don't expect Marcus Schillen to lie back and enjoy it. He'll react.'

'That's what I want,' he grinned. 'If I can rattle him, so much the better. If Todd Kranski's family come good over this TV business, then Marcus Schillen will be getting a visit. You've traced the family?'

'Sure. I've got a complete rundown. We'll talk about that later. But first I want to talk about Sandie. Did you speak to her like I said?' She expected the answer to be no, but was wrong.

'Yes. It wasn't easy but even I could see you were right about her.' Laidlaw's face was thoughtful as he recalled the uncomfortable ending to the recent lunch. 'I think I rather upset her but I didn't mean to.'

'Well, I'm sure it was for the best. And you've certainly made me feel a lot more comfortable. I'd hate to see her really hurt. Anyway, let's make a move. I'm taking you over to my place, *Le Bijou*. Maybe some tennis, then a swim, a work-out in the gym and some barbecued steak. Does that suit?'

'I was always keen on the pentathlon. Can't you think of anything else to make it up to five? Maybe some jogging or a game of golf?'

'I guess we'll reach five . . . one way or another.'

* * *

Fifteen minutes later Inge's white BMW Cabriolet paused briefly at the massive security gate built into the heavily walled citadel of her Highland Park home. The electronic trigger in her car set the mechanism in motion to reveal *Le Bijou*, which stood a hundred yards back, in front of it a large fountain, the water splashing down in a cascade of lights created by spots and searchlights which shone from every tree. 'You could see a spider's smile as it climbed up the wall,' he suggested.

The Dallas Dilemma

'We need real tight security round here,' she said. 'And what you see is only part of it. There are photo-electric cells crisscrossing the shrubs. Round Highland Park we even have our own police. If we didn't we'd be cleaned out.'

'Aren't you ever frightened here? On your own?'

As the car crunched to a halt on the gravel, having circled the fountain, she gave him a quizzical look. 'Honey, aren't you assuming that I spend a lot of time here *on my own*? But, hell, why be afraid? You can't spend your life like that. So someone comes in? They rape you? They shoot you? Probably better than plunging from 30,000 feet in a 747 or trying without avail to avoid a collision with a trucker.' She tossed her hair dismissively as she swung open the door. 'Hell, it may never happen, so why worry?'

'But you still have all the security.'

'Sure. The insurers insist on it.' She waited while he came round the car and then led him to the front door of the two storey building which stood seventy yards long and maybe half as deep. 'It was built fifteen years ago for the President of another drug corporation. Five years ago I traced some hot money nestling in the Virgin Islands and he was fired. It seemed real neat to buy this from him as a souvenir.'

'And where's he now?'

'He's done his time. I've lost track. Probably bouncing his way back. Just the sort that Drustein needs.' She laughed as the main door opened and Rob Laidlaw found himself standing in what she described as the lobby but which, to him, was more like an exhibition room at the British Museum. The highly polished wooden floor seemed to stretch endlessly in all directions while round the walls were suits of armour, totem poles, spears, blunderbusses, Chinese vases and giant cacti, all set out as if intended to be examined and savoured. 'I don't like them. They came with the place. But, with a room this size, what else do you do?'

'There'd be parking for thirty cars. Or you could play 'sardines'. That's if you invited the population of China.' She wasn't quite sure how to take it but she laughed anyway, grabbing his hand to lead him through the vaulted room until he arrived, limping and pretending to be footsore, at the other end. 'Gee, this conducted tour makes your feet ache.' He put on a harsh New York accent, the type he regularly heard near the Tower of London.

'Y'all ain't putting your feet up for a while yet. This tour's hardly started.' she replied in deep Texan as she pressed a button in the wall and a solid security door slid aside, revealing three acres of rolling grass, ornamental shrubs and trees, with a swimming pool and tennis court in the corner.

'Best of three sets first and then the swim?'

Laidlaw looked at her lithe figure and judged that he was beaten already. 'But I haven't got a racquet,' he suggested, as limp as a broken string, knowing that in this house there were probably at least three of Jimmy Connors' cast-offs, to say nothing of a team of ball-boys on call at the press of another electronic button.

'Bad loser are you? Say, that's great. That means you like winning. It'll be quite a game.' She led him through a maze of corridors, up some stairs and, after a left and a right, they were in her bedroom which seemed to combine the intimacy of a Mecca ballroom with the velvet luxury of a courtesan's boudoir. Dominating the room was a four-poster with full drapes available for privacy. 'Just as your predecessor left it too?'

'Nothing changed. *Le Bijou* is just a little bit of history, my own museum dedicated to bad taste and corruption.' As she spoke she was rummaging in a drawer and producing immaculate white tennis gear. His throat tightened as he saw the bobbing fullness of her breasts when she leant forward, noticed the curve of her buttocks sharply outlined beneath the scanty white dress.

'Where do I change?'

'Here, unless you're shy or unless you've only something *very little* to hide?' The white evenness of her teeth shone from the Texan-tanned face, her hair flicking round her cheeks as, with a single quick movement she unzipped her dress from top to bottom and let the entire ensemble fall to the floor, revealing the full, generous brownness of her breasts and firm, raspberry-like nipples which protruded with a vehemence which outdid Rob's imagination. And the panties, previously sketchily visible through her dress, were now revealed, their cut so brief that a flicker of golden hair could be seen. She had nothing else on as she licked her lips, suggesting to him just a touch of uncertainty.

Did she really expect him to play tennis after that display? He wasn't sure and so he acted impulsively and yet deliberately, slowly undoing each button on his shirt and, all the while, he was watching her, watching her eyes, watching her smile and then her eyes again. And then it was socks and shoes, each movement distinctive, positive, as first they and then trousers disappeared to leave him standing beside her, dressed now only in dark red jockey underpants. And as he'd stripped, he'd noticed again the licking of the lips, the slightest trace of nervousness, the first time he'd ever seen it. He'd noticed too the widening of her mouth, the merest tightening of her stomach muscles as his broad chest, his waist and then his thighs had been revealed. He took a step closer to her. 'Do you always play tennis like this?'

Her response was sudden, so sudden that he was almost caught unawares as she thrust herself towards him, forcing the coolness of her body against his, her arms linking themselves around his neck, her lips now nibbling at his cheek, then his ear and then slipping round once again to his mouth, this time to meet it fully open, firm and responsive.

As he ran his fingers through the sweet-smelling softness of her hair, he could feel the surge of her emotion, exciting him to press himself harder against her, forcing her head back till she was arched beneath the pressure of his own urgency. Suddenly she bucked, trembling so much that he had to support her, gasping, sighing and forcing her nails deep into his shoulders, her eyes tightly shut, her face contorted in wave after wave of contentment, her stomach muscles shuddering uncontrollably against the lean firmness of his own body. Only as the sighs subsided did her grip ease and only then was he aware of the talon-like scores which she had been making across his back.

'Sorry,' she said. There was a glint of emotion in her eyes as he held her now, gentle and limp against him. 'I couldn't wait for you. But thank you, thank you.'

For response he ran his right hand gently, smoothly over her back while his left turned her head, pulling it close until it nestled against the dark underside of his chin and curve of his neck. 'Don't say a word,' he whispered, 'just relax. All the best tennis lasts at least three sets.' And so they stood, neither saying a word until the fierceness of her emotions had subsided. Only then did Inge ease herself away from him, so that she could face him, once again demonstrating the gentle serenity of her face, still flecked here and there with the suggestion of a tear and the drying salt of her perspiration.

'Let's have the second set over there.' Her voice was soft, husky, as she nodded towards the four-poster. 'It's your turn.'

'Our turn,' he corrected.

'No, that's the third set,' she was quick to respond as she removed her panties with easy elegance and the assistance of a toe to flick them aside before she lay back on the bed where he joined her.

'Shall we make it a five setter?' He stretched to pull round the drapes.

Later, much later, Inge smiled dreamily, her eyes half closed as he lay full length beside her, crooking his head in her elbow. 'New balls please,' he murmured.

'Yes. And some ring doughnuts. I can do the most amazing things with a ring doughnut. But there's always tomorrow.'

* * *

Twelve hours later Rob Laidlaw was still recovering on the 32rd floor of the downtown, smoked glass skyscraper which housed Inge Loftin's law firm. At her desk by the window, Inge was sucking a gold pen between staccato bursts of conversation. Wearing a black suit with white blouse and a gold brooch, she was fiercely businesslike, the scourge of the drug manufacturers. Was this really Inge, who'd exhausted every corner of his imagination? Who'd insisted on 'just a few lengths of the pool to freshen up' before returning to bed for barbecued steak in overstuffed sandwiches?

'OK, Ralph but don't let me down. Fifteen minutes. Then call me back. Be sure that you do.' She put down the phone, her face creasing with happiness as she looked at him, remembering the extraordinary arousal to which he had brought her. Even now she couldn't believe that such feelings were possible or that they could occur again. She felt weak, childlike, a prisoner, captivated by the passions which he'd unleashed within her, and she wasn't sure whether she liked it. Usually she was in control, both of herself and her emotions. Vulnerability was a strange sensation.

'Ralph Macey's a good private eye though he needs his butt kicking,' she said. 'He's checking out some details about the Kranskis. More coffee?' She rose to pour and even an uninformed bystander would have noticed the suggestive intimacy of her glance as she filled his cup, but that apart, she gave not the slightest hint of what had passed between them.

'While we're waiting, shall I ring Marcus Schillen?'

'Sure. Go right ahead, though I doubt he'll see you.' But this time Inge was wrong. When Schillen's secretary told him that Laidlaw was on the line, Schillen had muttered to himself: 'just as I expected, right on cue' and had taken the call. Seconds later a meeting had been fixed for 5.00 p.m two days later, at Drustein's premises. In the burnished gold of his castle, Schillen had looked pensive as he anticipated the arrival of Laidlaw. He was glad he was well-informed. The day after tomorrow would be quite something.

Meantime, seven miles away, in Inge Loftin's downtown eyrie, Laidlaw moved to the window. 'This wonderful view over nothing,' he commented as she awaited Ralph Macey's call. 'Dallas doesn't win many prizes for beauty, does it?' adding 'can we see from here where President Kennedy was shot?'

Inge joined him, her movements feline and sensuous, with the gentlest rustle of expensive silk against soft skin. He stood behind her and rested his head against hers, looking across the untidy less well-developed fringes of downtown. 'You can see Deeley Plaza and the Texas Book Depository just there,' she pointed. Following her gaze he saw the familiar configuration.

'Folks are still arguing about whether to open up the Depository as a museum. Feelings still run high here. There are those who say that the conspiracy which killed him was organised here; there are the kooks who are *pleased* he was shot here; there are those who just want to forget the sheer hell of it all. But that's it anyway – that squat, red-brick building on the corner.' From their lofty vantage-point he had a sniper's eye view of the scene, could imagine the open Lincoln making its 120 degree turn from Houston into Elm, its slow manoeuvre setting up the simplest of targets for an experienced shot. And then the rapid acceleration with the mortally wounded President racing for the underpass and hospital as swarms of pigeons swooped and circled in terror at the gunshots. 'So long ago and yet so vivid,' she said.

'It's strange – looking at history. Almost unreal.' He fell silent, aware now that while she had been speaking, her body had been shifting back and forth, from side to side, rubbing against him with increasingly hypnotic rhythms. Without noticing it, he had been holding her tighter till once again he felt the changed pattern of her breathing, aware of the short, jabbing, eager bursts, her face pushing hard against his cheek. He twisted round so that his lips met hers, when the telephone rang.

Reluctantly she broke away. 'No, Ralph, I haven't been running!' She laughed, a big laugh, loud and mocking as she winked at Laidlaw before jotting down the details. 'Well thanks, I really appreciate that.' She put down the receiver and Laidlaw gently caressed her hair as he stood beside her, trying to read her writing. 'It's my own form of shorthand,' she said. 'No one's ever managed to read it. And they're not meant to.'

'That's what people say about my *best* writing.'

'We're in luck. Both Todd and Rachel's families come from East Texas and it's fixed for you to see them together. It's about an hour and a half out of town and real hicksville. Y'all need a checkered shirt, boots, a stetson and fiddle if y'all want to go visitin' up thar'.' She mimicked the style of East Texans. 'I guess,' she continued 'they've got electricity and johns with running water – that's if you're lucky. Small place called Pittsburg, quite unlike the city you'll have heard of.' She selected some papers from a drawer and put them in her briefcase. 'The Court Registrar's due in a few minutes so I've got to go down to our deposition-room for discovery, maybe to the Court-house now, put some lead into Bechrach, preferably where it hurts. Meantime, enjoy the drive to Pittsburg. Take it easy.'

'And this evening? More tennis?'

'Something like that.' She swept out of the room, leaving him wondering how he'd cope with the Kranskis. And with her.

Dallas

At 6.00 p.m. next day, he was surging through the warm waters of Inge's pool, where even twenty-five lengths didn't appease Laidlaw's irritation. As a child he'd always been encouraged to be positive and to forget might-have-beens, but it had been a day of if-onlys. He wished he could re-run it without the mistakes.

Forget it, Rob told himself. What was it his father had said? 'Show me a successful man and I'll show you someone who faces reality.' Not easy. Maybe I expected too much. He towelled himself dry and then stretched out on the flower-decked patio. Maybe Inge had done better.

The drive out to Pittsburg through the rolling green of the countryside had been pleasant enough, the scenery fairly reminiscent of England except for the 'nodding donkeys' pumping the oil. Only when he'd reached Pittsburg had things started to go badly. The four parents had gathered at the Kranski homestead, a small, timbered property, much in need of paint, a poor relation to the spacious luxury houses which lined some of the streets of the small community.

He had quickly established that Todd had been a local boy made good, his parents simple Christians, Lou Kranski working on the land, Martha Kranski bringing up five children on too little money. Rachel's parents ran the local drugstore. All four were in their fifties, warm, polite and friendly as they'd sat in the small yard, surrounded by trees.

Till the murder of their children, life had been uncomplicated and they seemed reluctant now to resurrect more bitterness, more sadness. Their children were dead, murdered. That was fact. Precisely by whom didn't really matter. Nothing was going to bring them back. Only Martha Kranski, well-rounded in both body and personality, seemed tempted to co-operate and ready to believe that Todd's employers could have set up the murders.

'San Antonio police ain't got nowhere, nor ain't likely to,' said Lou Kranski. His manner of speech was ponderous, much in keeping with his heavy jowls and stomach.

'But suppose that Marcus Schillen had them murdered, suppose Todd knew something was going on at Drustein and didn't like it.'

'Todd was a good son, doing well at Drustein. Never did talk much about what he did.' Martha Kranski smiled in reminiscence. 'Guess we wouldn't have understood anyway.'

Thinking back now, Laidlaw wished he hadn't made his next remark. 'I was just hoping that you'd have thought that your son was worth fighting for.' He knew as soon as he said it that he'd chosen the wrong words.

'Mr Laidlaw,' replied Lou Kranski. 'Todd and Rachel were worth everything. It isn't for you to make value judgements. Those kids meant everything to us. Their memory still does.' His voice rose. 'We have no lust for vengeance. The good Lord has taken them to Himself. Who did it and why the Lord will reveal if it is His will. So it ain't for you to come from England preaching to us Mr Laidlaw.' The words tumbled out, the speaker's face anguished. 'For what? For more false hopes, more pain? Don't you think we've suffered enough?'

Rachel's mother started to sob, forcing her husband to take up the attack. 'To achieve revenge. Is that what you want? Revenge for

The Dallas Dilemma

the victims of this drug? Well let me tell you, Mr Laidlaw, you're wasting your time. No way sir, no how. Matthew Chapter V, Verse 39: "turn the other cheek".'

Lou Kranski nodded. 'And Verse 44: "love your enemies".'

'I'm not sure,' said Martha Kranski. 'Mr Laidlaw here's giving us the chance to go for the truth. There's plenty support for that in the Bible.'

'No, Martha,' replied Lou. 'It's no use pretending. Mr Laidlaw here wants vengeance. The memory of our dead son deserves better.'

At this point Laidlaw had pushed aside the remains of the casserole of pork and beans. 'I'm sorry I've caused so much distress. I think I'd better be going.'

'I think that's a good idea.' Rachel's father was still smarting. After an embarrassed 'goodbye', he'd gone, seen out by Martha Kranski, who looked at him as if to say that she had done her best, making him wish that he had seen the two families separately, so that she had not been outnumbered by three to one.

He'd driven back badly, his mind racing on whether he should go ahead with the television broadcast if Adawi would put up the money. Had he the right to go ahead, causing the families more distress? Anyway, he'd avoided telling them about the broadcast.

On his return, the call to Adawi had not been entirely successful either. Damn it all! When was something going to go right! When were they going to get the break. His thoughts were interrupted by Inge's arrival.

'Hi!' she called. It was nearly eleven hours since he'd seen her, yet she showed no signs of having done a day's work, her face as radiant as in the early morning. 'Fix me a beer, can you please, honey?' she said after she had kissed him. 'We must talk in a minute. But first I need a swim.' In a couple of movements her clothes had gone and, entirely naked, she dived with scarcely a splash, to emerge fifteen yards away, her blonde hair swept back and clinging tightly over her ears and round her neck.

'Did you have a good day?' he called.

'No. Did you?'

'Disastrous. I bet mine was worse than yours.' She never heard, as she had started the first of several effortless lengths of the pool, the soft brown of her body powering through the water. When at last she got out and lay beside him, her nipples stimulated by the water, she was scarcely out of breath.

'I ought to swim more. I used to swim morning and evening all the year round. Anyway, tell me about your day.' As she spoke she nuzzled closer to him, he warm and dry, she still damp, her skin tingling from her exertion.

'If your day was half as bad as mine, let's just forget about it – for a while anyway.' He stroked the side of her cheek and saw a look of contentment appear as she placed her arms around his neck.

'Let's hope Ralph Macey doesn't ring this time,' she murmured into his ear.

By the time the long gentleness of their love-making had concluded, the sun had dipped behind the tree-line and there was a chill in the air as she lay across him, her hair dry but spread-eagled now. In contrast to the night before, they'd found their pleasure this time in a lingering, laughing intimacy, whereas in the shadowy depths of the four-poster there had been an almost black intensity in their noisy, contented sighs.

After another swim and a shower they set off for dinner in the discreet comfort of The Mansion restaurant, where the squelch of oil wealth could be heard with the footsteps of each new arrival.

'So you're going to prove that your day was worse than mine,' Inge said. 'You've told me about Pittsburg and the Kranskis. That's no

The Dallas Dilemma

problem. You said there was more?' As he listened, Laidlaw could feel her right leg rubbing against his calf and, for a moment, his mind was elsewhere, his eyes showing his pleasure, her puckish look reflecting her thoughts.

'If you'd only let me concentrate, I'd tell you. Do you behave like this with everyone?'

'Most everyone,' she laughed. 'I'd even try it on Ed Bechrach if I thought it would do any good. But what else went wrong?' She advanced her other leg to continue a mean game of footsy.

'Having tailed in Pittsburg, I decided I'd ring . . . someone I know with a lot of money. I thought they might put up some funds.'

'And?'

'The answer is probably yes.'

'So what's the problem?'

Laidlaw was uncertain what to say. 'My contact is paranoid about secrecy. When he heard that I was phoning international from a hotel, he was outraged.' That had been putting it mildly, particularly as by then Adawi had confided in him that the Shaikh's health was declining more rapidly. 'The Shaikh wants a result,' Adawi had said. 'If you want fifty thousand dollars for the reward, it's yours. But hurry. You don't seem to be achieving much. If anything.' The voice was scornful and then angry as he continued. 'Don't ever call me again from a hotel phone. Better still, don't phone me at all.'

Afterwards Laidlaw was uncertain whether he'd mentioned Ahmed's name over the phone. Was his line bugged? He couldn't be sure but the angry rasp of Adawi's voice had lingered. So had his warning about security.

'You mean this guy doesn't want it known that he's a rich benefactor?'

Laidlaw was grateful for the prompting. 'Something like that. But what if my room were bugged?' Laidlaw watched Inge's face change and even the persistent friendliness of the roving feet was quelled.

'Funny you should say that. When I was questioning today and getting nowhere, I wondered again whether Schillen had gotten hold of our strategy. I've got three para-legals helping. I'd stake my reputation on each of them.'

'And the secretaries?'

'Don't know the strategy,' she finished the sentence for him.

'I've told Sandie. You'd expect that. But then, what if I've been bugged? Perhaps I haven't been security conscious enough. Maybe I should be more aware about under-the-belt espionage. Maybe Marcus Schillen has had a little transmitter stitched into my shirt so that, even now, he may be listening. I've just never thought in that way.'

'You should. You'd better believe it. We're fighting a war against Drustein. There's much more than money at stake. If we can prove it, then Schillen is stone dead, finished. He knows that. You fight your way to the top like Schillen, you're not fussy about how you stay there. Today, even my unexpected questions were expected. No way could I throw Julius Weissman. So my vote goes for the TV appearance. We take the battle to him. I guess I'm sorry about the feelings of the parents but there's too much at stake not to take up that attack. And in the meantime, you'd better think hard about security, become as paranoid as your unnamed benefactor.' She smiled disarmingly, tilting her head slightly to one side. 'Meantime I'll keep trying to slug Ed Bechrach. He's had it too easy. By the time I've finished with him, even his ulcers are going to have ulcers.' She was about to continue when the waiter came over and said there was a call for Mr Laidlaw.

He hurried to the phone. 'Rob Laidlaw speaking.'

'I sure am sorry to break into your evening,' said Martha Kranski. 'But your hotel told me where you were.'

'Don't apologise. Can I just say again how sorry I am I distressed you. I hope Rachel's folks are feeling better.'

'Oh, sure. I guess we were all kinda jumpy. After you'd gone, me and Lou, we kinda got to thinking. I don't mind telling you, Mr Laidlaw, you sure took us by surprise. Maybe we just needed more time to see you were right.' She spoke quietly but with precision and Laidlaw was able to imagine the discussion which had followed his departure. He was able to recall her tired features which still showed the stress of her son's murder. It was a face which attracted sympathy – homespun, ready to smile, shining with good faith and honesty.

'I'm delighted. Does that mean you'll co-operate?' As he spoke he was aware of the irony of having upset Adawi in his attempt to raise cash. Now it seemed that the call could have been avoided.

'We'll put up fifty thousand bucks. That's half the life money on Todd.'

Laidlaw thought quickly. It should be enough to loosen some tongues, though not as much as he had hoped. 'That's just wonderful Mrs Kranski. But will you do me one favour?' Now for the difficult bit. He hesitated fractionally. 'I'm setting up a press conference for tomorrow. Would you come and join me, be on television? That'll be even better than money.' There was a long silence and Laidlaw did nothing to press her.

'Will that mean coming to Dallas?' She made it sound like Outer Mongolia.

'Yes, to the Hyatt.' He recalled his own feelings the first time that he'd faced the media, could remember the pounding heart, the obsessional fear that he would 'dry up' in front of the viewers and knew that he was inviting her to face an ordeal such as her imagination could not conceive. To relive the agony of her son's death was one thing; to do so in the glare of the camera was another.

She hesitated and the hesitation seemed endless to Laidlaw as he waited, anxious not to pressurise her, yet desperate for a positive response. Then he heard her. 'I'll come. Tomorrow? that'll be just fine. Be sure and let me know when.'

'I'll telephone you. And thank you but how did you persuade your husband?'

'I quoted him his favourite Matthew, Chapter V, but I relied on Verses 21 and 22. Are you familiar with them?'

With what Mrs Kranski took to be modest understatement, Laidlaw replied. 'I can't say that I could quote them offhand.'

'"Thou shalt not kill". Everyone knows that. But Verse 22 is more important. "Whosoever is angry with his brother *without a cause* shall be in danger of the Judgment". Now I told Lou that we had cause. There ain't nothing that says it's a sin to find out who did the killing and when we've done that, we can then move on to his verses and decide whether or not to love the enemy. You deserve help.' There was a catch in her voice as she spoke.

Back in the restaurant Laidlaw quickly recounted the conversation to Inge. 'Tomorrow's going to be quite a day,' she enthused. 'It's going to be the beginning of the end for Marcus Schillen. Don't ask me how. I just know it.'

'We must get moving fast. I want to hit the midday news.'

'Any particular reason?' enquired Inge.

'Oh yes. It means that Marcus Schillen will have heard the broadcast by the time I meet him.'

The feeling of buoyancy lasted the journey back to the hotel.

'Any messages?' enquired Laidlaw. He waited while the front desk attendant went away to check.

'Just the one call. A Mrs Kranski. Did she get through to you, sir?'

'Thank you, yes. That was all, was it?'

The Dallas Dilemma

'Someone else stopped by and asked for you.'

'For me?' Laidlaw was at first surprised and then concerned, thinking back to the call to Adawi through the hotel switchboard. 'Who was it?'

'The gentleman was here about half an hour ago, sir. Didn't leave a name. Just asked if you were checked in. Said he'd call again.'

Inge looked at Laidlaw and wondered why he was so anxious. 'What's the trouble, Rob?'

'Nothing, nothing. Just puzzled. Wasn't expecting anyone.' He was unconvincing. He spoke again to the desk clerk. 'What did he look like? You spoke to him yourself?'

'Yes I did, sir. I guess he was about thirty.'

'Was there anything about him, anything you remember?'

'Well, sir . . . I guess he wasn't from Dallas. Wrong accent. East Coast maybe.'

'Not a foreigner?'

'Now that you suggest it, it's possible. Gee, I'm not sure.'

'What did he look like?'

'Normal. A regular guy. Dark hair, dark complexion. Funny. I'd have put him down as a New Yorker until you suggested he was foreign.' The young man shook his head ruefully. 'I'm not being too helpful, am I? Didn't take too much notice of him. But then why should I?'

Laidlaw's face was grim. 'Thank you.' He tried to sound unconcerned. 'No doubt he'll drop by again. If he does, get him to leave his name.' Together, he and Inge went up to his room. In the lift he said nothing. Had it been a New Yorker? Or was it someone from the Middle East? Someone who had overheard his call to Adawi? Would the man come back? What had he wanted? He chewed his lip, his brow furrowed, his eyes fixed on the floor.

Besides Shaikh Ahmed and his physician, only three people knew the full truth. Adawi was well protected. That left two. Him. And Hugh Waddington.

'Rob, this is your floor.' Would the man have been in his room? The bedroom door was closed. Silently he slipped the key into the lock and then threw it open. The room was in darkness. He flicked the switch and saw that nothing had changed. It was undisturbed. Or so it seemed.

Inge closed the door behind them. 'You look real worried Rob. What's it all about?'

'I don't know what it means. It just might spell trouble. Don't, please don't ask any more.' Inge looked frosty as he poured himself a brandy while she had a Coke. 'Look. I don't want to stay here tonight. I don't think either of us should. Do you mind if we go back to your place? We can do the calls for the press conference from there.'

'Best excuse I've heard!' She was smiling again.

Dallas

The cat and mouse game was about to begin but who would be the cat, Laidlaw wondered as he entered Drustein's opulent headquarters. The seemingly endless corridor leading to Schillen's suite did nothing for his confidence but, still high from the successful clamour of the press conference, he remained buoyant.

He was greeted by the waiting secretary. 'Well, hi Mr Laidlaw,' welcomed Lucille Malone. 'Good afternoon,' he replied, slightly aloof, an Atlantic's width away from a response in the local jargon. Not that her greeting was over-familiar, for indeed it was not. The smile was fixed to balance the look in the eyes which was enquiring what the hell he was doing in Dallas, or why the hell he was knocking Drustein. It was obvious that she knew of the morning's TV broadcast and to some extent shared her boss's icy distrust.

'Mr Laidlaw to see you,' she said as she knocked and entered his room. She paused momentarily while the two men shook hands, watching Marcus Schillen's face, hoping to get some better inkling of what he was thinking, but whatever it was, he gave nothing away and, as she withdrew, she heard him offer the visitor a cocktail.

It would have been easy to say yes – a sight easier – but he resisted. 'No, thank you. Too early in the day for me,' he lied. 'But I'd love some orange juice. Or coffee. Whichever's easier.'

'Sure.' Ice cold orange splashed into the pair of matching crystal glasses and each took a sip, thoughtfully, as if savouring the flavour, yet each looking at the other, assessing, measuring, wondering how the first vital minutes would develop and who, if anyone, would land the first punch. As silence engulfed them for a lengthy few seconds, each was aware that set speeches, preordained plans and glamourous rhetoric contemplated earlier in the day were redundant. Whereas Schillen had originally dismissed Laidlaw as a piece of flotsam which could be sunk without trace, new reports from London and the latest TV broadcast had made him retrench.

Schillen took in the steadiness of the eyes, the steadiness of the hands, the thrust of the clean-cut chin, all the features which he'd noticed on the television and which now, in his presence, were even more prominent. He put down his own glass, wishing that he'd applied himself to finding out more about Laidlaw's pressure points. He'd have to work on that. 'I'm mighty glad that you've come over to talk to us,' he said. 'It's like meeting an old friend.' The smile and voice were plastic. 'If you're not on the BBC in England, you're building up coast-to-coast coverage over here. Since this morning, our switchboard has been jammed.'

Laidlaw shrugged dismissively, anxious not to appear flattered by compliments which meant nothing. Schillen's superficiality was exposed by sharp downward glances, darting from behind gold-rimmed spectacles, suggesting his true insecurity.

Laidlaw had been told that his own features inspired trust. Schillen's attracted, at best, deference to wealth and power. The close-set eyes and meanness of moustache broadcast his cunning. 'As you should know, Mr Schillen, what counts is the product, not the presentation. I've been selling a story of human tragedy, of heroes and villains. That's what people understand.' He fixed his eyes on Schillen. 'I stand for the truth.'

'And Drustein are the villains?' Schillen's smile was forced, his voice rising a couple of notes.

'Yes. The media work in colour but want issues in black and white. Drustein is black.'

'Well I sure hate to disappoint you but your storyline's not going to stick for long.' Schillen sat down, crossed one short, slender leg across the other and, without thinking, set his small desk globe spinning.

'Then sue me. I'd welcome that.' Laidlaw swept out an arm in challenge.

'We may just do that,' but Laidlaw judged that it was mere words. 'Let me explain. The villains, as you so quaintly describe us, are just as much the victims of circumstance as the unfortunate people who suffered through Lusifren.' As he spoke, his eyes narrowed in concentration, watching the globe spin before him. 'We feel for the victims. We really do.' Then the room was silent, except for the swish of the air-conditioning and the slightest whirr as the globe came to a halt.

Schillen looked up sharply, a decision made. He wouldn't mention Bechrach's idea of putting up their own hundred thousand dollar reward for information about the Kranskis' death. 'Make sure that any witness who crawls out of the woodwork comes to us first,' Bechrach had suggested, adding, 'and then we can fix him.' At that moment the idea had seemed attractive. Now, faced with the steely look of the Englishman, the plan seemed fanciful. 'Did you know we've issued a statement welcoming your initiative. You see what does concern us is that your abrasive intervention may have set back our own enquiries into the death of Todd Kranski.' Schillen's lie was convincing and hard to disprove.

He handed Laidlaw the text of the release. 'Here's our media statement.' He watched Laidlaw glance at the document. 'What it doesn't say, but what I can tell you, is that our own enquiries haven't disturbed the official verdict of murder in the course of felonious theft.' The drawl was unappealing.

'And the murderer? Surely your private eyes have identified him?' Laidlaw enjoyed the mockery, his tone reflecting the conviction that beneath that skim of integrity lay the sour milk of deceit.

'No. Not yet awhile. But say, that's quite some lawyer you've hired. Inge Loftin can crush granite, even when she's smiling. Perhaps you've noticed.' There was nothing in Schillen's look to give away whether the observation was loaded.

'She was recommended to me. Highly recommended.' As he spoke he tried to avoid the mental image of the granite crusher, recalling her soft and gentle in slumber as she'd lain beside him in the four-poster.

'Even Inge Loftin won't win this one. We have the "state of the art" defence. We'll drag out this litigation for years, as long as it takes.' He poured more orange. 'Tell me something of your Association. I guess you're a poor man's Ralph Nader? The consumer's friend?'

Laidlaw could feel the patronising pat on the head. 'With what we've now got on Lusifren, we won't be poor for long. Don't worry about us, Mr Schillen.'

'But I do. Drustein is a reputable, respected giant. People trust us. People trust me. With good reason. If I said it was Christmas Day tomorrow, folks would all be decorating their trees.'

'Rhetoric never impressed me. Maybe you'll convince yourself though.'

'Well, I guess you've been out of diapers long enough to know that over forty per cent of patients suffer some kind of adverse reaction to prescription drugs.'

'It's statistically impossible that your tests showed nothing.'

'I trust you're not suggesting fraud or malpractice?' Schillen's thin moustache stretched sideways with his razor-sharp smile. 'We are, I repeat, a major corporation with an annual turnover into billions.'

'Big need not be beautiful. As for dubious practice, I'm suggesting nothing but Inge Loftin won't miss much in your paperwork.'

'She's getting nowhere.' Schillen slapped his hands on the desk. 'And I'll tell you why – because there's nowhere to go. The trouble with Inge Loftin is that she's sniffed fraud so often that she smells it all the time.'

Ignoring the chance to comment, Laidlaw replied: 'unless you pay compensation, my Association will fight all the way – and here in Dallas.'

'And we shall resist. My lawyers tell me that you English can't sue in Dallas. And you'll never prove a case in England. Not with your laws. Remember the Eraldin case? The beta blocker problem?'

'Yes, but those victims were paid out. The manufacturers played fair. You should do the same.'

'Maybe they thought they would lose in court. We don't. Frankly, Mr Laidlaw, we at Drustein don't give a damn for what you believe. We carry a lot of our own risks without insurance cover – that's a measure of our confidence.'

Laidlaw's face glared out a message of anger but he kept his voice under control. 'I'm unimpressed.' He patted his file of papers. 'I'm concerned for victims. You can afford to pay out. I'm warning you, Mr Schillen. By the time I've finished with you, you'll have *no* reputation. Furthermore, you'll be uninsurable.' He leaned forward, spun Schillen's globe and pointed at it. 'Not here, not anywhere in the world.'

'Big ambitions for a small-timer, Mr Laidlaw. Now I suggest you listen and listen good. Before Lusifren went on the market there were tests on animals and animal tissue; there were carcinogenic tests for cancer-causing propensity; there were tests against side effects in pregnancy; there were physiological tests. There were behavioural tests. Then there was consent from the FDA for tests on volunteers and patients. And the records were lodged.'

'All of them?' scoffed Laidlaw. 'If my aunt had balls, she'd be my uncle.' His tone was disparaging. 'Anyway, you'll teach me nothing about the integrity of drug companies. Remember the Kefauver Commission? The Kennedy Commission? Both of them exposed the chicanery, greed and manipulation of corporations like yours. In this field, Mr Schillen, just count me in as a *magna cum laude* graduate.'

Schillen removed his glasses. 'I think I might get kinda mad at you, Mr Laidlaw,' he said. His voice was cold. 'I suggest we end the meeting now – we have nothing to discuss.'

Laidlaw decided to take a chance. 'Todd Kranski died because he disagreed with your policy. In more than one serious respect.' Laidlaw made as if he were about to volunteer something when in fact he had no such intention. The effect had been created. Schillen was riled, shifting his position and taking shelter behind polishing his glasses on his tie.

'What you're saying is lies, damned lies.' Schillen replaced his spectacles and his eyes retreated even deeper behind them as he thought back to the search carried out at Kranski's home, following the death. Surely Weissman had removed all the suspect material. Forget it. Laidlaw could do nothing. 'I can't say it's been a pleasure but thank you for calling. The meeting's now over.'

'So I suggest you switch off your recording system,' concluded Laidlaw, laughing at Schillen's reaction. The bug alert in Laidlaw's pocket had been softly vibrating during the meeting, confirming that every word of the conversation was being recorded by Schillen. Inge's intuition had been right.

'It's easier than taking notes.' Schillen's reply sounded defensive and would do so on the recording.

Laidlaw rose from his chair, so that he dwarfed the American. 'Let me warn you. It's not just *your* telephone lines which have been jammed, Mr Schillen. I've been getting calls too. Some of your former employees seem keen to sing a song.'

'You want to listen to kooks and disenchanted deadbeats who I've fired, you go listen to them. Me? I'd rather go listen to the ducks farting at the White Rock Lake. Less nauseating.'

'I'll listen to everybody.' Laidlaw stretched forward to shake hands and Schillen responded, albeit reluctantly. They shook hands and immediately Schillen looked down in surprise for now, nestling in his palm was a small bug, no bigger than a jacket button. From the look on his face Schillen might now have been holding a black widow spider rather than a listening device.

'What's this?' he exclaimed.

'It's a bug, Mr Schillen, found in my hotel room. I thought you'd like it back.'

'Like it back? You've got it wrong. It's got nothing to do with Drustein.' By Schillen's standards the words came too quickly, reminding Laidlaw of Lady Macbeth washing her hands after the bloody deed.

'Well, it's similar to the one found a few months ago in Inge Loftin's office. An interesting coincidence?' Laidlaw laughed and was about to leave the room when, as an afterthought, he turned again to face the corporation President. 'You've given me plenty of advice. Let me tell you something. If I were you, I'd think it politic to pay up now, before it's too late.'

'Politic? What do you mean?' Schillen's voice was edgy.

'Politic? Just a word we use in England. It means prudent. Take care, Mr Schillen.' Laidlaw opened the office door himself and, after a cheerful 'have a nice day' to Mrs Malone, walked down the corridor. It didn't seem as long this time as he fought back a smile at Schillen's reaction to the bug.

A sweep of Inge's office and Laidlaw's hotel room had revealed nothing. But it was a dirty war. Inventing the discovery of the bugs had been a good bluff. A few dirty tricks wouldn't go amiss. Not against Schillen who was already on the phone to Bechrach. 'Say Ed, what do you mean by setting up bugs on that bitch of a lawyer and this Laidlaw guy?'

'Not me.'

'Well somebody did. There's something very strange going on.' He put down the phone, wondering why he felt so uneasy. Oh yes! That was it. Politic! Why had Laidlaw used that word? Was it loaded? Did Laidlaw know about his political ambitions? Surely not. But he *was* well-informed. Knew rather too much about Kranski, was picking up information from former employees. 'Julius,' he barked into the intercom. 'Come in. We've got some hard thinking to do.' He spun the globe on his desk until the countries blurred and became as confused as the thoughts in his own head.

Dallas

Sitting in the Marriott Hotel, Laidlaw waded through the letters from cranks and glory hunters. As a precaution against the mysterious visitor, he'd checked out of the Hyatt but had resisted the temptation to base himself at Highland Park with Inge. As far as he could tell he hadn't been followed.

As far as he could tell.

It was uncomfortable being the nut in the nutcracker, jammed between the forces of Drustein and Middle East politics.

In the two days since he'd exchanged angry words on the telephone with Adawi, Shaikh Ahmed had further deteriorated and his private physician gave him a maximum of three weeks to live. The latest message from Adawi had been, as might be expected, peremptory. 'You're being paid a lot of money. I want action not words, Mr Laidlaw.' For Christ's sake! What did Adawi expect? Smash and grab tactics on Schillen? Hand over your confidential documents, Mr Schillen, or I shoot? The man was unrealistic. The approach had to be subtle.

Laidlaw was not alone in his concern about His Highness the President of the United Arab Emirates. In the White House, President Jack Hode had been silent for nearly two minutes while studying the single sheet of paper in front of him. By habit acquired in childhood, he was chewing the length of his forefinger, eyes narrowed in concentration. The contents were plain, unpalatable and yet had to be faced. If the CIA report were correct then Shaikh

Ahmed, a good friend of America, was dying. The prospect saddened him for Ahmed had a rare humour and his Western outlook had led to valuable rapport, but now the Ruler's indecision over Gulf security was trouble-some. Nine days had passed since they'd reviewed the question. 'Ahmed is not going to make any decisions now,' he sighed.

Narey agreed. 'Right. Shaikh Rahman seems certain to succeed him and he resents the laxness of the modern Emirates. There's no doubt he will stir up Shi'ite support and return the Emirates to inward-looking Islamic fundamentalism.'

'Which means goodnight America. We get our flags burned, mobs in the street shouting anti-West slogans; instability in the Gulf; uncertainty over oil prices; a domino effect into Saudi Arabia and elsewhere.' The President was looking at the blown-up map of the Middle East tinder-box.

'Reports keep coming in that these Islamic extremists throughout the Gulf are gaining headway. Kuwait and Bahrain are minnows in a sea of sharks.' Narey paused to emphasise the smallness of the two shaikhdoms. 'I think you should go for our plan, Mr President.'

The President gazed at the stars and stripes, a constant reminder that he represented the hopes of the people . . . and of people far away, be they street traders in the souk at Dubai or tearaway Saudi princes crashing luxury cars for a pastime. 'And your recommendation? Will it work? Will there be no come-back?'

Bob Narey, Director of the CIA was positive. 'Technically, this is an easy operation. Anyway, do you really have a choice? You have the three personalities in that country. Ahmed is dying, Rahman is unacceptable. Next in line is Shaikh Hassan who's pro-West but inexperienced. He'd need to be cosseted.'

'You'd better go ahead then.' The President's head was shaking

The Dallas Dilemma

even as he said it, demonstrating that he wished there were another course. Some of his predecessors might have used more profane language but his warning was nevertheless plain. 'Just make sure there are no foul-ups. The election's too damned close.' He watched as the cracked leather face of the Director broke into a creased smile, each of them knowing that the risk of a foul-up could never wholly be eliminated.

'I think I read you, Mr President.'

* * *

It was shortly after 2.00 p.m. local time in Dallas when the telephone rang in Laidlaw's hotel room. It was Sandie, and Laidlaw's banter died away quickly when he heard the breathlessness in her voice. Immediately he was concerned. 'What's the trouble?'

'They've murdered Hugh Waddington. Sir Victor's just called me.'

The flood of questions which tumbled through Laidlaw's mind all seemed trite. 'Where was it? How? And who do you mean by "they"?'

'God knows, though I thought you might!' Laidlaw was immediately aware of the accusation in her voice. 'It's all part of your mystery, isn't it?' Her voice trailed away into silence and Laidlaw knew that she was fighting back tears. 'He was such a kindly man. And now this. It happened at his consulting rooms. That's all I know. What are you going to do?' Sandie waited for a response and it seemed a long time coming, so much so that she repeated the question, wondering if he'd heard. 'What are you going to do?'

'I'm coming back. There's nothing I can do here for twenty-four hours. There's a whole team of private eyes following up the leads after the press conference. Set up an emergency meeting of the Committee but tell no one of my visit to England. I'll let you know where I'm staying but that'll be secret too. Depending on what Hugh Waddington said or didn't say, I'm in some danger.' He put down the phone. God! Poor Hugh Waddington! Was it those Middle Eastern bastards? They could be rough. If they tortured him. . . . He grimaced at the thought.

His hands shook as he poured himself a large drink and stared across the high rise and low level buildings of downtown, until their edges blurred and he realised that he'd got the shakes. Had 'they' found Waddington's records on Shaikh Ahmed? Had 'they' found out that he had only a short time to live? Anyway who were 'they'? He'd always been inclined to think the office break-in had been the work of Shaikh Rahman's supporters.

It didn't have to be.

If they'd got nothing out of Waddington, maybe he was safe. True. Only if his phone call to Adawi from the Hyatt had not been picked up. Wrong! They'd picked up his *visit* to Dubai. That's why they'd done over his office. Unless that really had been the work of Drustein. No, it had to be Rahman's supporters.

If only he could tell Inge. No. That was out of the question. It would only expose her to danger. Anyway, she was battling with Bechrach and he'd have gone before she was through.

Having booked a flight, he spoke to Ralph Macey. 'You won't be able to contact me. I'll phone you. Apologise to Inge for me. Explain why I had to dash.'

'Sure, sure. And should I give her your love?' Macey finished facetiously in his dry lingering voice.

Laidlaw's laugh was sheepish. 'I didn't say that. Bye.' He wondered how the hell Macey had got the drift. Had it been *that* obvious?

In the cab heading for the airport, through the downtown

snarl-ups, he wondered how Senator Harvey Loftin was getting on. When he'd told Inge of Schillen's startled reaction to the word 'politic', she had instantly determined to speak to Harvey. It was one of her best features. Not only did she know immediately what to do but she acted at once and, moments later, her ex-husband had been dragged from a caucus on Capitol Hill.

'Marcus Schillen certainly knows Jack Hode,' Senator Loftin had confirmed. 'I think it goes back to college days. Furthermore Schillen has definitely contributed to party funds but there's no buzz round the Hill that Schillen's got any political role to play. I'll ask around.'

A DC10 and a 737 landed noisily in a pair on the parallel runways, bringing Laidlaw back to the present. He was reminded of his own arrival just four days previously, full of hope, expectation and confident of success. What had he achieved? Nothing? No. It was better than that. Just. He'd lit some fuses. Leading to what? Something . . . or nothing? And ahead of him was London and a dead Hugh Waddington.

'That'll be thirty-five dollars.' The driver's words were a welcome relief from Laidlaw's chain of thought.

'There's forty bucks. Keep the change. Buy some new springs.'

London

Lunch at the Goring Hotel, tucked away discreetly near Victoria Station, was an elegant affair. The very Englishness of the cool, comfortable room was a relief after the long flight and the heat of Dallas. He'd landed five hours before, dehydrated by the brandies which he'd drunk to send him to sleep, feeling as crumpled as a tramp's jacket. He'd showered and changed, and smoothed out the tired wrinkles with a catnap. Then a visit to the police, before arriving at the Goring for lunch with Sandie.

'You weren't followed here?' he enquired of Sandie anxiously.

'Not so far as I'm aware. I'm not expert in spotting tails.'

'I think we're all going to have to be more careful. Waddington's death has moved me one place higher in the batting order.' He broke off to study the menu and then gave their order. 'Funny, only yesterday I was uptight about Drustein. Today, it's these other bastards who will stop at nothing.'

'And you're still not telling me who they are.' It was a statement.

'No. 'Fraid not. By the way, who knows I'm here?'

'I've told no one, not even Sir Victor. Have you seen the midday Standard?'

'Yes. They haven't got it quite right. They're speculating that the murder was linked to Waddington's wealthy Middle East patients.'

Sandie smiled admiringly at her smoked salmon. 'That looks

good. But isn't that right? Isn't it all to do with the Middle East somehow? That's where you flew to.'

Laidlaw's response was decisive. 'Don't ask any more questions. Don't speculate and don't tell anyone anything. We want to keep Waddington's death well removed from Lusifren.' Even as he spoke he was conscious that Detective Chief Inspector Pritchard *had* linked Waddington's death with Lusifren and had asked Laidlaw one or two penetrating questions about the similarities with the break-in at Laidlaw's office.

Sandie gazed at Laidlaw's bronzed features, wishing that she could ask the question which troubled her most. Like, had he been screwing Inge something rotten. But it couldn't be asked. 'Are you going to see the police?'

'Seen them.' He squeezed the lemon over his smoked salmon. 'We may be getting somewhere in Dallas. How have you been?'

She rotated her glass of Perrier, twirling the stem, watching the endless bubbles before she looked up, trying to bring a smile to her face. 'I've got to say it, Rob. I've missed you. It's no use pretending. Life just seems so dull and ordinary when you're not around. It's like going through the motions without any conviction at all. Without you the Association just splutters along.'

For a moment he clasped her hand across the white tablecloth. 'I'm sorry. I wish it could be otherwise but I can't pretend either. Inge has really ripped me apart. I just hope you'll feel differently with time. One thing: you're going to find someone really special. I'm sure of that. You're looking so stunning these days. I mean, for months you've looked like one of Mao's minions, a lost soul from Red China, all white face and boiler suit. Now your War on Want face has gone. Suddenly you look . . . very Beauchamp Place boutique.' He could see that she was not offended. 'I wonder what Sir Victor thinks about it. You were supposed to grate against me.

We were meant to be red and white wine, never to be blended into a mediocre rosé.'

The laugh came quickly. 'Sir Victor is somewhat bemused, I think. The trouble is that working with you has changed me. I'm seeing my old friends differently now. Once they were idealists. Now I see that in some ways they are simply extremists, trying to change society from a flat in Clapham.' She paused, looking downcast. 'Remember our last lunch – and how it ended. I was hoping that maybe. . . .'

Laidlaw noticed that she was playing with her food, pushing the lamb round the plate. It was only then that he realised that he too had been ignoring his cutlets. He poured more wine.

'I'm sorry. Perhaps I went too far. I didn't mean to, least of all did I want to hurt you. Let's change the subject before I put my foot in it again.'

'Although the press say that Waddington died of a single bullet, that was only partly right.' He looked grim at the recollection, the humour vanishing from his laughter lines. 'What they didn't say was that he had been extensively tortured, his body massively defiled.'

'Tortured? Oh my God!' exclaimed Sandie.

'That's right.' Laidlaw spat out the words, resentful, face drawn and tense with depth of feeling. 'Whoever visited him wanted him to talk. I wonder if he did. It would be a brave man who resisted what they did to him. I, for one, have no wish to have my private parts cut off and stuffed in my mouth.' He caught her eye, as she pushed her plate to one side. 'Sorry – I'm putting you off your lunch.'

'Did he say anything?' Sandie had spoken without thinking.

'That's a bloody silly question. How the hell should I know?' Then he smiled, trying to take away some of the sting. 'Sorry. I'm a

The Dallas Dilemma

bit on edge. Jet lag . . . and a touch of fear.' Fear. *He* was at risk. His body. Six foot, one inch. One careful owner for over thirty years. Now it was threatened. Could be snuffed out at an Arab's whim. A single bullet. Or worse.

'After Waddington, you're number one then?' She saw the look on his face and answered her own question. 'OK. Don't tell me. I can see.'

Laidlaw pushed aside his main course uneaten, his stomach knotted like a fist. 'Don't worry. I'm not looking for a medal on my coffin but everyone gets that moment when they face two doors marked "easy" and "hard". I can't take the door marked "easy". Anyway, what about the Committee meeting?'

'5.00 p.m. You'll be there?'

'No.' He shook his head. 'I've changed my mind. Now that I've seen the police, I don't want any awkward questions.' The head waiter approached the table and whispered respectfully that there was a call for him. 'I'll take it in the lobby.' He stood up. 'Don't let my Filofax out of your sight,' he said to Sandie. 'It's my lifeline.' Deliberately he avoided using his own room and knew that the caller had to be one of two people. Only Adawi and Inge knew where he was.

'Rob Laidlaw speaking.'

'Well hi!' said Inge. 'Good flight?'

'Fine. But unexpected. I'm sorry I couldn't say goodbye.'

'I'm glad you didn't. I'm not ready for goodbyes, just hellos.'

'I know the feeling.' Just the sound of her voice made him want to pull her close to him, to bury his face in the golden brown of her neck. 'You'll want to know about Professor Waddington?' Quickly he gave her the details. 'What about you?'

'Me? I'm getting nowhere. No change. Every line of questioning on documents seemed to be anticipated. Maybe they're clever, maybe they're just well-informed. I wish I knew. But there is *some* news. A Mrs Sophie Gossop wants to meet you in Las Vegas. Her daughter saw your broadcast.'

'I can hardly wait. Who is she?'

'No, Rob. Quit fooling. It sounds good. She called just after you left Dallas yesterday. Ralph Macey spoke to her. Her husband, Max Gossop, was senior chemist and pharmacist with Schillen and, wait for it, he was killed in England, crossing the road in Stratford-upon-Avon. The story is that he'd forgotten that you drive on the left and looked the wrong way. Anyway she wants to talk to you. The accident was four years ago. Maybe you can make some enquiries?'

'Stratford?' He mused. 'Probably much ado about nothing, but I'll try.'

'To cross or not to cross, that was the question,' she countered, jokingly adding 'you'll love Vegas! Refined, chic, nearly as cultural as Stratford. Sophie Gossop lives there. Spends her time playing the machines, hoping for a jackpot. Or maybe a millionaire. Anyway, Rob, we've got another lead besides. A man from Austin, that's our State capital, saw the broadcast. His name is Hiram Green and he was in San Antonio the weekend the Kranskis were murdered and he shot a lot of film. When he saw you and Todd's mother and the photos of the Kranskis, he re-ran his film and recognised Todd and Rachel. He'd got two shots of them and each time there was another man in view.'

'Which means that the Kranskis, the cameraman and the fourth man all went to the same places. With tourists, is that surprising?'

'You're tired. You've got to think positive. Ralph's trying to get a blow-up of the man's face. See if we can pin him on Schillen.'

Laidlaw whistled quietly. 'A mug shot of a murderer. Maybe we are getting somewhere.'

Back at the table Laidlaw briefed Sandie on the conversation and sensed her disappointment that he was returning to the States so soon. He pushed aside his cold coffee and then picking his words carefully, told her how to deal with the Committee. 'Tell them that I'm meeting Sophie Gossop at five o'clock on Tuesday at the MGM-Grand Hotel, Las Vegas. It could be a major breakthrough. Also get our solicitors in touch with the Stratford Coroner. Here are the details. Schillen seems to have been somewhat unlucky, losing one of his research team as well as Todd Kranski. Get the solicitors moving today.'

'As you like it.'

'Don't you start. I crack the bad jokes round here.'

Las Vegas

It really is an oasis. So thought Rob Laidlaw as the long flight westwards from New York touched down and taxied to a standstill at McCarran Airport, Las Vegas. Where, seconds before, he had seen only desert, rugged, sparse and awe-inspiring, there was now something at least as awe-inspiring and maybe as rugged, but this time man-made – a shrine dedicated to the worship of self-indulgence.

Out of the plane, into shimmering heat he was immediately in the unreal world of flashing lights and flash money. At Charles de Gaulle or Orly there would have been armed gendarmes; in Lagos there would have been chaos and local officials looking for their bit of 'dash'. Here it was bandits, one-armed all of them, rows of them, lined up like a guard of honour to greet the latest load of New York stumble-bums with their limitless pockets and limited brains. Laidlaw found it easy to ignore the temptation, aware though that he'd succumb in the end. Everyone did.

Just a glimpse of the Grand Canyon and a laconic message that the Hoover Dam was almost in sight was the nearest that the flight had come to sanity. Everyone round him was out to have a good time; everyone round him was going to have one helluva good time. Make or break, they were going to really enjoy themselves, these pot-bellied New Yorkers, the women with so many facelifts that their navels would soon be approaching the peroxide, strawberry-rinsed hair. They'd earned it, this fat and sickly torrent of anonymity, each seeking a chance to be a big shot.

The feeling of being out of step with the madness accompanied Laidlaw until he was dropped outside the sparkling portico of the MGM-Grand Hotel. Before entering he stood for a moment taking it all in. The hot sand-flecked wind blew across his face and within seconds he felt as if the grit had penetrated every part of his body so that it was a relief to reach his room, seventeen floors up, clinically clean and chilled by the efficiency of the air-conditioning. From there he could see the lines of hotels along the Strip, the Flamingo Hilton, just opposite, Caesar's Palace, The Dunes, The Sands and the rest. After dark, the view of the neon city was going to be spectacular.

He booked a wake-up call for 4.00 a.m., showered, lay back on the bed, yawned once and remembered nothing else until his call came. Through the window he saw the reflected glow of the night sky and, feeling refreshed, he stood by it, staring down at the punters filling the scene – at least as many of them as during the daytime. Nothing seemed to stop. The cascading patterns of lights, multi-hued, beckoned their invitations in a dozen different ways and the Strip was filled with a line of limos, taxis and saloons, cruising slowly, ever so slowly, taking the occupants to their next chance of paradise.

This was the world of Sophie Gossop, the place where she chose to live. This thought accompanied Laidlaw as he went down into the dazzlingly opulent foyer, which housed the Casino, a hundred and fifty yards long and easily fifty yards wide, the whole room lit by endless chandeliers, beneath which thousands of people milled about playing blackjack, craps, roulette and then the slot machines. At the airport there had been only the single lines, but here platoon after platoon were lined up, filling the air with the endless sound of cranked handles and whirling symbols. At one of them was Sophie Gossop. He checked his bearings and then breakfasted quickly on fresh pineapple and coffee while others around him were eating lunch, or maybe it was dinner. It didn't matter. Time here was an irrelevance unless you had a rendezvous. He looked at his watch and set off into the rows of machines, where the air was filled with whoops of joy and the incense of greed, mechanical Elysian Fields where dreams of a fortune could seem real.

He recognised her at once, seated at the appointed spot, looking just as he'd imagined her, aged maybe forty-eight, dumpy and shaped like the bucket of dollar chips she was in the process of losing. Behind tinted glasses, her eyes were expressionless. Ten years ago she might have been attractive, but now she showed the blowzy decay of the life she was leading. The glittering pink of her lurex dress had lost some of its sparkle from the endless hours of rubbing against the edge of her stool, carefully positioned so that she could feed her chips into two machines at once, mechanically pulling the levers, never looking to see if she'd won, just waiting for the bell to signal success. Biceps like a bison confirmed that she'd spent too many hours pulling the handles, rarely pausing even to drink from her orange-coloured cocktail, courtesy of the management.

'Sophie Gossop?'

'That's right. That's me. And you must be the guy from England.'

'I'm Rob Laidlaw,' he almost shouted above the metallic din which surrounded them. 'Shall we talk here? I mean do you want to go on playing?'

'Nope. I always stop at this time. We'll take a drink. That OK by you?' She eased herself off the stool, clutched her bucket of chips and pointed vaguely in the direction of a bar. 'Let's go over there. SR was all right. R was kinda moody.' Laidlaw wondered whether he was meant to understand, thought about it, decided

The Dallas Dilemma

he was completely baffled and then asked. She laughed before responding. 'Didn't your agent guy tell you? Those two machines are *mine*. I always use them, *every* night. R is the one on the left. That's the one I call "Rich". SR, the other one, I call "Stinking Rich".'

'And one day you'll hit the jackpot?'

'I doubt it. But I like to think so.' She eased herself on to a bar stool and crossed one plump thigh over the other. Her buttocks sagged over the edge of her perch. 'Vodka Martini, straight up with a twist and no olive. Make that two,' she told the bartender before smiling at Laidlaw. 'You've got an interesting face. Too open maybe, gives away what you're thinking. So I'll answer your question straight away. No, I'm not an alcoholic. No, I'm not a hooker and no, I'm not here looking for an easy lay, though I'm always being asked once the hour gets late and judgements get blurred. I'm here... because I like it. I like the climate. Dry, warm and good for my asthma. I've got an apartment about three blocks away which I rent. By day I lie by the pool; sometimes I take in a show but mostly I watch the movies on TV before coming here.'

'When did you come here?'

'After Max died four years back. I realised I had no reason to stay in Dallas. Our daughter was married and living in Fort Worth and there was all the life insurance money and the proceeds of the house. I couldn't face a normal life, certainly didn't want to marry again. Being married to Max was more than enough. Not that there was anything wrong with him. But he was married to his job, one of Schillen's slaves, dedicated to the success of Drustein, uncaring about the toll which that took on me, let alone him.' Though she smiled as she sipped her drink, the downturn in her mouth and the lines on her face showed she was well used to the sadness and bitterness which she obviously felt. As Laidlaw looked at her he liked her, wondering how many other Sophie Gossops there were out there, pulling handles, each of them an individual, each of them with a story to tell, and probably a sad one at that.

'I'm surprised you heard about my broadcast,' he said and then wished he hadn't, as her eyes expressed the nearest to anger she probably ever came.

'Hey, honey,' she retorted. 'I'm no zombie. *You* may think I live an unusual life. Maybe I do. But I'm not ready for the meat-wagon yet, not by a long way. And to answer your question, I heard about you from my daughter.'

'Sorry. I've never met anyone who talks to gaming machines before.' She liked the remark and as she laughed, stretching her make-up, Laidlaw once again got a hint of what she had looked like when first married to Max Gossop. It was a pity she had gone to seed. 'Well look, Sophie, you took the trouble to make contact. I suppose that you know something about the death of Todd Kranski.'

'Don't ask me about that. I don't know nothing. I'd guess he was murdered on Schillen's instruction. That man.' She felt like spitting but refrained. 'He's bad, real mean. And nothing will stand in his way.'

'Do you mean that Max did? Is that what you're saying?'

'I guess.' The loose skin in her cheeks seemed to sag, the wrinkles in her face spread as her tired eyes, peering out from behind black lashes, looked down at her cocktail, which she swirled disconsolately with a swizzle stick. 'I don't know why Max had to die. He was a regular guy, he'd have said; the perfect husband. And to Schillen, he was the perfect company man, loyal, hard-working and with a good brain.'

'But?'

'Wait Rob, I'm going to call you just that. You're as cute as you look. You're jumping ahead.' She sunk her drink and called to her pet barman for another. 'Hey Wilbur, fix us another couple of those lousy drinks.' She turned to Laidlaw again. 'You guess.'

'But he was honest. Is that what you were going to say?' prompted Laidlaw.

'OK, Mr Wise. You got it. That's right. I don't know what it was. But in those last months before he died . . . was killed over in your country, he sure was running scared. Goddamned petrified. Crept about the house, nerves jangling. You could almost hear his teeth chattering. He never told me the details, just said he was being pressurised to do something he didn't want to do.'

'Because it was dishonest?'

'I guess so.'

'But he was working on Lusifren, wasn't he?'

'Oh, sure. A key man. One of three. He was the head. For Chrissake, Lusifren was his *baby*!'

Laidlaw was about to change 'baby' for 'bastard' when he checked himself, uncertain how she would react. 'Did he know that Lusifren was a killer? That it could maim, cause untold damage?'

'I guess he did but he never told me that. I reckon that's what the pressure was about. He went to see Schillen one night. When he got back after a twenty minute drive from Schillen's place, he was still shaking with fury. I'd never seen him so upset. But he wouldn't explain.'

'When you heard later that Max had been killed in England, did you think then that he had been murdered?'

'It may sound strange – yet it never crossed my mind. Not until I heard about Todd Kranski. I knew Todd just a little. He was cute. A churchgoer. Maybe a little weak. Max and he used to have lunch together. They got on because they were so different. Max was no businessman. He was a scientist, dreaming up cures for mankind. As for that bastard Schillen – he had all the qualities which Max never had, the ones which made him the winner and Max the loser. Maybe, too, Max had a sneaking regard for the man . . . and besides all that, hell, we lived in some kinda comfort.'

She leant across and put her hand on his arm. It was warm and enveloping, like her own personality. There was no invitation in the move or, if there was, it was a cry for friendship from a lost soul. 'I like you, Rob, I like you a lot. In fact I like all you Brits. We get a few here. Not many, not enough. I like big men, not just big physically but with broad minds, flair and imagination. Those were qualities which Max never had, though he was a good man and didn't deserve. . . .' Her eyes, sheltering behind a wall of mascara, filled with tears but she brusquely declined his offer of a handkerchief. 'No, no, I'll be all right. Sometimes, at five in the morning, you get to feel this way. So when I heard about Todd Kranski I started to wonder if perhaps Max's death in England *had* been fixed. There was no evidence to suggest it at the time. The driver of the car which hit him said that Max just stepped out, having looked the wrong way first. Forgot that you drive on the left in England.'

'It happens.'

'Too neat. Ask Schillen. I'd say Max had got in the way of something. So when I heard about Todd, it opened up a lot of old sores. But what could I do? Who'd want to investigate the suspicions of an ageing broad in Las Vegas? The cops would just laugh. Anyway, what good would it have done me? So I did nothing, not until my daughter said that you were sleuthing out the death of Todd and Rachel. Rachel was a nice kid too. Real nice.'

Laidlaw was beginning to feel disheartened. Encouragement was fine but he had flown over five thousand miles and His Highness Shaikh Ahmed could scrub another day off the short calendar of his life expectancy. 'There's something else you're going to tell me. Something you've told no one else. I can see it in your face.' Laidlaw encouraged her, not really certain whether or not she had any more to tell.

'Say, Rob, you ought to be doing a cabaret spot here. You'd do great as a mind reader. I *like* this game. You carry on guessing.' She rocked precariously backwards on her stool, the lurex straining uncomfortably under the stress.

'I wish I could.' He helped himself to an olive. 'All I can say is that I'm attracted to the notion that both your husband and Todd Kranski died because of something they knew about Lusifren. When was that meeting?'

'About two weeks before he went to England.'

'You didn't go to England?'

'Me? No. Marcus Schillen thought Max needed a vacation and so he sent him a note two or three days after the meeting suggesting that he take a break as a reward for all he had done. Max liked Shakespeare and so Schillen paid for him to go to England. Fourteen nights in Stratford-upon-Avon.' She laughed bitterly. 'But he never got as far as Twelfth Night – that's the way someone put it to me.' She laid her hand back on his knee and nodded her head slightly. 'Schillen was real good about it. Paid for an attorney in England to go before the Coroner. Paid for his body to be flown home.'

'The least he could do. Was your husband suicidal?'

'It's possible. That interview with Schillen really depressed him. Schillen was right too – he did need a break and I was glad that he was able to go. I hoped it would do him good. But I don't think his death was suicide. He was a scientist. I don't know what that means to you, Rob, but to me it means a man of precision, a man able to calculate odds. If he'd wanted to kill himself, I don't think he'd have stepped in front of a car. It's not certain enough. He might have gotten himself two broken legs and a sore head. No. If he'd wanted to kill himself, he could have made up his own lethal and pain-free potion at any time.'

Laidlaw listened attentively and saw the force in what she was saying. 'Come on then. You've got a gem for me. Trust me with it. Todd, Rachel, your husband. They deserve that the truth comes out.'

'I can't tell you any details – that's right but there was one remark he made before he went to England. I didn't really understand it but he said there was a file which would be his complete vindication. He called it his "insurance".'

'And where did he keep that file? Have you got it?'

'No. He never brought work home. The file would be with Drustein.'

'How do I know what I'm looking for? How can this file be identified?'

'It had a number. And even now I can remember it. He called it file 353.' She coughed throatily as she laughed at the look of amazement on his face that she could remember the number. 'I used to smoke and cough. I managed to give up smoking but can't giving up coughing.' She rocked her head back to laugh, revealing a too perfect set of teeth which nestled behind her carp-like lips. 'Most days I wish it was the other way round. But you're wondering why I can remember No. 353. It was easy. Our home was No. 352. Max made a joke about the file "keeping him one up".'

'But why have you never done anything about this?'

'With Max dead, what did it matter? Look Rob,' she stretched out her manicured hands and grasped his arm. 'Max was a research chemist. Lusifren was just one project on which he had worked. He was concerned about his professional reputation, his integrity if you like. He didn't spell it out but I got the impression that the file was there to vindicate him if anyone attacked his reputation.

The Dallas Dilemma

No more, no less. So Max died. I left Dallas. He had no reputation left to protect. And anyway I've never heard anyone criticise him.'

'No, neither have I. In fact I'd never appreciated the role he'd played with Lusifren at all.'

'If you hadn't gotten yourself on TV, I'd have done nothing. But I just hope you can do something to fix Schillen.'

'I intend to. Shall we go into the coffee shop and eat? You want some breakfast before I go?'

'Sure, let's go eat. It's not breakfast time. Time means nothing in this place. Mostly I go to bed about 4.30 p.m. and get up around 10.00 p.m. *That's* breakfast time. Let's just call this a late lunch.'

'Fine. Call it what you like. It's now 6.00 a.m. here. That means it's 1.00 p.m. in London. It's lunchtime there too. I'll join you.'

Las Vegas

As Laidlaw waited at the airport for the 9.00 a.m. flight to Dallas, he decided to fill the time with a call to Sandie. Better than the mindless gambling which surrounded him, though he had won eight dollars at blackjack. 'How are things going?'

'Fine. I brought the Committee up to date, explained that you were putting great store by your meeting this afternoon with Sophie Gossop. Oh! And I mentioned that you might have another breakthrough with some witness from San Antonio.'

'Fine. Except that you got your timing wrong. I know it's teatime where you are but I've already met the illustrious Sophie Gossop. Like at five o'clock this morning.'

Sandie laughed. 'I should have known you'd be meeting strange ladies at five in the *morning*!'

'That's Las Vegas! Sophie Gossop doesn't live what our church elders would call a conventional life. She was useful. Anyway, what's the news from Stratford?'

'Just as I told the Committee, nothing much. The American was knocked over late on a November evening. It wasn't a "hit and run". The driver stopped. There were witnesses at the inquest. The driver had no chance. He said that Gossop stepped straight in front of the car.'

'Maybe it really was an accident,' mused Laidlaw. He was about to continue when he heard his flight being called. 'I must go. Thanks for your help. Hang on! I almost forgot. But you'd

The Dallas Dilemma

have told me if there had been any news about Hugh Waddington's murderer?'

'No news at all.' He put down the receiver and hurried towards the gate for the Dallas flight. How was all this helping Shaikh Ahmed, he questioned himself? How much nearer was he to the truth? God, please God, stop the clock! Give me time, time to think. As the plane droned eastwards, he was acutely aware of time slipping away, constantly reminding him that Ahmed's ailing body was not going to wait for him. Or for anybody.

* * *

Little more than three miles from the airport, Sophie Gossop was alone in her second floor apartment, putting together a few bits and pieces to take to the swimming pool – suntan oil, a novel and two swimsuits. As she pottered round the bedroom, moving here and there with dreamy indecision, her thoughts were on Rob Laidlaw and the information which she had given to him. He'd seemed bright enough to do something with it. She certainly hoped so, and then maybe she could see him again. Yes, that would be nice. Nothing improper, just that she didn't come across enough gentlemen, especially English gentlemen, around Vegas.

Her warm, pleasant thoughts were interrupted by a knock on the door. She wasn't expecting callers. Who could it be? Rob Laidlaw! Mmm. That would be neat, real neat. She opened the door just a fraction and two men burst their way in before she could stop them. Instantly the door was shut and the shorter man clamped a hot, smelly and rather grubby hand across her mouth. The other man was taller with a pork-pie hat pulled somewhat low over his grey sallow features. His jacket was dark, his shirt green, with tie to match, his stare unbending. His companion was squat and sufficiently overweight for his ungainly shape to be all too obvious through the cheap cut of his suit.

It was this man who held the Smith and Wesson which he now pointed at her in a hand which displayed the nervelessness of the true killer. 'Si' down, Sophie! We've some questions. And I suggest that you don't scream.' He released his hand from her mouth. The accent was West Coast, probably Los Angeles but with just a twang of Texas. The taller man pushed her so that she stumbled backwards, sprawling into the depths of her easy chair.

She was amazed at how calm she felt, was able to notice that her sense of outrage outweighed her sense of fear. 'Say! Who the fuck are you? Why are you here?' Her voice rasped in anger.

'Just listen, and listen real good. You just answer questions. Don't bother asking. Your husband was Max Gossop?'

'Sure. You win tonight's star prize.' So that's what it was about, she realised. Something to do with Rob Laidlaw's visit. Surely he wouldn't have sent them.

'You're meeting a guy called Laidlaw at five o'clock this afternoon.'

'No. You're wrong.' She was quick in her denial, swift also now to conclude that it was Schillen who had set this up. Had to be! Bastard! Heh! Wait a moment! They didn't know she'd met him already. They'd been mis-informed. Twelve hours mis-informed.

'Don't,' he swiped her viciously across the left cheek as he spoke, 'give me that crap. We *know* you've got this meeting. We have information.'

Sophie's eyes glared defiance, her head spinning slightly from the force of the blow. 'Don't you dare hit me again and don't tell me when I'm lying. You're wrong. There's no meeting this afternoon or any afternoon. You'd better get back to Big Daddy for more instructions.' She sat upright, crossed her arms and glared at the man, her small eyes wild with outrage, the black lashes flashing warning. A blow to her other cheek was delivered by the tall man standing behind her, the impact knocking her sideways, though she quickly recovered to emphasise that she was not to be cowed. 'Bastard. Leave me alone. Tell Marcus Schillen go fuck himself. What's all this Laidlaw shit anyway?'

'You're lying. You set up a meeting for this afternoon.' The thin man took a step forward and with great deliberation, centred the cold nozzle of the gun against her forehead.

'I've told you. You're wrong.'

'Quit stalling! You have two choices. I recommend the easy way, lady.' The words were nasal, clipped, the choice as stark as the gun now held against her. 'You just tell us what you were going to tell Laidlaw. Then you hoof it out of here. Forget Laidlaw. Forget *everything*.' The man nodded his approval at that option. 'The alternative is you don't tell us. That way you don't get to tell Laidlaw either. A simple choice, doncha think? So make it easy on yourself. Don't go putting us on any longer. That way you'll live. There's no way I'd risk being dead, just so I could talk to Laidlaw.'

Sophie looked at each man in turn, saw four eyes, each of them as unfeeling as a shark's. She knew they were serious. She hated them, hated their yellowing teeth, hated the squat man's moustache, the tall man's hollowed cheekbones and hawk-like nose. She shifted uncomfortably in the chair, crossed her legs and then clasped her hands together around her kneecaps. She had an idea. It might just work. Have to push them a bit further first before she started to waver. 'You deaf or something? I don't know Laidlaw. Don't know nothing.' She managed to sound uncertain and the men knew she was dithering. OK, Sophie, go for it. They don't know you've already seen Laidlaw. Invent something. Get them off your back.

'I'm counting to three.'

'Don't stretch your brains, kiddo. I'll tell you.'

'That's better! I knew you'd understand.'

'You're right. I *am* meeting this guy Laidlaw. I heard he wanted information about the death of Todd Kranski.' She broke into a throaty cough, while the man waited impatiently for her to continue. 'Todd called me up just before he went to San Antonio. The day before he was murdered. He told me he'd written a report which was so shit-hot that it would blow Drustein into orbit. One way ticket into oblivion, he'd said. All about Lusifren.'

'Where is it? Where is the report?'

'I can't remember.' She searched feverishly for the right thing to say, something which would satisfy them, something to make them go away. Invention and coherent thought didn't come easily. She sat sullen-faced which the intruders interpreted as a reluctance to continue.

'Come on, you goddamned bitch. Don't give us that shit!' Another blow sent her head spinning. The ring on the man's little finger tore a lump of flesh from her cheek and blood streamed down her face and dripped on to the sun-top which she was wearing. She glowered hatred at the two men. 'All right, all right. He told me he'd stuck the report in an envelope to the underside of his desk at Drustein's headquarters.'

'Why didn't you tell the cops about this?'

She paused, momentarily lost for an answer. 'Because I wanted no hassle. I've been on Schillen's payroll every month since Max's death. Still am. It didn't suit me to blow Drustein apart. Todd confided in the wrong person. He thought I'd major the story if anything happened to him. I guess I considered it but decided to put myself first. I need the widow's payments from Drustein.' She paused to plan the rest of her lie. 'That was until I saw Todd's mother, tears streaming down her face, appealing for help. I said to myself: Sophie, you're a goddamned bitch, living on Drustein's money if you believe, really believe that Schillen had Todd murdered. I guess I wondered whether he'd had Max killed too.' She unclasped her hands and noticed that they were shaking. She quickly put them together again, interlocking the manicured fingers so that the trembling was stilled. The squat man had moved from his previous stance in front of her and was now out of sight. The gun, held by the tall man, was again at the forehead, the sardonic look still on his face. 'That's everything. I can't tell you any more. Now go! Get out! Get out of my room, get out of my life.' Her voice rose. 'That's everything. That's what I was going to tell the Brit.'

'But you won't, will you baby?'

The reply tumbled out. 'I guess not. No, of course I won't. Sure, I promise. I'll leave Vegas, go anywhere, do anything. Catch the next plane to most anywhere. All I want is my pension and a quiet life.'

The tall man nodded and shook his head. 'Understandable. Very touching.' There was a sneer in the voice. 'But it's unacceptable. Can't have you going round even *thinking* unkind thoughts about Marcus Schillen. I guess we've got the answer to your pension problem though. You won't be needing it.' He nodded to the squat man who, with a sudden sharp movement, brought the garrotte viciously round the woman's neck from behind, tightening it instantly and retaining pressure until he was sure that she was dead. It was the hand of experience. He'd lost count of his victims.

By the time Rob Laidlaw's plane was approaching cruising height, Sophie Gossop lay dead, sprawled across the purple and green carpet. By her side lay a dollar chip, one with which she had 'got lucky'.

Dallas

Even before Laidlaw's Dallas flight touched down at noon, the murder of Sophie Gossop was common knowledge. A suspicious neighbour had seen the two men leaving. Sophie wasn't one for men visitors, singly, let alone in pairs. The neighbour and Sophie had exchanged keys, and so the woman entered the apartment, only to draw back in horror, hands in front of her face as she saw the strangled features of her friend sprawled across the carpet, her hands clenched, her lips purple, her nose and mouth stained with blood.

Within half an hour the whole block was full of police, sirens wailing and an ambulance positioned and ready. Reports were flashed out on teleprinters, though another homicide was scarcely news in Vegas. A million buck payout from a fruit machine? Yes sir, now that *was* news.

None of this was known to Rob Laidlaw as he tried to convince his time-clock that it was not evening and that he was not hot, sticky and uncomfortable as the cab took him across town to Inge's home. Instinctively now, he peered through the rear window of the cab, trying to assess whether he was being followed. Could it be the Oldsmobile? Maybe it was the Lincoln which had been following at a steady distance for the past three miles. He felt on edge, eyes restlessly trying to survey all four directions at once. With the thermometer lipping 84 degrees in the shimmering heat of midday, the streets were almost devoid of people and those who were about moved purposefully to the next air-conditioned haven.

The Dallas Dilemma

Once they had turned into the quiet, tree-lined Highland Park, the open Lincoln had disappeared and a blue Buick Regal was the only car in sight as they cruised sedately up to the electronic gate of Inge's house. As he waited for it to open, the Buick passed by, the two front seat occupants glancing casually towards the taxi. Who were they? Probably nobody, he convinced himself as the gates swung open and he saw Inge standing at her front door, wearing sunglasses, a smile and little else. 'You look like you've just flown to England and back – solo and using your arms as wings.'

'Thanks for the compliment. With 5.00 a.m. trysts and enough different time zones in the last two days to make a Swiss clockmaker go cuckoo, I feel like it. But hey, it's great to see you.' He kissed her gently, touching her as if she were porcelain, almost scared that time and absence had changed something, until she held him firmly and he responded, whispering gently in her ear. 'We never even said goodbye.'

'Or hello either. I'm glad you're back. I've really needed you.' She wriggled closer to him again. 'And not just professionally either. Say, why don't you get yourself showered while I fix a salad for us down by the pool. Unless you'd rather eat inside. It's kinda humid.'

'No. By the pool will be fine.'

'Were you followed?'

'I doubt it.' To convince himself he shook his head vigorously. 'No. I'm pretty damn certain.'

'Fine,' she commented. 'I hope you're right.' He said nothing in reply but kissed her again, the touch bringing back memories of a few days before. 'And when you come down,' she continued 'I'll want to know all about Vegas.'

'And I'll want to know why you're not in the office or, better still, hurling a few fast ones past the slippery Mr Bechrach.'

'I'll tell you that now. Ralph Macey's coming out at 3.30 with this movie, taken by Hiram Green down in San Antonio. Ralph says we're not going to be disappointed but, before he arrives, well I thought you and I had a little catching up to do, a few experiences to share.' She waved him towards the stairs, posing herself like the naked statue of a Greek goddess which stood on its plinth by her side. 'See you at the pool.' She turned away, profiling the bronzed breasts and firm tight lines of her stomach and buttocks, the latter covered by what with exaggeration could have been called a blue bikini bottom.

'You're looking great Rob,' she enthused as he joined her by the pool, clad now only in swimming trunks.

'I've washed off half the Nevada Desert. You could make sand castles in your shower. Grit everywhere.' He looked around him. 'Funny, already it's getting to be like I haven't been away, haven't been in England, New York and Vegas at all.'

'Welcome back anyway. Try some Chablis. It's the genuine thing, straight from California!' She extracted a bottle from a cooler, knowing what he thought about the mechanised simulation of French wines in California.

'If it's cold, I'll drink it. The other half of the Nevada's down my throat.' He sipped it, and sipped again. 'But, having said that, it's not bad. The Californians are learning.' She'd positioned the two recliners half in the shade, half in the sun and upon each was a small tray with crab claw salads and a finger bowl and as they ate, they talked, covering a lot of ground quickly, using their own shorthand, each too astute to pad out the essentials, each knowing just what needed to be said and what could be disregarded.

'You're so concise,' she said. 'You could paint "The Last Supper" with a single stroke.'

'Why waste words but, seeing as you are in the mood for

compliments, brevity depends on the intelligence of the listener. So I've told you about Vegas and Waddington. Tell me what you think about this file 353.' He stopped caressing her neck and pulled her close to him.

'All-rightee,' she responded, dropping a cherry in his mouth. 'The highest file number used by Drustein is 347 which means that there are at least six more files, not only undisclosed but which, according to Bechrach, don't exist.'

There was silence for a moment as they both thought about it. 'Why not ask for 349 or 351?' suggested Laidlaw. 'Don't mention 353; don't let them know which one we're really after. Just establish the principle that Drustein have been dishonest in their disclosures.'

'Sounds good, Rob. Do you want a job?'

'I could never work for you. Far too distracting.'

'You don't seem to have been distracted much recently.'

'Is that a reprimand?'

'Call it an invitation. Ralph won't be here for another hour.'

* * *

If Ralph Macey suspected what might have been happening immediately before his arrival, he had the diplomacy to keep his mouth shut. Not that his mouth was really shut at all. It rarely was. Laidlaw had put him at about fifty, and was five years on the wrong side but most people made a similar mistake. The agent's face was shaped like the full moon and along the way it had attracted more than a few of the craters, dark and shadowy, which were creeping through his forehead to where hair had once been. Now he had almost as many hairs on his face as on his head. His wild grey eyebrows were like an unkempt garden, while the sun-tanned crown sported silvery-white hair which tufted sideways like a pair of ship's stabilizers. The overall effect was eye-catching, so much so that Laidlaw wondered how the man could ever make any observations without being spotted from miles around. But a glance at the cuff-links, the tie-pin and the Gucci shoes showed that Macey had both money and taste. His strength was probably subtlety, his success based on far more than mere snooping.

Laidlaw was eager to get under way and they went inside. 'I'll call you Rob. OK by you?' Macey enquired and, without waiting for an answer, continued with another question. 'Do you know San Antonio? No, I'm sure you don't.' He answered another question as he set the ageing projector running. 'What you're seeing now is the movie taken by Hiram Green from Austin. He and his wife were celebrating twenty-five years of whatever it is you celebrate when ending the first part of a life sentence. Seems they were staying down there, just like the Kranskis. Every weekend San Antonio's full of them – second honeymooners, old-fashioned kids looking for romance. The Kranskis were looking for God knows what. Just a devoted couple. No kids. Loved each other crazy. The Greens were looking to re-live their honeymoon with moonlight strolls by the river and a few highballs to speed them towards another twenty-five years of matrimonial bliss.'

'Come off it, Ralph,' laughed Inge. 'Just because you never married.'

'Too right. But I don't reckon I made a mistake. My idea of romance isn't a packaged weekend in San Antonio . . . or Waikiki. Give me an evening with the Dallas Cowboys and maybe get to date one of the cheer-leaders afterwards.'

'You're not twenty any more,' said Inge. 'Forget the cheer-leaders and get on with the movie. What are we looking at?'

Laidlaw peered at the screen. 'That must be Mrs Green, the one scratching her backside and then putting on the fixed smile for the camera?'

'You've got it, Rob. That's her and you'll see plenty more of her. And her ass. Not a pretty sight. Adult viewing only. Say, come to think of it, she's always scratching. Most every shot.'

'Just tell us when there's something interesting to look at,' said Inge feigning a yawn and sharing the joke with Laidlaw. 'Wake us up when Donald Duck appears.'

Green's film of the river, the Alamo and the Tower of the Americas seemed interminable.

'Mrs Green obviously enjoyed being the star. Have you noticed how she puts on that Marilyn Monroe pout?' asked Inge.

'I tell you, if she'd starred in *Bus-Stop*,' replied Laidlaw, 'no bus would have stopped for her.' He and Inge were still running on a high and, as they sat close in the darkness, he felt her shiver as he ran his hand gently across her thigh. 'What's more,' he continued, 'our friend Hiram Green took more shots at the Alamo than were ever fired in the real battle.'

'OK you funsters. Now you'd better start looking,' Macey interrupted them. 'The Greens have finished shooting the Alamo from every goddamned direction and, having crossed Broadway, having bought a Davey Crockett hat, are now admiring the water cascades at the Hyatt Hotel.'

'And there's Kranski.' Laidlaw beat Inge to the observation, but only just. Instantly recognisable, he'd come into shot, walking with his wife, a well-matched couple, he fresh-faced, casually dressed in 'Reeboks', jeans and polo-shirt, she in sun-top and skirt. They were arm in arm, not talking and seemed locked in their own thoughts. Whilst everyone else was stopping to wonder at the genius of the architect who had designed the tiers of water tumbling and sliding through the hotel lobby, the Kranskis never stopped.

Yet no – they were *not* alone in failing to stop, one other person had no interest in the cascades.

'See him? There's your man.' All three stared at the flickering pictures of the short, squat man dressed in an over-tight suit and white shirt. 'Now we move on. This is later the same afternoon,' explained Macey. 'They're outside the Arneson River Theatre and Green was shooting a backdrop of trees and water. Just watch this.' Down the steps came the Kranskis, talking animatedly this time. For a second the camera picked them up full face at about twelve yards, as they hovered, uncertain which way to turn before heading to their hotel. Seconds later, the squat man appeared, hands deep in pockets, head down, sauntering apparently unconcerned as he descended the dozen or so steps. At the river, he followed the same route. 'I think we owe a vote of thanks to Hiram Green for being suspicious. And I reckon he'll get the money.'

'Hey, hey, hold on Ralph!' Inge's voice was sharp and penetrating. 'All this movie proves is that Mr Green, Mrs Green, a short ugly guy and the Kranskis visited the same high-spots.'

'For Chrissake, Inge! That's the lawyer in you talking. We're not trying to persuade a jury. We're looking for a lead, a clue. And. . . . .' He paused for a moment to produce the blow-ups taken from the film. 'This guy,' he stabbed his finger, 'is an Angelino who just happens to live in Dallas.' Macey's crumpled face beamed in self-satisfaction as he poured himself another bourbon, confident that he had yet to play his best card. 'Y'all better wait till Ralph tells you the real big one.'

'OK. Shoot.' said Inge.

Macey was unabashed. 'This hood is called Arnie Travers. He's small time, well-known downtown, pretty much of a gofer. Been in jail for violence. Did three years. And, wait for it – you'd better believe it, the janitor at the building where Ed Bechrach has his law

The Dallas Dilemma

firm recognised him at once. Said that Arnie had been in the building yesterday.'

'Your imagination's running away with you Ralph,' intervened Inge. 'Just for the benefit of Rob here, who doesn't know the building where Bechrach has his offices, just how many different corporations are in there?'

'Well, it's thirty storeys. Your guess is as good as mine. But I reckon 2,300 people work there.'

'Exactly.' Inge looked at Macey with the type of dismissive stare which she normally reserved for the benefit of the jury. Now the only jury was Laidlaw, who was inclined to share Macey's enthusiasm.

'We've got nothing better, Inge,' he said. 'I'm impressed. It's got that sniff about it. Where's that famous instinct, Inge? I vote we give Ralph his head, give him a chance.'

'I'll tighten it up, real good, you see if I don't,' responded the agent. 'And . . .' A telephone interrupted him and Inge answered with the remote handset. The watchers saw her intense concentration, the pursed lip, the rapid note taking, yet apart from the occasional muttered 'you're kidding', Inge said nothing. She put the phone down, staring at Laidlaw with eyes which had turned cold and more than a touch fearful.

'That was my office asking if I'd heard. Sophie Gossop is dead, murdered this morning. Strangled in her apartment.'

Feeling as guilty as if he were the murderer, Laidlaw swallowed hard. The paintings on the wall of Inge's study seemed foggy and blurred, his senses reeled as he shook his head in slow even movements from side to side as he struggled to understand what was going on. 'It can't be right. She was fine when I left her.' The words were senseless, spoken out of shock, and neither Macey nor Inge knew how to respond.

'They don't know who did it – but there's talk of two men who were seen leaving her apartment, identities unknown. You never went to her apartment, did you? And I don't want any bullshit. If you went there, then we must know.' Inge was serious.

'No. It was like I said, I interviewed her at the hotel. She never invited me to her apartment. I guess she left me around 8.15.'

'Time of death?' enquired Macey, now following up his own line of thought.

'Probably around 9.30, which tallies with the sighting of the men. Her apartment had been turned over as if the men were looking for something.'

Laidlaw nodded his head. 'But who? Who knew? I don't know what to say. I liked her. She was kind, warm and outgoing. Yet she was sad. No, maybe that's not right. She'd had a sad life and was reacting with a show of bravado, living an upside-down lifestyle. To her, Dallas had been just one boring routine.' He clasped his head in his hands. 'Do you know, can you understand, how responsible I feel? Either I was followed to the meeting or someone found out she had responded to the broadcast and twigged her importance.' He paced restlessly between the ornaments. 'Do you mind if I have a drink? I feel pretty shaky.'

'I guess we could all do with one. I'll fix them,' said Macey whose glass was always empty. He filled the lead crystal glasses with bourbon on the rocks all round.

Inge put her hand on Laidlaw's arm. 'Rob. I know how you must be feeling. Maybe the man was Arnie Travers. Sophie's murder is going to be the turning point. It means she had something to tell; it means what she told you was true, was vital.' She took the tumbler from Macey and sipped without apparent enjoyment.

Laidlaw acknowledged that he'd heard, but stared emptily at his glass. 'Why kill her after I'd seen her?' It was a good question.

'Malice, a vendetta?' prompted Macey. 'Maybe she wouldn't tell them what she'd told you. Maybe they were expecting to find some papers. The question is whether she *did* talk to these men before she died.' Macey drained his glass and seemed ready for another.

Laidlaw was instantly reminded of another conversation when he and Sandie had debated whether Waddington had revealed any secrets before he'd died. His sigh was long and audible. Death seemed to be stalking him.

'Rob says that she had no papers, that all Max's documents were held by Schillen.'

Laidlaw thought for a moment. 'In that case, Sophie can't have said anything, otherwise there was no point in searching the apartment. After all, if they'd thought that she had helped me, there wouldn't be any papers there to give.' He felt pleased at applying some logic. 'Should we tell the police?'

'Not yet. Let's leave it to Ralph to show around the photo of Arnie when *we're* ready. Maybe whoever saw the two men leaving the apartment will recognise him. We've got our own job to do. Let the police get on with theirs for the moment.'

She came over to where Rob was standing, examining a Ch'ien Lung green jade bowl as if he really were interested in it. He wasn't. 'I just thank God that you caught that flight and I sure hope that you weren't followed here. If Sophie talked, then those men will be reporting to Drustein that you know about file 353.'

Laidlaw put down the ornament, all twenty thousand dollars' worth of it. His smile was wan. 'Suppose her death was coincidence, nothing to do with Drustein?' His tired mind was prepared to rationalise its way out of anything. As he looked at her, tall, cool, the set of her jaw showing her determination, he noticed also a glimmer of pity. Her voice however reflected harsh reality.

'I don't think so, Rob.' The reprimand was gentle.

'I've got two ideas,' volunteered Macey. 'And they're both good. First: who knew about the time and place of your meeting? Second: maybe Bechrach briefed Arnie Travers when he visited his office yesterday. He'd have easily had time to get to Vegas.'

'My guess is that he'll be back in Dallas by now.' Inge's observation was not reassuring. She nodded thoughtfully and found that she had been stroking Laidlaw's arm. 'Ralph, it's worth a few phone calls to find that out. See if Travers was in Dallas this morning. He'll need a good alibi.' She turned to Laidlaw. 'Think carefully. Who knew about your meeting?'

'I told *you*.'

'Sure. Who else did you tell?'

'No one apart from Sandie. Oh . . . and she told the people on my Lusifren Action Committee.'

'And no one else?'

'I told no one else. We don't know who Sophie Gossop told.'

'And your Committee . . . they knew you were meeting Sophie this morning?' probed Inge.

'Yes. . . .' Laidlaw's response had been quick, made without thinking. He almost physically jumped in his seat, his eyes reflecting the startling thought which had gone through his mind immediately afterwards. 'No! Wait! Sandie thought the meeting was this afternoon. I told her it was at five. She hadn't realised that Sophie Gossop wanted to meet me at 5.00 a.m. and told the Committee the meeting was at 5.00 p.m.'

Macey's southern drawl became almost hurried as he intervened. 'I told you my ideas were good. OK. So they thought the meeting was this afternoon.'

'Your modesty is as becoming as ever, Ralph.' Inge's face was a mask. 'I don't like where this is leading us.' A shaft of sunlight lit her hair as she turned to face Laidlaw, who had flopped into a swivelling leather chair and seemed to sink deeper into it as if retreating into a shell. His face showed disbelief as he spoke. 'Sandie? A spy? I won't have that. One of the Committee? A fifth columnist? I can't believe it.'

'Well I can. It could explain a lot of things. Think of the value to Drustein if one of your Committee were reporting to them. It would be worth more than a handful of bucks.' It was Inge's turn to be dogmatic. 'Schillen's mob could easily identify a weak link and then make an offer they couldn't refuse.' She walked to her desk and then sat on it, ball-like, wrapping her arms round her endless brown legs as she spoke. 'It's been done before. Committees are great for democracy. The trouble with democracy is that everyone has their say, everyone has the right to know. If we rule out Sandie, then an inducement to one of your Committee would have ensured a steady flow of information.'

'Oh god!' But which one would it be?'

'We'll work on that but I'd say it sure hangs together,' said Macey. 'No wonder Bechrach could side-step Inge's questioning. He'd have known from London just what your strategy was.'

Laidlaw was deflated. 'So what do we do? Tell the Committee nothing?'

'Tell them nothing unless we *want* them to know. I've got an idea. Let's set something up. Let's set *someone* up.' She swung herself off the desk, sat in her chair and scribbled down a torrent of notes.

Laidlaw looked across at her, admiring the neat boldness of the hand, wondering at the electric speed of thought as she roughed out her strategy, never once pausing as she wrote. Sophie Gossop dead! Strangled! Waddington tortured. Both had been trying to help him. Max Gossop dead. The Kranskis dead. He wished he'd never heard of Adawi. Wished that rubbing his tired eyes would wake him up and there'd be Inge. Keep the dream. Forget the nightmare. And still in the background he could hear Macey rabbiting on. Crowing about his success.

Nobody was listening. Nobody cared about Shaikh Ahmed. Nobody knew. It's up to you Rob. You and nobody else. Pull yourself together. No one else is going to fight for Shaikh Ahmed. You've got to be cold, calculating. Be like Inge.

He looked across at her, still the lawyer, brisk and efficient, even though she was clad only in a brief towelling wrap and bikini bottoms. He felt increasingly irritated by Macey's presence and wanted him to leave. All he wanted was to be alone, with Inge. To feel her strength. To share some burdens. To reassure her. To be reassured. Out of the question. Macey was pouring himself another drink and explaining to no one in particular his genius in tracking down Arnie Travers.

'I'd like another drink please,' Laidlaw said to him and watched the big man clumsily pour into the glass. 'Thanks.' The bourbon filled his mouth with its warmth as he wondered which of his Committee was Judas. If any of them. Or could it be Sandie? Vulnerable because he'd spurned her, upset her? It was impossible. He sipped thoughtfully.

Shaikh Ahmed was another day nearer death, another chalkmark scrawled on the slate.

'Listen to this,' Inge smiled at her audience. 'You'll like it. The aim is to get Schillen so cornered that even he can't fight. 'My plan's gonna give us game, set and match.'

Dallas

Not for the first time that morning, Marcus Schillen found that his foot had been scuffing the carpet, a lifetime's habit when under stress. He looked down at the fluff which had accumulated beneath his heel and then thoughtfully rolled it back across the indented line which he'd created. He poured himself some coffee but didn't drink it, only remembering its existence when a thin, cold film had appeared on the surface.

The call from the White House had not been reassuring. Jack Hode was not a man to panic but his tone of voice revealed concern at the erosion of his lead in the opinion polls. 'I'm still gonna win but we don't need any problems between now and the election. Marcus, that flight to Washington DC's as good as yours so long as I'm returned. But only. . . .' and here President Hode had deepened his tone, just as he did in his TV broadcasts, 'if you're out of trouble over Lusifren. There's polluted air gathering over Drustein like an LA smog. I don't want it drifting my way. Can't you close a deal over the claims? Don't tell me! I know you can keep it running for years but, as a friend, I'm telling you I need your help.' He had grimaced as he had spoken in the Oval Office. 'You won't need reminding that if that lawyer finds out something . . . unpleasant, the end could come much quicker.'

Marcus had been forced to agree. 'I'm hearing every word Jack. But to make a pay-out now, when we're not liable, would rip the guts out of Drustein. Hell, you know the way it works, once we're seen to have a soft underbelly, there'll be a deluge of claims from a bunch of rednecks. A pay-out now could cost us 500 million bucks. The way I see it, Jack, is that we go on fighting – get Drustein's name cleared. Maybe . . . just maybe make a small payment in a few years time.'

'You know your own business Marcus. I know mine. I'm just warning you. You get to hear things up here in DC. I just hope they're not true. That's all.'

'Like what?' Schillen was quick to ask.

'No point telling you, Marcus. Not if there's nothing lurking in your closet. Talk to you later. Bye.'

Schillen was still worrying when Ed Bechrach came on the line. Whereas Hode had sounded calm in delivering his warning, the words which tumbled out of Ed splashed panic in all directions. 'But are you telling me, Ed,' said Schillen 'that this Laidlaw guy has really got a breakthrough?'

'That's right. There's to be a meeting this afternoon at the Parkway Tower Hotel. That's near the junction of Mockingbird and North Central.'

'Sure, I know where it is. Our usual informant, is it? Well, I guess he's reliable. Helped us out over the Sophie Gossop tip. So what's going to happen?'

'Information is that Laidlaw is meeting a vital witness who'll name Kranski's killer. I've checked with the hotel. Laidlaw's got a reservation. The meeting's for 3.45 p.m.'

There was a long silence as Schillen stared across the open expanse of green towards the snarled traffic in the distance. In his mind were Jack Hode's words of warning. 'You say this witness can name Todd Kranski's killer?'

'Yep. For Christ's sake, what can we do? Whoever this witness is, he's got some video which he's bringing . . .' the words trailed away.

'Cool it, Ed. No video will show anything. It was *dark* when it happened. What's more, your report said to me there were no witnesses.'

'Well, I don't like it. I wouldn't count on it.' The defeatism in Ed's voice conjured up an image in Schillen's mind of the lawyer shifting from position to position, hunched up, first leaning on one elbow and then on the other, unable to find a way through an increasingly hopeless case. He'd seen him like this before. 'I'll tell you something else. That Inge Loftin's been on the phone. She's demanding to see files 349 to 351.'

'That bitch again! But steady – strictly speaking no files of those numbers even exist. They've never been mentioned. All references to them have been destroyed.'

'I know. So how the hell did that smart-assed lawyer find out? You know she and Laidlaw have really got me worried.'

'Ed – that's goddamned obvious. It's about time you grew some balls. Just when I need you, you're behaving like a real asshole. Quit panicking. At least the bitch hasn't asked for 353. So she doesn't really know anything.' Deliberately, he silently counted to ten. 'Mind . . . if they get hold of the San Antonio link, that's your problem. Just like that *other* matter. You'd better sort it.' Schillen listened with displeasure to the heavy sigh from the lawyer and knew that he had to go further. It was time to finger the man's jugular. 'Don't forget the odd favour that I've done for you, Ed. Now you won't let me down, will you?'

Again the sigh. 'I'll do what I can. What do you reckon about these files? I mean, hell, what if she asks for 353?'

'She hasn't. So why worry about it? Stonewall about the rest. Ask her to put her request in writing. Deny any such files exist. Say you've got to consult your client. For Chrissake, Ed! You're the lawyer. We must be paying you for something. Now get on and do it.' Schillen slammed down the phone.

On that discordant note the conversation had ended, leaving Bechrach popping an Alka-Seltzer into a glass and Schillen scuffing his feet in frustration. 'No callers at all,' he'd told his secretary over the intercom before locking the office door to create absolute privacy. Then he slid back a painting to reveal a wall safe, from which he pulled a stack of files, each carefully numbered, each buff volume apparently innocuous, yet the production of any one of them, most of all 353, would spell the end for Drustein, the end for Schillen, political aspirations and all.

He returned to his desk, refreshing his memory on the details, weighing up how best to deal with them. Two hours later he knew. There was no choice. 'Those files just don't exist,' he instructed Bechrach. 'Don't rush to tell Inge Loftin. Do what I said before. Stonewall. Say she was misinformed. Play for time. You got that?'

'I got it. But she won't like it.'

'So who cares. We're not organising a hen party to a Broadway show.'

* * *

At 3.00 p.m. Laidlaw had checked in at the Parkway Tower and moments later Macey had joined him in Room 209. Laidlaw lay back on the bed reading the paper, trying to concentrate, while Macey examined his Luger, an old friend which had once saved his life. 'Which of your Committee knew about this place?' enquired Macey.

'Peter Shaldon,' replied Laidlaw. 'He's the best prospect. He's suffered badly and was very short of cash. If I'd had to bribe someone, he's the one I'd have gone for. Sandie said that he was always asking questions, checking on what we were doing. At the time we weren't suspicious about him.'

'Sure. He had a right to know.' Macey threw the Luger onto the bed. 'Some chick, that Inge! Perhaps you've noticed.' The bramble-bush eyebrows rose in jest as Macey spoke. 'This scheme, it's real neat.'

'So long as you trust Sandie.' Laidlaw saw no hostile reaction.

'I do' confirmed Macey.

'So yes, Inge's idea of getting Sandie to tell each member of the Committee about a meeting with a key informant, but telling each of them a different time and place was. . . .'

'Inspired. Sure, Inge's cute. What she needs, really needs, is another man in her life. I was thinking of volunteering.'

'Don't let me stand in your way.'

'Jeez. I reckon I just could make a play for that.' The grey, wiry stabilizers of hair shook as Macey laughed at his leg-pulling. But then he was serious as he slipped the Luger back into his jacket. 'I guess we should quit dreaming of those legs and just check the plan. The Quality Inn rendezvous was an anti-climax but, like you, I just fancy our chances on this one.' His face was motionless, his strength of purpose obvious. 'Have you ever fired a gun before? Ever shot someone? Ever killed someone to save your life?'

Laidlaw shook his head. 'No.'

'I hope you don't have to. We'll just have to make sure that Arnie Travers doesn't get in here. They say he only needs one chance, one bullet. You want a gun?'

'No. I'll leave the heroics to you. I'd rather not think about it.' He picked up his newspaper, all the while feeling the growing knot in his stomach, wondering whether to be reassured by the Luger. He scanned the columns quickly, taking not much in and dismissing most as irrelevant until, at the foot of page two, a small paragraph caught his eye. No doubt in Washington, New York or London, the story would have been front page news, but the death of Shaikh Rahman, Vice-President of the United Arab Emirates, in a helicopter crash was of little moment to the *Dallas Morning News*. Whilst flying from Abu Dhabi to Al Ain, a rotor blade had fractured and the helicopter had crashed in the desert, bursting into flames and killing all occupants instantly.

Laidlaw had been about to exclaim when he remembered that he could say nothing to Macey. He laid down the paper and shut his eyes. Had it been an accident . . . or was it sabotage? And if it were sabotage, then who had removed the pretender to the Presidency? Who stood to gain? The telephone by the bed interrupted his thoughts. 'Rob Laidlaw,' he said as Macey craned forward to listen in. 'Thank you. Tell Mr Hackett I'm just finishing my shower. I'll call you back in about two minutes. Please ask him to wait till then.' Laidlaw put down the phone.

'Your man's here on time,' he said to the private eye. Ned Hackett was a stooge hired by Macey to carry a video intended to look like the vital evidence to be delivered to Rob Laidlaw.

'The honey's in the pot then. My other guy, Joe Lockyer, is in the lobby. He can take care of himself if there's any action. Otherwise he'll be taking photos.' Macey moved to the door. 'I'll go down. If Arnie Travers is there and he gets in that elevator with Hackett, then Hackett's dead.'

'Remember what Inge said. No violence. Low key if you can. All we're trying to prove is the link from my Committee to Bechrach. We're not here for a shoot-out.'

Macey grinned. 'Pity.' He slapped the bulge in his pocket. 'Make my day. We'll see. Anyway, don't open the door. Not unless you're sure it's me. Understood?'

'Understood.' Laidlaw watched the door close and waited. The second hand on his watch ticked interminably as he gave Macey time to reach the lobby. At last. One hundred and twenty seconds.

The Dallas Dilemma

Macey should be down by now. And Hackett. And Lockyer. And Arnie Travers. That's if Peter Shaldon was the source of the leak. He picked up the phone. 'Send Mr Hackett up, can you.' Now there was nothing he could do. Just wait . . . and imagine. He double-locked the door.

* * *

In the lobby Joe Lockyer enjoyed a good view of Hackett's arrival but he gave no sign of recognition. The lobby was not large and the main seating was shaped like a square in its centre. Mid-afternoon. It was a quiet time, the surge of check-ins not due for another hour or two yet. Sitting near him and within easy earshot of the desk was Arnie Travers, instantly recognisable, half-reading a paper but watching every arrival. His muscles seemed to bulge from every seam of his white linen suit, the restless movements of his eyes reflecting his inner tension. Now Lockyer watched as the squat, ungainly mobster prepared to deal with Hackett. Slowly, Travers folded away his paper and slipped his hand into the pocket of his suit. Lockyer had no doubt that he was handling the weapon with which he intended to silence Hackett for ever. And seize the video. Prevent it reaching Laidlaw.

He saw Hackett take a seat after being asked to wait by the desk clerk and then a movement caught his eye as the elevator doors opened and his boss, Ralph Macey, appeared. Lockyer felt better for seeing him, though he pretended not to notice his arrival. Macey paused near the elevator to study a street plan fixed to the wall. 'Mr Hackett,' called the desk clerk. 'Mr Laidlaw says to go on up. 209, on the second floor.' Hackett acknowledged the instruction and moved towards the elevator, the video-sized brown parcel in his left hand. Macey drifted away in the other direction in case

Travers had any ideas of frogmarching Hackett elsewhere. Without even bothering to look casual, Travers rose to his feet and walked pigeon-toed into the elevator recess, off-set and out of sight of the front desk. Side by side stood Hackett and Travers, watching the numbers flash as the elevator sped down through the floors to the lobby.

Lockyer watched the elevator doors open and Hackett moved forward, making as if to enter, with Travers poised to follow a mere two steps behind. Now! This was the moment! Now Hackett's life depended upon Lockyer as he aimed the camera at the two men standing fifteen feet away, both with their backs to him. 'Hi Arnie,' he called. Travers' reaction was immediate, his head turning so that the camera caught him full face with Ned Hackett right beside him. Surprised by the flash, Travers was indecisive. Then he lunged for the parcel in Hackett's fist but, perhaps realising that he had been set up, changed his mind. From behind them, Macey appeared, Luger pointing at Travers, cutting off that line of escape. There was only one way to go and that was the way he'd come. Ill-suited for running, he nevertheless made a dart out of the recess, Lockyer's camera catching him as he passed the front desk and out into North Central. He didn't stop until he reached his Corvette in the parking lot, eighty yards away, before jumping in, firing the engine and lurching dramatically away to disappear into the throng of the afternoon traffic heading downtown. Sweat dripped from the dark skin of his forehead as he congratulated himself on his escape and puzzled as to why no one had followed him.

Back in Room 209 Macey and his team joined Laidlaw. 'Sweet, real sweet,' said Macey. 'No violence. Inge will be pleased. The only shots came from Joe's camera. Got more mug shots of Arnie Travers than the Dallas cops have ever had. So . . . Shaldon's your guy. There's the leak on your Committee.'

The Dallas Dilemma

Laidlaw added tomato juice to the vodka. 'Don't you feel sick that he could do this?' asked Macey.

'Everyone's got their price. I guess the approach to him was too subtle and too big for him to resist.' He picked up the phone. 'I'll ring Inge. She'll be pleased.'

'Do I get to keep the video as a souvenir?' enquired Hackett. 'I reckon I deserve it. That sweat and garlic as friend Arnie stood beside me! I was just thinking it was probably the last smell I'd ever have on mother earth. Then I heard Joe call out. It was a sweet sound. Even from him.'

The craters on Macey's face erupted in mock anger. 'Keep the video? You're too young. It's an old Linda Lovelace movie. Maybe I'll send it to Arnie Travers, show him what he missed.'

* * *

The floodlights silhouetted Rob Laidlaw as he stood, massive bunch of flowers in hand, outside Inge's front door. Unusual, he thought. Normally, once the electronic gate had swung open to let in the taxi, she was there waiting for him. He shifted from foot to foot until the door opened. 'Hello darling,' he said, half stepping forward, the words choking as a tall, rather saturnine man, with gold-rimmed glasses filled the doorway. He was unsmiling, jaw full yet pointed. Illogically and instantly Laidlaw feared the worst, imagining Inge, throat cut, spreadeagled across the stairs.

'I'm Harvey Loftin. We haven't met.'

'Oh . . . er . . . I'm Rob Laidlaw.' He wanted to shake hands but found that, with his briefcase and the bouquet of flowers, it wasn't possible.

'Sure. Inge's expecting you. You'd better come in.'

'Inge asked me to drop by. Needed some help.'

'Is that you Rob?' Laidlaw heard her voice and footsteps echoing across the lobby. She threw her arms round him and added to his embarrassment by kissing him loudly and with relish while, from the corner of his eye, Laidlaw could see a flicker of bemusement on the face of Senator Loftin. She took the flowers from him, suggesting that he 'go freshen up and then come down for a drink on the patio', yet she seemed nervous, a little on edge.

Laidlaw hovered, not sure what to do, where to go. Inge's divorce wasn't through and he felt uneasy at the thought of his clothes lying around her bedroom. 'Don't you mind about me,' said the Senator. 'Inge's told me all about you. I hear you're doing one helluva job.' He put his arm round Inge's shoulder and continued. 'And you've chosen the best goddamned lawyer in the whole of the US of A. Bar none.'

Harvey Loftin, with fifty-one years of life behind him, spoke with casual confidence. It was easy to imagine him practising electioneering speeches in the barn-like space of this lobby, perhaps modelling himself on the statuesque pose of Thomas Jefferson, whose bust stood on a plinth next to a wax model of a pouting and busty Mae West. Laidlaw could see why they voted for Harvey. With his lean body, clean cut face and close-cropped grey hair, his mix of respect and charm could be blended to suit every occasion.

'Harvey's got some news from Washington,' said Inge. 'I think you'll be *very* interested but it'll keep till you join us outside.'

'I shan't be long,' said Laidlaw, turning to the staircase and, as he ascended, passing the wall poster of King Kong, he could just hear the Senator telling Inge that he thought Rob was 'a real regular guy.' He permitted himself a gentle smile as he headed for Inge's bedroom, feeling like the nervous fiancé just approved by his future father-in-law. Harvey Loftin seemed old enough.

Twenty minutes later, as the sun started to drop behind the

tree-line, he joined them. 'Hi, Rob,' said Harvey, thrusting a mimosa in his hand. 'I was just saying to Inge that it was like old times being back here. Trouble was, I had to spend too much time on Capitol Hill. Inge too was the victim of her own success here in Dallas. Our lives grew apart. I guess that's why we broke up. That and *anno domini*. I have a few years on her, a few too many maybe.' A rare and rueful smile flickered and died.

Laidlaw accepted the drink, uncertain how to respond and so took refuge in the business in hand. 'I gather you've picked up a lead in Washington.'

'Sure. And I'm going to tell you about it right now.' No doubt out of nothing else but sheer habit, he fixed his 'I'm telling you most sincerely' look on his face. Laidlaw admired the positive jut of the jaw, the steadfast look from the eyes, the crinkling and creasing around his cheeks. The man inspired confidence. 'I've got to move on in half an hour as I'm speaking at the Trade Mart at nine. It'll be a night for wearing a smile and a white tuxedo, but if it helps to keep Jack Hode in the White House, then I guess it's worthwhile. I'll come straight to the point, Rob. I made a few enquiries around Washington about Marcus Schillen. Politically, the name meant nothing at all. I was beginning to think your hunch about Schillen, when you used the word 'politic', was a no-hoper. Then two nights ago I was having dinner in The Palm with Larry Parker who, as you know, is as close to the seat of power as the mole on the President's butt.'

Laidlaw laughed at the line which he'd heard before from someone else describing the President's right hand man. Not since the days of Haldeman had there been another aide so influential in the White House as Larry Parker. 'Anyway we got talking. The usual Washington scene. The opinion polls, Central America, the Russians, the Saudis, Iran, who's sleeping with whom and whether it's doing them any good. Or, come to that these days, any harm. But eventually I slipped in the name of Marcus Schillen. Well, just like you saw Schillen react to the word 'politic', so I saw Parker's eyes widen and then flicker. I knew at once that I was on to something and was able to log-roll him, exchanging some info about a Democrat's indiscretion I'd picked up which just could be useful in the run-in to the election. I could see that Parker still didn't want to tell me. It really is top secret. So I had to be just a little bit indiscreet myself. I told him that there was a gathering storm over Drustein – fraud and maybe more. Far worse than anything reported in the newspapers.'

'Fine. No harm in that.' Laidlaw shifted position to keep the sun from his eyes and wondered whether his glass had a leak, so quickly had it become empty. He replenished it himself from the jug as the senator continued his story. 'On the basis that Parker wants to be kept informed, he told me in the strictest confidence, and to be passed on to you and Inge alone, that if the President is re-elected, then Marcus Schillen will be appointed Deputy Chief of Staff working with Parker in the White House – and that's real power.'

'Wow,' said Laidlaw. 'We've got him! I can just see his eyes water as we squeeze.' He took a generous gulp from his mimosa. 'It's incredible.'

'Incredible? I guess it is when you've just heard it. It's not when you analyse it. Hode and Schillen are old buddies and Schillen's a major supporter of the Republican Party – pitches in ten thousand dollars regularly. Better than that, Schillen's tough and he knows big business, an area where the President's notoriously weak.'

'So, who gets the axe?' enquired Inge, quick to realise that this was just as sensitive.

'Parker wouldn't say. My guess is that if this story were to break between now and November, it would blow the election wide open. This is why Schillen's appointment and the change-over is being kept utterly confidential. The polls say it's close but the Presidential wagon's rolling and rolling real good, so what the Democrats need is to flush out some real scandal.'

He helped himself to another drink. 'If,' he continued 'it leaked out that Hode was appointing Schillen and then the Lusifren fraud were revealed, Hode's judgement would be shot to hell. The headlines in the Washington Post would run and run. Just like Watergate, just like the Iranian arms deal.'

'Hode's been pretty good at his PR hasn't he?' Inge was phlegmatic, matter of fact and showing none of Laidlaw's almost boyish enthusiasm. She was still probing, testing the news from each angle, just as she had done in a multitude of law suits.

'Sure. This campaign's been kinda strange. There's been no real issue. That suits the President. Now the Democrats, hell, they need an issue. Remember Raymond Donovan, the Labour Secretary under Reagan? The timing of the attack on him was impeccable. After forty-four months of rumour, suddenly, just five weeks before the election, he was charged with fraud, pushing the Republicans onto the defensive, giving the Democrats the chance to run a sleaze factor campaign. Coincidence? You won't convince anyone in Washington of that. Now, if they only knew it, the Democrats have got another Donovan.'

'Only better. This one's fraud and murder. So what are you saying? What's the message?' Laidlaw's adrenalin had taken over.

'Parker and I had breakfast together this morning. For the moment, Schillen's got the benefit of the doubt from his buddy in the White House. Though only just. The President has requested that, if you're bringing Schillen down, you wait till after the election.'

'Request?' Inge's tone was hostile.

'You're right. As usual. I guess you can say it was as near to an order as the President could manage. After the election, even if you're not ready to bring Schillen down, he wants your evidence, confidentially. Doesn't want it before the election. You can understand why.'

Laidlaw assessed the position. The afternoon's events at the Parkway Tower had been the dynamite. Now Harvey Loftin had produced the detonator. So when to detonate? 'Thanks, Harvey.' His face and voice had become abstract as his thoughts drifted to the image of a failing Shaikh Ahmed, wizened, skin like parchment now, lying on his couch, sick and unable to move. His interest required action now. And there was the helicopter crash. He'd almost forgotten that. Where did that fit in?

'What have you got on Schillen? You said fraud and murder.' Harvey Loftin tried to make the question sound casual. 'Can you tell me the details?'

'I suppose Larry Parker put you up to that one,' Inge intervened sharply. 'No matter, we can't tell you.'

Loftin raised his hands to fend off the attack. 'Sorry. I shouldn't have asked. No, as a matter of fact, Larry didn't ask me to find out. I was just interested.' Neither listener believed him and each guessed that he was anxious to have some snippets to peddle. The slight baring of teeth towards a smile showed that he had not been offended.

'Anyway, time for me to leave,' he continued. 'Got to ooze out some old phrases and make them sound new, rally the faithful to the sound of Old Glory. Do you know, Rob, that tune used to bring tears to my eyes? That and all the rhetoric about our great country. Sixteen years in Washington has changed all that. I guess I'm getting old.' He extended his hand in friendship. 'I guess before I hit the sack tonight, I'll shake a few hundred more. Pressing the flesh – a real vote-winner!'

After he had gone, it seemed strangely quiet round the pool. Inge was silent, prowling round the water's edge, glass in hand but not drinking. Her head down, her frown etched deep across her forehead, she was obviously lost in thought. Laidlaw debated the reason for her concern. Was it something Harvey had said? Was it the comparison between himself and the man she had married or had she sensed that there would be a conflict ahead? The splash as she dived into the water interrupted his thoughts and he watched as she swam vigorously, arms and legs thrashing the water. He felt apprehensive, a prickly sensation gathering near his nape and spreading to settle in the pit of his stomach.

She came out of the pool, the droplets glinting in the floodlights as she stood briefly shaking herself, her wet hair clamped round her ears. He threw her a towel and she dropped down beside him on the swing chair. 'Decision time then Rob.' Their faces were only inches apart and, as she turned to face him, he could see the face of the granite crusher referred to by Schillen in that seemingly distant interview.

'You mean to pounce or not to pounce?'

'Sure. It's no contest. The time to strike is *after* the election. We wait until Schillen's about to catch the flight. Then we pounce. At that stage, he'll sign anything for a hush-up.' Her face, shadowy from the lights round the pool, was determined. 'What's more, that suits Hode. Not a critical point but I don't want a Democrat in the White House.'

Laidlaw's response was just as fervent. 'You're wrong. We can't wait. If Hode loses the election, Schillen won't be appointed anyway. Result: pressure point gone.' He put his arm on her shoulder but it was shrugged away: this was business, not pleasure.

'You seem to forget that I represent two thousand claimants, each of them relying on my judgement. I guess you'd better think about that. And think hard.' She swatted angrily at a bug. 'You're my client too. *My* clients do as I advise. That's what I'm paid for. I'm representing your Action Committee . . . and what a leaky bucket that's been.' Her voice started to quaver. Laidlaw had never seen her like this. He could see that she wasn't used to having her views challenged. 'Every move I've made, Bechrach was there before me, making *me* look foolish.' The vibrato revealed her anger and frustration. 'We do it *my* way. I'm not playing games, Rob.'

Laidlaw's jaw sagged. Such was the strength of her will that he felt drained, defenceless. Yet he was sure she was wrong. Very much so. 'For Christ's sake don't go on about that leak. Do you think I can forget that Sophie Gossop was murdered because of me? Because of Peter Shaldon? I'm living with it all the time. And don't forget I've still got to decide what to do about Shaldon.'

'He set up the chain for murder. Why not go for a murder rap?' Her tone was contemptuous, untypically irrational, her face showing the stress of the torment which she was feeling inside.

'Be sensible. I can't judge him too harshly yet. We don't know what pressure Drustein put on him.'

'Don't expect me to be reasonable. OK. So I'm giving you a hard time. Take heed. No one, including you, can undermine my career, taint my judgement. Nothing ever has or ever will.'

Laidlaw looked across at her, tried to catch her eye but she gave him no chance. He paused for a moment and then spoke quietly and without rancour. 'Sometimes Inge, we all make mistakes. Even you. This time, I'm afraid, you are wrong, hopelessly wrong. Schillen's got to be bombed out of existence as soon as possible. I'm sure of that.' Again, he looked at her, trying to see what impact he was making. 'I hope you're taking notice of this Inge? It's too important to sulk.'

'I'm listening.' Her tone was not encouraging.

The Dallas Dilemma

'I'm glad. So hear me out. We've got the link from my Committee to Drustein. That's corruption for a start. It's pretty obvious that Arnie Travers was going to silence what he thought was a key witness in the Parkway Tower. We know that the same Arnie Travers appeared in San Antonio. Almost certainly he was the murderer of Todd Kranski and his wife. We've got the link between Travers and Ed Bechrach.' He shivered as a slight breeze rustled through the trees surrounding them. 'At this moment we've enough to make Schillen write the biggest cheque for the victims in the history of pharmacy.'

'No. I'm the lawyer. I'm the best judge of evidence. We haven't got what we need. If we let Schillen sizzle a while longer, we may yet get hold of file 353. If it's as hot as Sophie Gossop believed, then we can negotiate from real strength.' Her eyes narrowed. 'Negotiating deals is my job. We do it my way. Clients who don't do as I say aren't clients for long.'

Laidlaw hesitated. Yet he was still sure that he was right. Was he certain that it was not the urgency of Shaikh Ahmed's needs which was influencing him? No. It wasn't that. It was a factor but no more. Should he tell her about Ahmed? No. Not the right time, not the right moment, not with that venom in her voice, that malice in her eye. 'My Committee will appoint another lawyer. I'll do it my way. I shall visit Schillen in the morning.'

Her face froze, shaken at his determination. 'I didn't realise you were such a bastard. Is that your last word?' Her stare was scornful, her long, elegant fingers pointing at him with disdain. 'Here's your warning. If you play my cards and foul up my clients' damages claims, I'll drag you through every court in every country. Everywhere. I'll sue you and your Association for every last dime – to the very last dime.' Her brown skin was flushed, her breath coming unevenly, the muscles round her mouth solid and tense.

So this was the granite crusher as defined by Schillen. Her voice dropped. 'I wouldn't have believed you could do this to me Rob. You of all people.' She leapt to her feet, her hair flailing. 'Go! Get out! Now!' She was close to hysteria. 'Our attorney-client relationship is ended.' She pointed him towards the house. 'And that goes for everything else.'

At first Laidlaw didn't move, not understanding her wrath and astounded by its intensity. 'I'm sorry it's come to this,' was all he could mumble.

'To hell with being sorry. Just cut the crap, grab your things and go.' She was in no mood to exchange sentiments and strode angrily towards the floodlit portico. He followed like a whipped pup trying to keep up with its master.

In the bedroom, its luxurious spaciousness full of memories for him, he flung his belongings into his case while she sat on the four-poster bed, legs crossed, saying nothing, staring emptily in the direction of an Impressionist painting of a clown which hung above her dressing-table. 'Goodbye then.' He looked at her, seeking from her eyes some last chance of reconciliation. He remembered Sandie's warnings.

'Screw you.' she yelled at him. 'Screw you, Rob Laidlaw.' Her words were still reverberating, his thoughts jumbled as he descended the stairs, realising that he had no transport. He looked up and saw her on the open landing, her face black and scowling as she stood, hunched over the bannister like a vulture awaiting its moment.

'I'll need a taxi.'

'Then call one. No, on second thoughts, I'll do it myself. It'll be quicker. I want you out of here. The atmosphere's kinda polluted with you around.'

Moments later he was standing on the gravel drive watching the

The Dallas Dilemma

taxi arrive when a thought struck him. He turned to Inge. The flush had gone from her face but the wrath remained as he stood close to her so that the driver could not overhear. 'Just suppose President Hode axes Schillen *before* the election, tells him he doesn't want him. As I think he will. Where's your pressure point then? I'll tell you. You won't have one. You'll have nothing.' He moved towards the cab. 'I'm going now but when I'm gone just think about it. You . . . the great negotiator giving up control to Jack Hode. Putting your clients' future at his whim.' He opened the taxi door and climbed in. 'But you're the expert. You know best. Goodnight.'

He settled back into the soft battered depths of the leather seat and had shut the door when Inge banged on the window. 'Wait Rob! Wait!' Then there was a pause. '*Please* wait! You may have a point. We must talk!' She turned to the taxi driver. 'Sorry but we won't be needing you after all.' Laidlaw hesitated, caught in two minds, debating whether to play it rough. Easy to be macho, to leave her in a swirl of dust and regrets of her own making. But Shaikh Ahmed had no time for posturing, no time for the dramatic gesture, no time for common sense to be lost in emotion.

Slowly, he stepped out with a sardonic grin on his face and shrugged his shoulders at the driver. 'Like the lady said, cabbie. Here's ten bucks for your trouble.' Together he and Inge watched the yellow cab cruise through the gates and away into the night. Her voice was quiet. 'Gee, I'm sorry Rob. I don't know what came over me. I'm usually so controlled. I guess it was a mix. I don't like my professional judgement being challenged and I guess I don't want to bring down the Republicans, least of all both Harvey and the President. But the way you played it . . . oh boy, that really hurt. That and my feelings concerning this thing you won't tell me about. I felt sure that was colouring your view.'

They heard the gates at the end of the drive shut and were alone once again. 'If it makes you feel better, I wouldn't have gone to Schillen, not without talking to you. I couldn't believe what I was hearing, couldn't believe that the last half hour was Inge Loftin at all.' It wasn't quite true. He hadn't had time to decide what he'd have done next morning.

She flung her arms round him and cried gently on his neck. 'You see, Rob, maybe I'm not quite as strong as I appear. Having Harvey around churns me up. I feels waves of regret, resentment and guilt. That's the truth of it. Before you arrived he tried to turn back the clock, tried to get me into bed. Can you believe it? Then he was uptight when I refused. I don't want him to suffer any more. I tell you, it's been like a cauldron inside me all evening.' He gently wiped a tear from her cheek. 'The trouble is, Rob, you stir such deep emotions in me. You create such intense feelings. The harmony's so great that when we became out of synch, something snapped.' She saw him nod in his gentlest, most quiet way. 'I suppose what I'm saying, Rob, is that I'm sorry. I was wrong.' It wasn't a word she often used.

Laidlaw held her by the shoulders so that she was squarely in front of him, her eyes half-closed against the glare from the floodlighting. 'Let's forget it.' We've got something special.' He saw her eyes widen. They were soft and damp, childlike. 'Consider yourself hired as my attorney again.' His arm around her shoulder, he led her back inside, determined now to tell her about Ahmed. The time was right. Now she'd be ready to understand.

'Rob, I'm sorry. I should have told you. There was a message for you. A man telephoned but wouldn't give his name. The message didn't make much sense either. He just said to tell you that it was imperative that you achieved results at once. He said you'd understand.'

'Oh yes. I understand all right.'

'And?' She looked at him, her face one large question mark. 'You don't look very happy about it.'

'Neither would you be. I'll explain later. First though we must summon Schillen to a meeting tomorrow morning.'

'And if he won't come?'

Laidlaw patted her on the bottom as they walked towards the kitchen. 'He will. You'll persuade him. You'll make him.'

'And when we've called him?'

'I'll tell you what's behind my interest in Lusifren. It'll take a time.'

Dallas

At precisely 7.30 a.m. Inge's secretary buzzed through that Mr Schillen and Mr Bechrach had arrived. 'Show them in,' said Inge. 'We really have made them jump, Rob. I vote we enjoy ourselves at their expense this morning.' Laughter lines creased her face for a second but then she was serious as the visitors were ushered in. Schillen, the smaller of the two, looked overly petite when removed from his own empire. Inge, immaculate and clinically calm, watched as he glanced round the room, sizing up the situation. His eyes and voice revealed his testiness. With a curt nod he shook hands with Laidlaw but Inge ignored any sign of courtesy and simply beckoned him to a chair, where he sat uneasily, crossing and uncrossing his legs, the overhead lights catching the glossy blue sheen of his expensive but brash suit.

'Well, I guess this is important. It had better be.' Schillen's platitude was intended for Inge although his eyes flickered between Laidlaw and outer space as he spoke.

Laidlaw said nothing in reply, leaving it to Inge to puncture Schillen's aura of confidence with a smartly placed Exocet. He felt fatigued, maybe the more so because of Inge's exuberance. Physically, the long hours, the constantly changing time zones, the deadlines, the fear of the unknown, had sapped his reserves. There were too many niggling worries. Who had been the mystery caller at the Hyatt? Who had killed Waddington? Had he been followed to Inge's? In contrast Inge was loving every second.

'Coffee, Rob?' Inge handed him the cup and snapped him into the present as she turned to Schillen. 'We want a settlement of every Lusifren claim. Do you agree to that or do you need persuading?' As Schillen helped himself to juice, Laidlaw watched the weak, restless look on Bechrach's face and could read in those eyes that the lawyer had slept not at all.

'I'd need a lot of persuading.'

'OK, listen and listen real good.' She slapped the three inch thick file on the desk, flicked open the cover and started to turn the pages, slowly and with definition, so that each movement was as persuasive as the slow turn of a knife in the gut. 'Here I have the evidence which will send each of you to jail. And then to Death Row. And don't look surprised. Don't play the innocent with me. I'm not bluffing.'

'You can't prove a thing. We're clean,' retorted Schillen, shoulders hunched as he leant forward, elbows on the desk. Laidlaw watched him struggling to retain the panache expected of him, noticed Bechrach steeling himself not to fidget in the face of Inge's stare.

'The Lusifren claims will be settled. On my terms. But shall I say it again: the State of Texas is once again using the death penalty. Electric chair? . . . Or you may opt for an injection.' Rob watched admiringly as, like Mademoiselle Guillotine, she chopped her right hand forcefully into the palm of her left in a gesture of severance and finality. The ensuing silence was deathly. The colour drained from Bechrach's face, leaving it a paler shade of green.

'Riddles. Talking in riddles.' Schillen's cough accompanying the remark was nervous, the bluster obvious. 'The Lusifren claims are worthless. They won't stick and neither will all this crap you're talking. Jail? Murder? You don't look crazy, just sound it.'

'But I'm not, Mr Schillen. In contrast, perhaps you are . . . at least you must be if you go on denying the truth.' Inge's response was immediate. 'I guess I was optimistic in thinking you wouldn't adopt the role of Brando. So take it straight. We continue this discussion on one basis only.' She clasped her hands together, eased her chair forward so that, until Schillen flinched, their faces were only inches apart. 'Just accept that we can pin the murders of the Kranskis and Sophie Gossop on you. What's more, we can show that you arranged for Max Gossop to be murdered in England. Because he was a nuisance. An inconvenience.'

As he listened, Bechrach was seeking saliva for his dry mouth while Schillen was wiping his hand down the seam of his trousers, a colossus turned pigmy when removed from his lair. Again, there was silence, a mind-ticking silence, which Inge was happy to prolong, a skill learnt long before. She waited until Schillen was about to speak and then cut him dead by looking away and turning to Laidlaw. 'Do you think they'd like to see the movie? Of Arnie Travers in San Antonio? Or the movie of his visit to the Parkway Tower?'

Laidlaw shook his head doubtfully. 'They might enjoy the movie though maybe they'd prefer some reading. What about the Statement confirming that Travers was a regular visitor to Mr Bechrach's office.'

'Sure. Or maybe Travers' confession.' She flourished a piece of paper, a dangerous but calculated bluff.

'And the fingerprints. They could read about the fingerprints found in Sophie Gossop's flat. Don't forget them.'

'No, I wouldn't do that,' she replied, keeping the dialogue moving, just the way they'd planned it.

'You're wasting your time lady. Smears. This is fantasy, tedious fiction of a very low order.' Schillen's voice gave away that he was not as bold as the words sounded and, despite the air-conditioning,

The Dallas Dilemma

a bead of perspiration had appeared just in front of his ear and was trickling down his cheek.

Inge laughed and ignored Schillen's assertion. 'Tell you what, Rob. Shall I read over the confession from your committee man, Peter Shaldon? Tell them how Drustein bribed him with two hundred thousand pounds to leak information to them. Or shall we tell them that the information he passed led directly to the murder of Sophie Gossop? I wouldn't want them to forget that, would you Rob?' She spoke contemptuously.

'We're wasting our time Inge. It seems that they don't want to listen. Tell you what. Maybe they'd prefer to talk a little politics – just like they do in the White House.' Laidlaw couldn't conceal his pleasure as he watched Schillen's jaw drop in shock. Inge nodded but decided to press on with other matters.

'Sure. We could discuss politics but maybe we could talk about why they marketed Lusifren knowing of its side effects.' The lines on Schillen's face deepened, the cheeks appeared more hollow, melting into despair. The Schillen of old would have stormed out. Now he was transfixed, uncertain. To walk away was a path to disaster. To stay, sullen and silent, was to admit defeat. The dilemma was disconcerting.

It was Bechrach who spoke. 'I hope you can substantiate these wild allegations.'

'Like hell you do. Quit trying these defamation threats. I'm telling you now, Ed Bechrach – your career is finished. Over and out. You're a disgrace to the Dallas Bar Association. You're a disgrace to humanity.' She rose from her chair and walked over the pale blue carpet, passing the tall pendulum clock and the Impressionist painting. 'There you are gentlemen. The exit. The fast track to the State Penitentiary.' She held the door, mocking them, challenging them to leave, arrogant in her superiority like a bullfighter taunting a dying bull. 'It certainly won't lead to the White House.'

As he watched her standing there in her white silk blouse, burgundy coloured skirt and flesh-tone stockings, Laidlaw wanted to applaud her. Better still, he wanted to go over and pull her to him, to relish the generous curves as she threw out her taunting, teasing message. Still she stood by the door, a lioness, queen of the jungle, tossing her hair defiantly as she pushed the door shut, a predator of infinite cunning, yet full of feline grace. She returned to her chair, all eyes upon her. 'Well, I guess you guys are smarter than you look,' she said. 'It's now 7.45. At 8.00 we take a visit to your office. There you will produce file 353 as gathered by Max Gossop. We know what it says.' She paused to glare at each of the men individually. 'Oh yes, we know what it says – thanks to Sophie Gossop. She'd told us most everything. The cruel brutality of her death was in vain.'

'These murders are nothing to do with us. And 353? There is no 353. Never has been.' Schillen's glasses bobbed on his nose as he shook his head over-vigorously.

Inge groaned. 'Schillen. You're just an asshole. Don't make me mad . . . or I'll call the police. Or maybe another number in Washington.' She wondered just when one of the listeners would take the Washington bait. Bechrach was looking enquiringly at Schillen, seeking guidance but there was none coming.

'What do you mean?' enquired Schillen, smoked out at last.

'You don't know?' She mocked him. 'Maybe your attorney doesn't know. For his benefit I'll explain.' There was a glint of her white teeth as she smiled at the lawyer. 'You see Ed, Schillen's been holding out on you. After the election he's going to be Deputy Chief of Staff at the White House. That's if President Hode is re-elected.'

Bechrach's face revealed that his surprise was genuine. 'Say Marcus, is this true?' He waited for a response but Schillen could manage no more than a flicker of an eyelid.

Inge spoke slowly, with deliberation, giving her listeners ample time to realise the crippling effects of her knowledge. 'You see Mr Schillen, you can lose the President the election. The gap between Republicans and Democrats in the polls is down to one and a quarter percentage points. In the run-up, public opinion is volatile. I mean when it comes out the way you've run Drustein – who'd give a dime for Jack Hode's judgement then? The President chose a fraudster? Jack Hode wanted to appoint someone who was a murderer? Your friend Jack would be a joke from coast to coast.' She pointed to the newspaper on her desk. 'If you don't come clean now, your name will be on everyone's lips, not just here but everywhere in the Western world. The friend of the President who brought him down. The man who let in the Democrats, the man who drove Hode into the political wilderness.'

Schillen was about to speak but she waved him silent. 'Some epitaph for you.' She rose and stood in front of him, one hand stroking the side of her face, the other outstretched to finger-wag him. 'He's your friend yet in your own lust for power and glory, you've repeatedly assured Jack Hode that you were clean. Clean!' She scoffed. 'You've never been clean in your life. You've defiled everything around you. That includes you Ed Bechrach. As a pair you are putrid.' She leant forward, flattening her palms on the desk, her golden hair swinging forward in immaculate harmony. 'Hode is sitting on a time bomb. It can be defused. You know how. *Your* future is short. Hode's can still be long. Don't kid yourself that you can do a deal with me. Did you ever read Charles Dickens? No? No worry. You'll be getting plenty of time for reading. I commend him to you, not least the character Sidney Carton in "A Tale of Two Cities", where Carton sacrificed his own life to save another's. It was, so he felt, the best thing that he'd ever done. Today, Mr Schillen, you have your chance to be Sidney Carton. It's your chance of saving Hode from public ridicule and electoral disaster.' She strolled slowly around the desk, passing behind the visitors, her back straight and stiff, her head held high, haughty and proud, her breasts prominent beneath her blouse, her slip rustling in the silent stillness of the room.

'Non-cooperation today means that this file goes to the police, to the *Dallas Morning News*, the *Washington Post*, the *New York Times* and to the desk of Jack Hode at a date and time in the run-up to the election which will cause the maximum devastation. Sorry. I should have also said a copy will go to the Democrats. It'll be the best news they've had since Watergate. Better than the dealings over Iran.'

Schillen waited to make sure that she'd finished. 'And if I co-operate?'

'Once the compensation is secured by bond and *all* your sensitive documents have been revealed, you will ring the White House and speak to Hode personally in my presence. You will tell him the truth and decline the job. Now, much as I want a Republican victory, if you don't co-operate, I won't hesitate to bring down Jack Hode. You see, even a denial by the White House wouldn't save Hode – not in the final days of a campaign. In the next month it doesn't matter whether the story is true or not. Compared with inflation, unemployment, arms deals with Russia, you might say that a presidential error of judgement in offering a key post to a murderer is a minimal matter. But in the tinder box of October and November, it'll be a story which won't die. Every link between you and Hode will be scrutinised. Every donation to party funds, official or unofficial, will be revealed. The story will linger like the stench of trash on a summer afternoon. Why? Because despite denials the public will *want* to believe it. Besides which, it's true.'

Schillen turned to his lawyer and was met with Bechrach's

The Dallas Dilemma

eyes, questioning, seeking out instructions from his mentor, for he'd known nothing of the pending appointment at the White House. Schillen was alone. Like filth on a running tide, omnipotent in its surge, Schillen had been fast, powerful, sweeping all before him. Now the tide was on the turn and, like that filth, Schillen was washed up, impotent and alone. His instinct told him to lie, to fight, to deny. But he couldn't. It was beyond that. Since the first days of Drustein, his fortress had always been impenetrable. Now as he looked first at Laidlaw and then at that bitch of a lawyer, their faces hard and determined, he knew that the castle had turned to sand, its defences useless in the tidal wave of hard facts.

Schillen looked at Bechrach and shrugged.

'What's all this White House stuff, Marcus?' Bechrach again sought an explanation.

'It's true, Ed. I couldn't tell you, couldn't tell anybody.'

'Then how, in God's name, did Inge Loftin know?' Bechrach was in a panic and was talking as if no one else were present.

'You'd better ask her.'

'Don't bother.' Inge snapped a lock on the idea.

'OK,' said Schillen. 'You want a deal.'

'No *deal*. A deal involves give and take. Today Mr Schillen, the market's against you. You do the giving . . . and no taking. The figure is eight hundred million dollars – equal to about four hundred thousand per victim on average, though the severely afflicted will each receive at least a million. Less than a jury might award but well within Drustein's capacity in conjunction with insurers. What's more, this sum must be bonded by close of business today.'

'Eight hundred million! That's crazy! *That* must be negotiable?' enquired Bechrach.'

'Sure it's negotiable,' Inge laughed. 'Upwards. So don't

start hassling me. We're leaving now to see file 353. No 353, no settlement.'

'I'd guess we'd better go,' said Schillen, easing himself out of the chair like a broken stick insect. 'File 353's at my office.'

'Fine.' She pressed a buzzer on her desk and spoke to Ralph Macey, who'd been waiting in the ante-room. 'We're going over to Drustein's. I want you to come with us. You can switch off the recording now.'

Dallas

Strange things were happening the other side of that door, decided Mrs Malone, as she sat at her desk trying to concentrate. They had been in there for three quarters of an hour, Schillen and Bechrach looking as if they hadn't slept for a week. 'No interruptions,' had been the order from Inge Loftin, whom she recognised from newspaper photographs. Laidlaw she knew anyway, but the other man, Ralph Macey, was unknown. The only time she had been allowed to enter the room was to replenish the coffee facilities and, during those few seconds, she had seen that the painting of the San Francisco skyline had slid three feet along the wall, revealing the safe.

The Englishman and Inge Loftin were sitting side by side at a small desk with a stack of files in front of them, none of which she recognised. Schillen and Bechrach were sitting across the room and Schillen was on the phone. On hearing the name 'Buzz', she knew that he was talking to Drustein's insurers, but about what she could only guess as she withdrew to gaze aimlessly at her VDU.

Her thoughts were interrupted as the phone on the desk rang. It was Inge Loftin, precise in her instructions. 'Within the next half an hour two people will be arriving and can be admitted. They'll be Buzz Crossley, whom you know, and an Angie Kerton. You're to let them in just as soon as they arrive.'

Inside Schillen's office Inge put down the phone, leaving the secretary realising that her boss was not in charge today, even within his own little kingdom. 'Angie Kerton's just about the best pharmacist I've come across,' said Inge to Laidlaw. 'She'll read the reports made by Max Gossop and understand them in seconds.' Her voice was low as she continued. 'What about the rest of 353? How far have you got to go?'

'I'm just starting on these memos between Max Gossop and Schillen. They're all dated in the few weeks before he died in England.' As Laidlaw went back to his reading, Inge herself slit open another envelope, nearly an inch thick, with stereotyped reports, but their interpretation was obscure, a job for Angie Kerton. As she slipped over the pages she heard Laidlaw give a low whistle. 'What have you got there, Rob?'

'Let's move into the secretary's room and clear her out. Then I'll tell you.'

'Oh! The cuckoos are going, are they,' observed Schillen, a flicker of confidence returning now that he was back in his own lair.

'Right. But it's you who's in cloud cuckoo land. We'll be back,' retorted Laidlaw. He gathered up the papers and leaving Macey in charge they moved into the side office. 'If you'll excuse us, Mrs Malone, we'd like to take over your room for a few minutes. Do you mind?' Laidlaw's face was all smiles and charm but it cut no ice with the secretary, who left her desk and headed for the corridor with ill-concealed irritation. Laidlaw closed the door behind her, his eyes blazing with excitement, his cheeks flushed with rage at what he'd just read. 'Bastards! You wouldn't believe what those bastards in there really know.' The words were clipped and spoken with grim determination. He leant back against the wall as if trying to relax but then surged forward, flourishing the documents. 'There's a *cure*! Those evil buggers in there have got a *cure*! Do you see what that means?'

Inge moved over to him, her coolness in stark contrast to his almost incoherent rage. 'Just sit down Rob. What are you saying? A cure for what?' She guided him to a chair and almost physically pushed him into it, pulling away the papers from his tightly clenched fist. 'Now, just count to ten and start again. Or do you want me to read the papers myself?' She kissed him almost patronisingly on the forehead, before seating herself in front of him on the secretary's desk.

Laidlaw laughed apologetically. 'Sorry. When I do get this out, when I make you understand what I've just read, you'll see why I'm so angry. So much suffering, so much pain and death could have been avoided. But those cynical bastards in there didn't care.' He stared at the floor for a moment, saying nothing, his breathing heavy with anger. 'OK. I can get it together now. Max Gossop reported to Schillen that the percentage of adverse side effects from the Lusifren trials was excessive. But by then the company was too many million bucks down the research road for Schillen to turn back. Gossop's report on the side effects problems was filed in 353. Naturally the FDA were never told. Schillen's reaction was to ensure that favourable appraisals from doctors and specialists were obtained at any cost. After Gossop's death, Weissman made a number of payments into accounts in the Virgin Islands for various medical consultants.'

'Bribes, no doubt.' She nodded vigorously. 'So that's how Drustein got its licence to market Lusifren – fraud and concealment.'

'Armed with that licence, approval in England from the Committee on Safety of Medicines came easily.' He sighed deeply and then leant forward to clasp each of her hands as he continued. 'The adverse side effects had been revealed when testing on mice and monkeys but still Schillen ordered the tests to continue on humans. Volunteer patients were deliberately subjected to the serious risk of illness as they underwent courses of treatment. In the heat of the chase, Drustein regarded the volunteers as mere fodder.'

Inge looked out at the man tending the flowers by the car park, unaware of the drama taking place inside. 'Nothing you say surprises me. It's what I suspected but now we have the evidence. What about the cure?'

'This is where it gets *really* nasty. Max Gossop, as their principal pharmacist and a scientist of considerable distinction, stumbled on an antidote to the *major* side effect of heart and blood supply damage. Remember that the worst problems from Lusifren have been heart trouble. Gossop appreciated these difficulties from the reactions on animals and in the course of his research also achieved amazing results, according to his report, on this antidote. On Schillen's orders some of the human volunteers who suffered artery damage from taking Lusifren were secretly used as guinea pigs for the *antidote*. They got better, never knowing how ill they'd been due to Lusifren. Gossop's formula worked on clearing the cholesterin. Now do you see what I'm getting at?'

'I'm starting to. But we've heard nothing of a cure before. Are you telling me that Lusifren victims who were given this antidote lived – or perhaps didn't even suffer?'

That's right. Schillen's notes show that the cure was hushed up for two reasons. Firstly it was impossible to reveal the cure without disclosing that they knew Lusifren should never have been licensed. To scum like Schillen, that alone was reason enough to keep the information secret.'

'And the second reason?' enquired Inge.

Laidlaw's voice lowered. 'Schillen had entered a secret deal with a small Swiss drug company in Basel for them to announce Gossop's cure as their own breakthrough in return for payments to him deposited in a Zurich bank account. Well over three million dollars has changed hands.'

Inge had quickly grasped the situation and projected the story.

The Dallas Dilemma

'So Schillen had realised at once that there was no way that Drustein could ever announce a cure without a heap of suspicion. But this Swiss corporation bought Max Gossop's research.'

'Yes, and a manuscript note from Schillen, dated just two weeks ago, reveals that the Swiss corporation is working to get clearance to market "their" drug in Europe. The greed of that bastard in there knows no bounds.'

'Maybe eight hundred million isn't enough, though I thought I'd pitched it plenty high enough.' She shook her head at what file 353 had revealed. 'No doubt Angie Kerton can check all this out. She'll be here any minute.'

'Christ. Do you understand? His Highness Shaikh Ahmed need not now be dying, Middle East politics needn't be in turmoil. Maybe the old boy's too far gone, but hell, with an antidote now, he might live. It would be a miracle. And for all the others too.' He paced up and down before concluding. 'And do you see? Once this Swiss company introduced the cure, Drustein's liability for fantastic damages would dwindle away. The heart victims in particular would be getting better. No wonder he was holding out.' He crashed his fist onto the chairback. 'If Schillen were to walk in here now, I'd tear him apart.'

'If *I* touched him, *I'd* feel soiled.' Her eyes darkened and even though she was ice cool, her brows were knitted in concern. 'Take it easy Rob. I feel just the same but it's a time for calm.' She spoke softly, in contrast to his outburst. 'We'll talk to Angie. If she can make up some pills to Gossop's prescription, maybe Shaikh Ahmed can live.'

Laidlaw felt sheepish at the way his emotion had again taken over from logic. 'God! If I could save his life. Unbelievable, truly unbelievable.' Still shocked, they were just words spoken without thought. She came over to him and for a moment they held each other tightly.

The muscles around Laidlaw's mouth were still twitching in anguish. 'So what do we do now?'

'We get the compensation fund established with Drustein's insurers. That's top priority. We'll get Angie Kerton working. We'll call the White House.'

'And the police? I got the impression that maybe you wouldn't go to the police until after the election, maybe not at all if he confessed.'

'Did I give that impression?' Inge's smile was wolfish. 'I'm glad.' She stroked his brow, softly, easing away the worry lines. 'But I also told him there would be no deal. The cops'll be here just as soon as the deal's signed and the money's been bonded – all eight hundred million of it.'

There was a knock at the door as Mrs Malone came in. Her eyebrows showed her irritation. 'Mr Crossley and Miss Angie Kerton are here. Do you want them now?'

'Sure. Show them in.' She turned to Laidlaw. 'I think we'll divide up. I shall have to deal with the insurance aspect. I'll introduce you to Angie. You'll like her. You take her through 353 and the other documents and get her working on the pharmacy. I'll go with the insurers, Schillen and Bechrach into the boardroom. It's going to be one long telephone call all day. I want the deal closed before the meeting breaks up.'

'Fine.'

Moments later, with introductions over, Schillen led them through from his office into the shiny chrome and smoked glass room. Though it was bright and sunny outside, the room was chilly from the air conditioning and darkened by the windows. Schillen's face was grim as he took his seat at the head of the long table, wondering as he did so whether this would be for the last time. He looked at Buzz Crossley, at Ed Bechrach and finally at Inge Loftin

The Dallas Dilemma

as she sorted out the papers in front of her and flicked her hair into place. She was well organised, everything in its place, every dagger drawn.

Was there really no way out? Was this really the end of his career? Was a lifetime of achievement, of fame, of wealth, really crumbling around him? Boom, boom, boom! The drumming in his ears added to the turmoil in his head. He felt dizzy, light-headed and wondered about his blood pressure. This was no way to end his career. To sign a document admitting defeat; to be frog-marched from his own headquarters in disgrace. To where? To jail. To trial. To conviction. A death sentence. Death Row. Appeals by his lawyers. More appeals on every possible point of law to every possible court. Maybe seven years of appeals, of raised hopes, of dashed hopes. Seven years of humiliation, seven years of retribution. Maybe a reprieve. Oh sure! A reprieve to life imprisonment. They'd carry him out dead. And for why? Because of her.

He looked again at Inge Loftin, his eyes narrowed and dangerous. *There* was the answer. *There* was the reason. *There* sat the person who had brought him down. No White House. No more meetings on Wall Street. No more excitement of stock rises and new deals. No hope of laying Lucille Malone after an evening cruise along the Potomac. Because of that bitch of a lawyer.

'Check the room for bugs, would you Ralph,' Inge Loftin said. He was looking somewhat off balance this morning, having obviously slept on one side so that one stabilizer tuft of hair was pressed down against his ear while the other projected jauntily at its normal ninety degrees. Add to that his drooping eyelids from a night on the town. He was a sorry sight.

'Sure.' No sooner had Macey spoken than Schillen opened a drawer in the top of a desk. From there he pulled out a recording unit. 'Here. You'd have found it anyway. It's voice activated.' He closed the drawer and put on something close to an angelic smile as he handed over the bug.

'Well thank you, Mr Schillen.' Inge was surprised at the cooperation. Schillen bearing gifts was out of character. She was suspicious as she twisted in her tubular steel chair to talk to Macey. 'Just carry on looking Ralph. Just because Mr Schillen has volunteered one doesn't mean there aren't any more.' She smiled at Buzz Crossley who seemed bemused by the atmosphere. 'I don't think we want our discussions recorded.'

'I agree,' Buzz Crossley, the puzzled Vice President of Drustein's insurers was quick to reply. There was something odd in the atmosphere, a tension which he did not understand. Still it wasn't every day that his insured gave instructions to close on a deal for eight hundred million bucks to be cleared in a day.

Everyone fell into an embarrassing silence though Inge was not embarrassed. She watched as Macey fumbled his way round the room until at last he proclaimed himself satisfied. 'Thank you Ralph. I suggest you do the same in Schillen's office.' All eyes were on Macey as he made his way to the door, his lopsided hair and rolling gait giving him the look of a 1943 bomber limping back to base after a night raid on Berlin.

From the corner of her eye as she started to explain to Crossley what she required, Inge could still watch Schillen. He seemed more relaxed now, was taking off his jacket and pouring himself coffee. It was odd. What had she missed? Perhaps she was imagining things. Anyway . . . concentrate. Get that eight hundred million bucks signed over. 'You've got the bare outlines of the deal, Mr Crossley. You start your phone calls. I want cleared funds today or an irrevocable bond. While you do the phoning I'll draft the documentation.'

The four occupants settled into their task, Schillen contentedly listening while Crossley telephoned and Inge and Bechrach haggled over the small wording of the agreement. Securing eight hundred million dollars in less than a working day wasn't as simple as buying a six-pack at a Stop-n-Go.

Dallas

'That's the formalities completed then.' Buzz Crossley pushed the signed terms of settlement across to Inge. 'Some sweat. Can't remember when I made so many phone calls but you got it, all eight hundred million dollars are now bonded.'

'Thank you Mr Crossley. I really appreciate it. I won't ask for any more favours today. So if you want to go?' She saw him smile in relief as he nodded his goodbyes and left the room, unaware of the background to the deal. His job of securing the money to Inge's satisfaction was over.

'There's your client's copy of the agreement.' Inge pushed the perspex folder, the pages just out of the word processor, over to Bechrach's side of the table. The laugh in her voice and the hint of a smile round the corners of her mouth said it all. Of everyone in the room she was the least jaded, thriving on the demands of the last ten stress-filled hours. Her eyes sparkled, her cheeks radiated power and mastery. In contrast, the faces of Schillen and Bechrach were shrivelled and lined.

'Can we all go now? I've got a corporation to run, brokers to call.'

'You *had* a corporation to run, Mr Schillen. The only running ahead of you will be around the exercise yard of the State Prison.'

It was then that hopes that Inge Loftin might yet do a deal surfaced again. He had to try. 'There's something in this for you. Name your price. One million? Two million? Paid anywhere. A

The Dallas Dilemma

bank account in Switzerland? The Dutch Antilles? It can be arranged. Just let me keep running my corporation. I mean, I thought we understood each other. Talk to the White House. OK. I've told Jack Hode I don't want the job. Settle the claims for eight hundred million bucks. That's done.' His voice was strained, cringing. 'For Christ's sake leave me something. Leave me Drustein.'

Inge laughed, head thrown back, hair flying. 'Jesus! I've never met a man who can make my flesh creep the way you do. You're more crazy than even I guessed. No deals! I said no deals! We settle on my terms. No dirty little kick-backs!'

Schillen's muscles clenched, his teeth bared in fury. 'You double dealing bitch. You hinted at a deal.'

Inge's eyebrows raised, her mouth pursed before she replied. 'Did I?' Her face was innocent. 'I think you deceive yourself. If you think. . . .' She broke off as Rob Laidlaw, carrying his papers, knocked and entered without waiting for an invitation.

'Sorry. I thought you were breaking up,' he explained. 'That is . . . I saw Buzz Crossley leaving.'

'We were. It was just that Marcus Schillen was putting a proposition to me. Money in a funny bank account. All I had to do was let him carry on running Drustein.'

Laidlaw looked at Bechrach and Schillen, a sneer of contempt on his face. 'I've just been speaking to Scotland Yard. Peter Shaldon was charged this morning.'

Bechrach rubbed his hand around his mouth. There was a nervous lick of the lips and the eyes seemed even more evasive than ever.

'Shaldon's information led to the murder of Sophie Gossop. Which reminds me that Julius Weissman was arrested this morning and at twelve noon Arnie Travers was picked up in a bar in South Dallas.'

'And I expect he talked?' prompted Inge, encouraging him to go on.

'He denied everything . . . for about half an hour I am told. Then he blamed it all on Ed Bechrach. That's where the instructions came from, both for the Kranskis and for Sophie Gossop and I reckon it won't be long before they pin the Stratford murder of Max Gossop on you as well.'

'I guess we've got him.' Inge had listened intently to the information, watching the shifty lawyer's reaction, appreciating every cheek-blanching moment. 'You've made your own will, have you Mr Bechrach?' She enquired innocently, hoping to prod him into an outburst.

'Well, don't look at me folks,' said Schillen. 'Nothing to do with me. If Ed here's been fixing up murders, then that's his affair. I know nothing!' He shrugged his shoulders. 'Jeez, Ed. Why did you do it? What got into you?'

For a split second there was silence. It was long enough for Schillen to know that he'd blown it, to know that he'd made the biggest mistake of his life. If ever there was a track he'd want to replay, re-record, then this was the one. Start again. Say it differently. Say it without blaming Ed. For Chrissake, what got into you Marcus? Ed doesn't need kicking. He needs support. Especially now. Just what you've denied him, visibly distancing yourself from his troubles.

Bechrach was now ready to snap. He sat in his chair, eyes lowered, hand on forehead. He'd heard enough. Yet no way was he going to carry the rap for Schillen. Hell no! The split second ended. 'You lying bastard, Marcus.' The voice was high pitched in frenzy. 'Everything I've done has been for you, to your order. You know that. If I'm going down, then you're coming too. My God, what I've done for you, only to be deserted when I needed you most.' He

The Dallas Dilemma

looked up and eyes of hatred fixed the corporate President sitting at the head of the table. 'But I'm not going to be alone. You're coming too.' He repeated the warning through gritted teeth. All eyes were on Bechrach, his face taut with emotion, his eyes staring in fixed penetration at his mentor.

'All right,' said Schillen, his voice quiet, his pace measured. 'I guess that's it then folks.' It was said so calmly, so casual was the tone that when he bent as if to gather his briefcase from the floor, it looked like the raising of the white flag of surrender. Inge relaxed.

'Right, Rob. I suggest you step out and get the police. They're still in the building, are they?'

'Some took Weissman downtown to Police HQ but there'll be others. I'll go and fetch them.'

'Hold it.' The voice was abrasive. 'Wait just there Laidlaw.' It was Schillen who had spoken and when Inge looked, her glance took in the open drawer in front of him and the .38 automatic pistol in his hand. Instantly she understood why he'd volunteered the bugging device from his drawer. It was to conceal the existence of the gun.

Too late now for self-recrimination. She looked at Schillen. She looked at the gun and knew at once that he was serious. Schillen was a man with nothing to lose now.

'I was just thinking of popping out to fetch the cops,' said Laidlaw wondering from where he'd got the ability to jest in the face of a handgun.

'And I was just thinking of shooting you first. But no. I think I'll start with Ed. I feel nice and relaxed now. I can see the three of you. The three people who've brought me down. Well, I can tell you I've got a full chamber. There's a bullet for each of us. I'm prepared to die. You've left me nothing else. First though, I shall have the pleasure of seeing you die.'

Laidlaw sat down, replacing his Filofax and documents on the table. 'Don't you think there's been enough killing?' he asked.

'Maybe. A few more won't matter, especially when they're you.' Grey, cold eyes accompanied the menace of the words. Slowly he turned the gun to Bechrach who, like the other two captives, was seated just a few feet from the gun. 'I'd like to say I'm sorry Ed. You know, give you a decent epitaph. But you don't deserve it. You always were scum. Right to the end.'

He squeezed the trigger and while Inge and Laidlaw watched aghast and helpless to intervene, they saw the reflex of self-protection before the bullet struck Bechrach slightly to the left side of his temple. The force of the impact rocked him backwards until he collapsed with a groan sideways to the floor.

There he lay. Motionless.

Then there was just a moment when Laidlaw might have dived at Schillen, catching him after the gun had fired. He hesitated. With Inge between him and the head of the table it was risky and even measuring the chance lost him the opportunity anyway. Schillen, face white with concentration, moved the gun and Laidlaw saw the muzzle face him. He thought of Waddington; he thought of Max Gossop, Sophie Gossop, Todd Kranski and Rachel Kranski. He saw Bechrach lying in a widening pool of his own blood. So why should he be different? Why should he be the lucky one to survive?

Rob, the luck's run out.

Then the pistol swung away from him to point at Inge but Schillen's words were aimed at Laidlaw. 'I heard you were screwing the ass off this bitch. I'll take her next. You can see her die as well.'

He aimed the gun at her head. This time Laidlaw acted without thinking, throwing himself sideways, barging Inge heavily to her right. As the bullet from Schillen's gun passed the Englishman's shoulder and buried itself in the soundproof wall, the boardroom

The Dallas Dilemma

door crashed open and a policeman in plain clothes was immediately in command, a revolver in his hand. With twenty years experience, he took in the entire picture, saw the corpse, saw the gun in Schillen's hands, saw the cowering bodies of Laidlaw and Inge Loftin. Surprised, Schillen swung his aim towards the intruder but before he had time to press the trigger, a bullet struck him, penetrating his heart. The gun fell from Schillen's hand as his arm slumped lifeless by his side.

Cautiously Laidlaw raised his head from Inge's body and unwound his arms from where he had grasped her in the despairing lunge. 'It's all clear, sweetheart. The US Cavalry has arrived.' He gave a weak grin to the policeman. 'In the films I've seen, they don't usually leave it quite so late.'

The policeman stooped to check the bodies. 'Next time y'all must send out the smoke signals sooner then.'

* * *

In Julius Weissman's office, empty now that he was being quartered somewhere downtown, Rob Laidlaw relaxed on a chaise-longue. He checked Adawi's number from his index and then dialled straight through. As usual with Adawi there were no preliminaries. As soon as the word 'cure' was mentioned, Adawi was insistent. 'Fly now. Bring pills with you. It's urgent.'

Laidlaw's sigh was helpless. 'I can't. They're not even made up yet. Our pharmacist's doing her best but they won't be ready until sometime tomorrow. I'll fly them to London.'

'Meet me there. Time is *very* short now.'

'Any news on why Shaikh Rahman's helicopter crashed?' Laidlaw was in two minds whether to ask but unusually Adawi was forthcoming. He told him.

A few moments later Laidlaw replaced the receiver and joined Inge along the corridor in Schillen's office where she was just finishing her statement for the police and also a press release for the horde of journalists who had been baying for news in the downstairs lobby for the past two hours. 'Ah, Rob! We're free to leave now.' She smiled at the two detectives who'd interviewed her.

'Fine. Thank you Ma'am. Y'all take care now.' It was the traditional throwaway line, so often said without thinking.

Laidlaw laughed. The words seemed to have a special irony but Inge's thoughts were elsewhere as they walked along the deserted passageway to the elevator. 'That blighter Adawi wasn't interested in our safety at all. Didn't seem to care that we'd escaped death by divine intervention. Least of all was he grateful for what we'd done. Not a word of it.'

'Gratitude! You don't do your job for gratitude. Neither do I. We give it twenty-five hours a day for our own satisfaction. The day you go to work expecting thanks, you might as well give up.'

'Well don't forget what you said yesterday. I'm *your* client. I'm grateful.' As they stood waiting for the elevator to arrive he kissed her on the mouth.

'*And* you're a lover . . . *I'm* grateful for that too.' Suddenly she trembled, shaking all over quite involuntarily. 'I'm only now realising just what you did for me. You risked your own life to save mine. How can I ever thank you?'

'You being alive is thanks enough.' He clasped her tightly and started to add something when the elevator door swished open but Inge held him back. 'Look. I'll give the press statement. We say nothing about Angie Kerton and no mention of any cure. We mustn't raise false hopes. By the way, when did Angie say that she would drop by with the tablets?'

'You make her sound like Moses. I hope she's quicker than he was. She reckons it'll be tomorrow.'

They stepped inside and the elevator started on its descent. Inge put a hand on each of his shoulders and looked Laidlaw square in the eyes. She was still trembling, the reaction to what they'd been through setting in. 'This divine intervention? Do you really believe that, Rob?'

Laidlaw bit his lips and shook his head thoughtfully. 'No. I can't believe in that. I suppose the cops heard the shot and then barged in.'

Inge looked doubtful. 'You think so? Seems strange to me. That room is sound-proofed. Schillen mentioned that earlier on.'

'Well in that case we were just lucky. Deservedly so.'

'They wouldn't have saved my life. That was you.'

'You deserved that.' He was about to kiss her again when the elevator glided to a stop.

'Save that for later. The press would love that one for their front pages. I'm not giving them the pleasure.' The doors opened and they faced a throng of shouting, jostling newsmen. She knew that they would want to talk about the shootings but deliberately she talked of what interested her first. 'Gentlemen. Is this what you've come to see?' She flourished the document settling the litigation. 'Eight hundred million dollars. That's the settlement figure. Signed by Marcus Schillen and Ed Bechrach. Just about their last act before they died. Quote me as saying it's the best thing they ever did. Today's a great day for all the victims of Lusifren.'

'Eight hundred million? Is that your fee?' someone shouted from the back to a burst of laughter.

'Is it true that Julius Weissman is on a murder charge? Did you see Ed Bechrach killed? Would Schillen have shot the cop?' From all corners, shouted questions filled the air and it took twenty minutes to half-satisfy the throng. Then a whispered word from Inge to the security guards and they were escorted into the early evening air and to the cool silence of Inge's BMW. They slammed the doors and with a screech of tyres sped away towards North Central.

'Quite a day,' Inge enthused. 'In twelve hours we've destroyed Drustein, seen the end of Schillen, Bechrach and Weissman. Better still, we've clinched eight hundred million bucks and yet not spilt a word about the White House link.'

'And we've discovered the cure.'

'Sure. How hopeful was Angie?'

Chemistry didn't come easy to Laidlaw. 'If I've understood her, Gossop had discovered a formula which attacks cholesterol and other lipids which clog the arteries. She described Gossop's goo as a rapid healer, de-clogging the arteries and giving the heart a chance to work properly.'

'Maybe too late for the Shaikh,' observed Inge. 'I suppose for you that's the most important thing. I've achieved everything I needed. I can see it's different for you.' Inge cut across an ageing Packard and ignored the blast of horns.

'Don't remind me. Adawi gets nearly hysterical on the subject.'

'Because without Shaikh Ahmed as President he's out in the wilderness, I guess.'

'Which brings us back to Moses again.' Laidlaw was elated. 'I just don't know what happens to Adawi in that situation. Anyway, think positive. We'll shove so many of these pills into the old boy that you'll hear him rattle in Dallas.'

'Sure. Just so long as it's not a death rattle.' Her every vowel, every consonant was laid back, drawled from the wide expanse of her Texan accent. 'Hey, Rob! What about the helicopter crash? Did you ask Adawi about that?'

The Dallas Dilemma

'I should have told you.' Laidlaw grasped the dashboard as Inge made a ninety degree bend seem like a Roman road. 'Someone had tampered with a rotor blade. He didn't know who. Papers found in Rahman's offices proved that he was plotting a coup. What's more, under interrogation, one of his aides had confessed to planting the Jebel Ali bomb.'

'So Shaikh Rahman approved the killing of his own father.'

'So it seemed. Shaikh Rahman was a zealot. His father stood in the way of a return to strict Islamic principles and goodbye to Western decadence.' Laidlaw found that he was speaking slowly, his mind tired, his thoughts less than orderly. 'You realise there would have been a coup already against Shaikh Ahmed but for one thing?'

'Being that Rahman knew that his President was dying.'

Laidlaw turned to her, a look of admiration on his face. 'You've guessed. I suppose it was obvious really. Adawi told me that one of Rahman's aides has confirmed that they'd found out about Ahmed's health. They'd known for months that something was wrong, but they didn't know exactly what. When Shaikh Ahmed visited London to see Waddington in Harley Street, they'd followed him. Apparently I was followed when I was in Dubai. That's why Rahman's people broke into my office – to see if they could find out the *nature* of Ahmed's problem. They only found out from Waddington when he confessed under torture, and then of course they finished him off. Once it was known that Ahmed was soon to die anyway, Rahman decided to resist the pressure for a coup. He could afford to wait.'

'Except that someone, still unknown, took him out of the game.' Inge had stopped shaking now.

'What we still don't know is the identity of the visitor to my hotel. Adawi had no idea. Maybe that'll always be a mystery.'

The BMW passed the Southern Methodist University. 'And now, back home you'll be a national hero. Overnight your Association will be Establishment. And doesn't your Queen still knight people or you get funny orders of the Garter?'

Laidlaw's laugh was dismissive. 'Later I may appreciate the publicity. Now all I want is to save Ahmed. Lusifren's caused too many deaths already.'

Inge stretched out an arm and ran her finger down his cheek, before resting her hand on his thigh. 'Relax. There's *nothing* more you can do now.' She brought the car to a halt, a swirl of dust rising above the bonnet in the evening air. From a neighbour's house came the sound of classical music, drifting lazily over the high brick wall which surrounded 'Le Bijou'. She saw the seriousness in his eyes, could see the determination, the frustration, the pain written large across his face. She pressed a button on the dashboard and the giant gates at the mouth of her drive slammed shut behind them. For the first time that day they were alone, really alone. 'Come on in. We can forget the lot of them. Now it's just us. Us until morning.'

* * *

As the morning sun rose over the green fields of East Texas, lit the Panhandle, burnished the wide open spaces of West Texas, so it cast its first gentle rays across Inge Loftin's luxury mansion. It was barely 7.00 a.m. and their eyes were half awake, half asleep, sharing their bliss and saddened by the prospect of separation. As they lay in the hush of Inge's room, there was no doubt about their unison – an affinity so powerful that they'd been drained of all emotion.

Inge looked across at the stirring figure next to her and then shifted slightly, leaning up on one elbow, her long hair falling like a shadow across the tenderness of her face. 'Time to wake up Rob. Angie'll be here with the pills soon. And then I'll take you to the airport. We've really got to move now.' She leant forward to kiss him, her eyes full of questions, her mind tormented as she studied his smile, almost naive in its openness. She watched as he stretched, muscles rippling as they adjusted to the day. Then his eyes were fully upon her, kind and unquestioning. She found herself being pulled towards him, unable to resist the strength of his grasp, and he hugged her with all the intensity of a last farewell.

Her voice was husky. 'You remember what you asked me last night? Well I think the answer has to be no. I've my career here. This is my life and I'm still a little bruised from the last time round. And you've got your life, your career, just opening out anew in front of you. Whatever we feel, we can't jettison our past or our present, however promising a future together might seem.' Even as she spoke she could scarcely believe what she was saying and found her voice breaking with emotion. So she tucked her face between his head and the pillow, whispering: 'in different circumstances I might say that I'd live with you, maybe even marry. But I want you to know and remember that you have given me more happiness than I could possibly have dreamed of. You may find it hard to understand, but you've given me that marvellous feeling of floating, of being cocooned from the rest of the world.' She found that she was crying in the pillow. 'All of these things have been mine – thanks to you.' As if it would stifle the tears, she clung even tighter to him, digging her nails into his shoulders, rubbing her cheek against his and burying her eyes even deeper into the pillow. 'We've got to go our own ways. We've each got to fulfil our ideals, be true to ourselves and I could no more do that in London than you could in Dallas.'

She expected him to speak but he said nothing. She could

imagine the quiet, thoughtful eyes moving slowly as he measured what he'd heard and how he should respond. She pulled away from him and she could see the depth of sadness which had momentarily hollowed the darkness of his unshaven jaw. Laidlaw knew what he wanted to say, almost wondered whether she was willing him to say it, but for several moments he continued to say nothing, trying to find the right words. 'I didn't realise that I loved you or how much I'd come to depend upon you,' he said as he placed a hand against either cheek and caressed her gently, so that he could look at her across the narrow divide of pillow. 'I'll always love you – I hope you'll remember that. And giving you happiness has just been too easy. But I'm going to see you again, not once but often, as we sort out how best to look after the victims. And everytime I see you I shall ask you again, in the hope that one day you'll change your mind. And if you do – then you'll know where I am and you'll know what I shall be thinking.'

Inge swallowed. 'Come on Rob. You mustn't miss that plane. Shaikh Ahmed depends upon you.'

* * *

The flight to Gatwick was comfortably uneventful or, if it were eventful, then Rob Laidlaw failed to notice, having bolstered himself with a bottle of wine and three brandies. He only awoke when Inge was four thousand miles away and the B Cal DC10 was circling over the grey dawn of a Sussex morning. The previous day in Dallas had been long and frustrating as Angie Kerton had struggled with Gossop's formula, finding it more difficult than she had expected. It was not until the evening that she'd delivered the bottles and he'd caught the London flight.

After a vaguely successful attempt to wash away a fuzzy head,

The Dallas Dilemma

Laidlaw sat back, concentrating on what he had to do. Find Adawi. Hand over the pills. Maybe even fly to Dubai in the Shaikh's personal DC9. Or maybe just wait in London. Either way it was out of his hands. Just wait. Just hope that Gossop's formula could really work. If Angie were right, it was feasible that the Shaikh could be saved. Just. Only just.

The man at Passport Control barely looked at him as he walked through and collected his suitcase from the carousel. The stride was still jaunty as he advanced towards the Customs area and, after a moment of hesitation, he headed for the green channel and was walking through when a rather senior looking official, a 'two ringer' rather than the usual junior officer with only one gold stripe, suggested that he stop.

'You're passing through the green channel, sir. Are you familiar with the Customs regulations?'

'Yes, I'm sure I am.' If his voice sounded doubtful, then it was only the uncertainty as to what the regulations really were which clouded the issue at all. He had no doubts. Not a bottle of Scotch too many, no gallon of aftershave buried in his suitcase.

'We'd like to undertake a thorough examination of your baggage sir, so, if you don't mind coming this way, please follow me.'

Laidlaw gave his shoulders a shrug of unconcern. 'If that's what you want, fine, of course I'll come.' Inwardly he was puzzled. This was no routine spot-check. What in hell's name was going on? Why me? Christ, the Shaikh could do without any delay. Still, he had nothing to declare. So just keep smiling. It would all work out.

'Right, sir,' said the Customs officer. 'In here.' He showed Laidlaw into a small cell-like room in which there was already another officer, apparently even more senior than the other. It was this man who spoke next.

'It's Mr Laidlaw, isn't it? I'm Surveyor of H M Customs.

Yes I recognise your face from the newspapers. Congratulations on this Drustein business and welcome back to England. I'm sure you've got nothing to be concerned about as a result of this spot-check.'

'I'm sure too. But I am in a hurry. So, if you'd please be quick about it.' His mind was on Adawi, waiting furiously just yards away, the other side of the barrier. Laidlaw watched as the suitcase was deftly and courteously emptied. His razor, washing kit, his bits and pieces, were soon all piled on the table top, his dirty clothes looking fit to be disowned. Then it was his leather briefcase. Out came notepad, Filofax, his paperback. And then two brown bottles of pills.

'And your pockets please.'

Unconcerned, Laidlaw removed his wallet, pens, comb, passport, keys and money, stacking them in front of the two officers. One studied the wallet, counting the money and looking at the credit cards with apparent interest while the other looked at the bottles of tablets destined for Shaikh Ahmed. 'And what are these, Mr Laidlaw?' enquired the Surveyor.

'Just some pills which I got in Dallas.' He thought that would be enough, that the interrogation would then be over.

'But what are they? What are they for? I assume they are for you?'

'I've got them for a . . . friend.'

'And who's that?'

'I'd rather not say. It's confidential.'

'Now come, Mr Laidlaw. I don't suppose this is anything serious, but it just could be. You must co-operate with us fully. What are these pills? Who made them? What are their ingredients?'

'There is no trade name. They were specially made for me. Or at least at my request, for someone else.' Laidlaw felt increasingly

The Dallas Dilemma

flustered, could feel his cheeks reddening and a dampening around the hairline as the small room seemed unbearably humid.

'You're not smuggling drugs, are you?'

Laidlaw laughed with conviction. 'No. That's absurd. Of course not.'

'What's the matter with your friend? What's it all about?'

'He's a very sick man, he's dying in fact. He needs these pills urgently. I heard about them in Dallas and decided to get some.'

'Well, who's your friend? We'll need to check up with him.'

'I'm afraid I can't tell you. It's confidential.'

'Now, Mr Laidlaw, I've been reading about you in the papers. It seems you've been doing a great job for a lot of people. But that doesn't mean that I mustn't do *my* job. You've already said you're familiar with the regulations about which items have to be declared. You didn't declare these. For all I know they could be a dangerous drug. And your answers have been far from satisfactory.' For the first time there was an edge in the man's voice. 'Unless you can tell me now who the drugs are for, who made them and what it's all about, then I shall have to send them off for analysis.'

'Confiscate these pills! You can't do that. It's a matter of life or death.' Laidlaw was almost shouting in desperation as he wondered if everything was going to go wrong at the last moment. What minutes before had seemed trite, a mere formality, was now a nightmare, swirling round him. Should he come clean? Should he tell the officers? Or should he say nothing? 'All right. I can't tell you the precise person. It's a matter of international importance. You'll just have to take my word about that. Can I just say they were specially made for a world leader who's dying? Will that do?'

The Surveyor shook his head slowly, the face severe, the grey complexion topped with thinning grey hair. 'No, sir, that won't do. I need a name and full details. Otherwise it's meaningless and, if I may say so, somewhat unlikely.' He held the tablets up to the light, removed a white tablet, sniffed it, turned it and then crushed it between his fingers. 'I don't like the look of it. We shall have to have it analysed.'

'Analysed? How long will that take?'

'A day, maybe two days. It just depends.'

'For God's sake. This is a matter of life or death. My friend needs these pills, straight away. I'm not kidding. He really is a world leader.' Laidlaw hoped that the sincerity in his face, in his voice, would get through the glazed indifference of the official. 'He'll die without these pills. Look, he's a Lusifren victim and this is an antidote, specially formulated. It's not available on the market.' It was a last desperate chance.

The two Customs men looked at each other and there was something of a look of pity about them, as if wondering whether Laidlaw were ready for the men in the white coats.

'I'm sorry sir. We shall have to keep these pills and have them analysed. We'd like a full statement from you and then you'll be free to go. It may take a little while.'

Laidlaw mopped his brow. He could feel the perspiration round his temples, trickling down his back, down his front, down his buttocks and behind his knees. Confusion was closing in on him pummelling his tired body and muddled mind. 'Look. It's simple. If you've got fax I'll get the formula faxed over by Angie Kerton who made up the prescription in Dallas. It could be here in minutes and that'll help your analysts. I *must* be allowed to take these drugs away at once.' It was obvious he was getting nowhere. 'What's more, I'm being met by two friends. They must be told that I've been delayed.'

'That can be arranged.' It was matter of fact, disinterested. 'As for the fax, yes, it might help but we have procedures, our own procedures to go through. I doubt the analyst will have prepared his report until tomorrow at the earliest. But I'm happy to tell you, Mr Laidlaw, that you will be free to leave before then. Shall we get on with the statement?'

* * *

'You're free to go now. We'll let you know when the pills have been analysed.'

'It's urgent. Don't you see, it's urgent.'

'So you've told us, sir. Now, if you'll just sign here for your belongings.' The Customs officer had no wish to appreciate the urgency.

Moments later Laidlaw was free. He saw Sandie and as she spotted him, he could almost hear the whoop of joy as she ran round the barrier to greet him. 'What held you up? Three hours, for God's sake! Oh! Sorry. I should have said you've done brilliantly. Fantastically.'

His voice was flat, despondent, the more so in contrast to her enthusiasm. 'Good to see you, Sandie and thanks for waiting. No doubt they told you I've had the utmost hassle with the bloody Customs. They thought I'd cornered the heroin market. Do I look like some kind of junkie? Anyway, they've confiscated some pills I was carrying.' She looked puzzled, still unaware of the race to save the Shaikh. As he was talking he was looking round. 'Have you seen Adawi? Ah yes. There he is.' Laidlaw had spotted the solitary man, slumped behind an Arabic newspaper which almost hid him from view. 'Sandie – I must talk to Adawi on my own. It'll be the last time. It's a promise. In future, we share everything.'

As usual, Adawi was neat and dapper in his Savile Row suit and from his cuffs and fingers came the glitter of gold. His voice was testy, his face crumpled like a discarded paper bag in a heavy scowl of irritation. 'What kept you? Where are the pills? We should have taken off over two hours ago. You had my orders.'

'No – I haven't got the pills.' He almost choked on the words, gasping nervously as he spoke. 'The bloody Customs have seized them. They thought they were dangerous drugs. They're having them analysed. We won't see them for a day, maybe longer, maybe never.' Laidlaw watched Adawi's face, expecting the dark skin to blacken with further anger as a preface to a bitter onslaught. But it never came.

'So what do we do?' Adawi's shoulders sagged with the downturn in his voice.

For a moment Laidlaw was taken aback at the defeatist attitude. Where was the Adawi of just a few short weeks ago? 'I've been thinking about that. I'll ring Dallas and get Angie Kerton to send more, one lot by air courier direct to London for you to take to Dubai. Another batch could be sent to New York and then maybe could go to Dubai in your diplomatic bag. One lot or other will get through, probably both. I suggest you wait in London. When the pills arrive, I'll let you know. It's 10.00 a.m. now. They can't be here for at least twelve hours – possibly longer.' 'I'm very sorry that it's all gone wrong.'

Laidlaw was surprised at the charity, the response coming as near to gratitude as he had ever heard. 'You could have done no more. His Highness is very weak you know but I'd told him what you had done. He wanted me to give you this letter. Now, go ahead and get this Kerton woman to send over more pills to here. And to New York. I'll organise a diplomatic bag at Kennedy Airport. Meantime, I need some rest.'

Laidlaw suppressed his annoyance, feeling helpless as if he alone were now fighting the war to save the Shaikh's life. 'Me too.

The Dallas Dilemma

I'm bushed. But I want to see this out first. *I'm* not giving in.' Was he the only one to feel the urgency, the heart-pounding frustration at the prospect of being baulked with success in sight? He beckoned to Sandie and explained that he had a call to make and hurried away once again, leaving her staring at Adawi with something bordering on malevolence. Just after midnight Laidlaw was back at Gatwick, awaiting the incoming flight from Dallas. Angie Kerton was aboard, the pills with her. Another supply had been sent via the diplomatic bag out of New York on a Gulf Air flight and they too were heading for Dubai. Laidlaw looked round the Terminal restlessly. Where was Adawi? Had the man given up the fight? What had got into him? The flight had now touched down.

'Would Mr Laidlaw please come to the information desk.' The announcement summoned him, and he collected a message to ring the Emirates' Embassy.

Adawi was there and spoke first. 'I tried to stop you going to Gatwick. His Highness died two hours ago. I shall be flying to Dubai as soon as possible. We shall speak again.' Adawi had put down the receiver, his voice distraught and with no word of farewell.

Laidlaw walked aimlessly round the concourse, vaguely aware of other passengers awaiting their flights, vaguely aware of the 'ding-dongs' of other announcements, the bookshops, the restaurants, the bars, the cafes, vaguely aware of life. Images of the ageing Shaikh's frail hands, the gnarled fingers, the falcon by his side, seemed to haunt him with every step. Defeat! He'd lost! He'd failed! Angie Kerton's journey would be in vain. It had *all* been in vain. At least for Shaikh Ahmed. True. But on the other hand, even if the Customs hadn't stopped him. Even the original pills wouldn't have saved Ahmed. Suppose, just suppose that. . . . No. Forget it! There was no place for 'if onlys', especially not now.

From his pocket he took out again the Shaikh's letter, written in simple English, though the hand was shaky and the signature feeble. 'Thank you for what you have done. To have brought about the downfall of Drustein, to have seen the end of the hateful Schillen, to have revealed a cure. What more could you have done? I shall die with peace of mind. Truth and justice have prevailed. I believe in that. I believe in you and what you can do. I believe too that the future of my country is secured. The death of Shaikh Rahman has changed destiny. Shaikh Hassan will succeed me and with time will be a wise ruler. Now my own life is unimportant – even to me. Make sure that my wealth is applied to your Association. I have made arrangements. There must be no more tragedies like Lusifren, no more deaths. That is your task. You will succeed. May your God bless you.'

'Well here I am.' The unexpected voice broke him out of his trance. 'I've got the pills.' As if in a dream he looked up and saw the smiling face of Inge Loftin. 'I thought I'd come myself. Save Angie Kerton the journey. London's so attractive at this time of year, don't you think?'

EPILOGUE

President Hode swung his chair round so that he could comfortably place his feet on his White House desk. Receiver in one hand, he waited for a moment and then heard the Prime Minister's familiar voice on the scrambler. 'Good Morning, Prime Minister! I'm just calling to thank you for what you did. I didn't want to involve you but I guess you understood the importance?'

The Prime Minister's voice was soft and fawning. 'Jack, of course I understood and anyway, coming from our oldest friend and most important ally, it was a request which I could never refuse. I'm just sorry that you had to take the decision. It must have been hard.'

'Sure, it was tough. But there was no other way. Once the CIA reported that Shaikh Ahmed was dying, we couldn't risk that commie Rahman taking over. The whole balance of the Gulf would have been jeopardised. But once he'd had this, er . . . helicopter accident. Most unfortunate that was. After that my staffers told me that the West could be reassured. Now with our friend Ahmed gone, Shaikh Hassan will take over and he'll be a good ally to the West. The CIA have given me favourable reports of him even though he's inexperienced. We'll hold his hand. No doubt we can bank on you giving him full support.'

'Of course. Just as you say Jack. But tell me, something went wrong with your plans? Is that right?'

'Right. Your man Laidlaw. He's some guy. Better than some of your Cabinet, if I may say so. No, no, Prime Minister, it was a joke. I didn't mean anything.' He sensed a frosty transatlantic intake of breath and was quick to retrieve the position. 'As you must have understood, once we were aware of the link between Laidlaw and Adawi, we had him watched everywhere. Furthermore, we'd had him wired for sound. A bug in his Filofax.'

'When did you find out his link with Adawi?'

'When he visited Dubai. Observation there is a matter of routine. We weren't alone in following him. Rahman's supporters must have been watching too. Anyway when Laidlaw moved to Dallas, naturally we heard his call to Adawi. This fitted in with other information which the CIA were receiving. One of our FBI agents visited his hotel and, on establishing he was out, planted a bug there in his Filofax.'

'I suppose I should object about the infringement of the rights of one of my citizens.' It was a rare joke from the Prime Minister.

Out of past experience, Hode took her seriously. 'Maybe. Let me tell you this. That bug saved his life. He doesn't know it, come to that, he must never know it. He just thinks it was chance, good fortune, God on his side which led the police to crash in on Schillen's office when they did. Well, he must go on thinking it was divine intervention. You and I know different. You and I know it was the Filofax and the information which it was transmitting.'

'You were going to tell me how Rob Laidlaw made the plans go wrong.'

'Right! Once our Filofax friend taught us that he'd gotten pills which might have kept the Shaikh alive as a cripple, there was no way that we could risk that. No way. The scenario was that the Emirates would then be run by a semi-invalid, semi-senile, decaying old man kept alive by some wonder pills. His own paralysis would paralyse his own government.'

The Dallas Dilemma

'So you decided to prevent the pills reaching him.'

'Sure. From listening to Laidlaw's conversations with the Shaikh's adviser, Adawi, we reckoned that it was only a matter of time. Days at the most. That's when I asked for your help to arrange for your Customs to stop him.'

'They did a good job.'

'And I am grateful to you, Prime Minister and maybe we saved our good friend, Shaikh Ahmed false hopes and more suffering.' He paused to emphasise the point. 'Certainly that's the way I'd like to think of it.'

'I understand Jack. And I hope you do well in the election. We want you back.'

'I guess I will. It's written in the tablets.'

* * *

Thank you for reading THE DALLAS DILEMMA

Read **HARD PLACE** — sign up here for my newsletter to receive your FREE copy!

Follow this link: douglasstewartbooks.com

HARD PLACE

Detective Inspector Todd "Ratso" Holtom of Scotland Yard is as tough as they come and must destroy the drug-running empire of murderous kingpin Boris Zandro. Ratso knows the dangers, but if he doesn't stop Zandro, the political fallout — in London, Washington, and beyond — will change the face of the world as he knows it.

Copy this link to read HARD PLACE, the acclaimed Det. Ratso novel!

douglasstewartbooks.com

BOOKS BY DOUGLAS STEWART

Fiction
The Ratso Series
Hard Place
Dead Fix
Deadly Hush

Other Mystery Thrillers
Deadline Vegas
Undercurrent
The Dallas Dilemma
Cellars' Market
The Scaffold
Villa Plot, Counterplot
Case for Compensation

Contributions
M.O. – a compendium
Capital Crimes – a compendium
Death Toll – a compendium

Non-Fiction
Terror at Sea
Piraten (German Language market)
Insult to Injury
A Family at Law

ABOUT THE AUTHOR

Born in Scotland but brought up in England, I have lived and worked as a lawyer and writer in London, Las Vegas, Cyprus and the Isle of Man. *Deadly Hush* is my sixteenth book and the third in the Ratso series. *Undercurrent* was selected by WH Smith as their Paperback of the Week. Another book topped the charts for 24 weeks as did an anthology to which he contributed. Whether fiction or non-fiction, my books reflect my love of distant and exciting locations.

AUTHOR'S NOTE

This is a work of fiction. All characters are fictional and bear no resemblance to any person living or dead. Any resemblance to actual persons, living or dead or to events is entirely coincidental and unintentional. In particular, the names, characters and incidents are from the author's imagination.

Copyright © Chewton Limited, Douglas Stewart

The right of Douglas Stewart to be identified as the author of this work has been asserted by him in accordance with the Copyright, Designs and Patents Act 1988 and all other current legislation.

You may not copy, store, distribute, transmit, reproduce or otherwise make available this publication (or any part of it) in any form or by any means (electronic, digital, optical, mechanical, photocopying, recording or by any other manner whatsoever) without the prior written consent of the author and of Chewton Limited. Any person or body who does any unauthorised act in relation to this publication may be liable to criminal prosecution and civil claims for damages.
All rights reserved under International Copyright Conventions. You have been granted the non-exclusive, non-transferable right to access and read the text of this e-book on screen. No part of this text may be reproduced, transmitted, downloaded, decompiled, reverse engineered or stored in or introduced into any information storage and retrieval system in any formal by any means, whether electronic or mechanical, now known or hereinafter invented without the express written consent of Chewton Ltd. Without written consent, no part of this book may be used or adapted for any purpose whatsoever (including for any visual or audio media) by use of what is generically known as Artificial Intelligence (A I).

Fourth Edition published in 2024 by Chewton Publications
© Douglas Stewart 1988

Printed in Great Britain
by Amazon